THE BILLIONAIRE'S MASK

Edited by:
Kimberly Braulio
C.B. Moore

Cover and book design by:
A.M.C. Bartolome-Turingan

ISBN: 978-1-641-53386-7
First Edition, April 2021

For you

CHAPTER ONE

Y ou must never enter Master Brandon's bedroom or his study. He's not a very patient man. He allows no one in his room. You can do whatever you want in the house but never go inside his private space unless you are permitted to do so. Do you understand?" Ms. Lennie warns. It is clear in her pale cerulean eyes how serious she is.

The head housemaid's hair is ash-colored and seems as if it has been tied in a bun forever. She has a strong countenance and is about five-foot-five. If I had to guess, I'd say she is in her late fifties.

"I understand." I gulp and nod.

I always do research before job interviews, so I know a little about the 'Master.' He's twenty-eight, a self-made billionaire, and the sole owner and chairman of Grethe and Elga Enterprises, a telecommunications and electronic consumer company headquartered in Manhattan.

But his family background, where he graduated, and his face are all a mystery. No single soul has seen him in person. He never shows up anywhere public and never attends any important events. I can't help but wonder why.

Does he have a disease? Is he allergic to sunrise? A vampire? I want to know.

"Um, Ms. Lennie? I just want to ask..."

"Yes, Miss Hart?" she turns, acknowledging the hesitation in my voice. We stop in the middle of a long stairway.

"Does he really not come out?"

She meets my gaze. "One more thing: this is the last time you will ask me *that*."

Is that a yes? I swallow again.

As we continue to the curve of the staircase, I can't help but admire the mansion's grandeur. I didn't know mansions still existed in New York City, but that's not so surprising if you walk to the posh end of the Upper East Side.

The house's neoclassical architecture enchants me. Although it's undeniably old, modernity is still present. The enormous chandeliers brighten the hall, and the floors are so clean it seems as though no single speck of dirt has ever touched them. Yet I can't miss the dark gray draperies covering the tall windows, as if they're there to prevent the light from coming in. And the silence of the surroundings is deafening—making the place seem lonely and empty.

However, the walls display expensive art pieces and oil canvases. I lean close to one—a beautiful scene of a majestic pine tree covered in snow. But what captures my attention the most is the portrait of a handsome young man hanging in the center of the space. He has dark hair, chiseled jaws, piercing gray eyes, a perfectly aligned nose, a mouth made for kissing, and an utterly stoic expression.

"Ms. Lennie, who's he?" I mumble.

She spins and throws me a warning look but doesn't answer. After a long walk, we stop in front of a hand-carved wooden door on the second floor. Ms. Lennie draws out a bunch of keys from her pocket and chooses one.

"The Master wants you to use this room. You're fortunate. The rooms in this passage are for the guests," she says as she unlocks the door and hands me a key. "Here's your duplicate," she explains. Her expression is still blank.

Does she even know how to smile?

"Thanks. I'll just settle my things inside." I smile, wondering if she would smile back. Predictably, she didn't.

"Your job starts tomorrow, but I'll meet you in the living room in one hour. I'll give you a house tour."

"Of course. Thank you." I smile, then open the door.

I step into my room, dragging my luggage behind me, and my eyes widen the moment I lift my head.

"Goodness gracious! This room is for a princess!" I exclaim, then cautiously lower my voice, anxious someone might hear me. I look around, astonished at the realization that I am meant to be alone in such an enormous room. I don't need so much space, but God, it's incredible.

Unlike the gloom in the rest of the mansion, there is light here. The room has white walls and is impeccably appointed. The floors are made of Italian marble, a stone fireplace occupies the far wall, and there's a sitting area with two small, padded loungers. Also, the curtains aren't gray, but baby blue! The queen-sized bed is covered by a spread cheerfully patterned with yellow flowers, and the pillows look fluffy.

I'm in love! It's as if they knew my favorite colors. But the thing that startles me most is the MacBook glowing on the desk. I wonder if I'm allowed to use it.

Considering the extravagance of the room, I have to check what's up with the bathroom. And as expected, the bathroom is luxurious. My highest hope was a clawfoot bathtub or something I could relax in. Then my eyes spot a Jacuzzi! I want to collapse in amazement.

It is all too much to take in for an assistant cook, but who am I to complain? My new boss is probably generous to compensate for his mysterious lifestyle.

I remember that Ms. Lennie wants me to meet her in an hour, so I quickly unpack my things. I pull out my few articles of clothing and hang them in the wardrobe or tuck them away in drawers. I lay my cosmetics and accessories on the bed; among them is the heart necklace Mom gave me.

Oh my God. Mom! I immediately grab my phone and call home.

"Hello?" a cute, high-pitched voice answers right away. It's Martin, the one who cried the loudest when I said I was leaving home for a while.

"Hi, it's Alayna."

"Alayna!" he squeals excitedly. "Are you at work yet?"

"Yeah, I just arrived," I answer, staring at the necklace. "Is Mom there?"

"Yes, but I want to talk to you!"

I chuckle. I imagine him pouting. "Fine. Did you miss me?"

He giggles. "I miss you! When are you coming home?"

"Very soon, but I want you to make sure you have good grades at school and show it to me when I come home, okay?"

"Then you will give me a chocolate cake?"

"As many as you like, but you have to share it with other kids too, okay?"

"Yes, because Mira wants it too!"

"Very good. But can you give the phone to Mom for now?"

"Okay," he says, sounding sad. "Mom! Alayna's on the phone!" Martin shouts, the second youngest of twelve adopted siblings. I chuckle again at hearing his voice. I hear his little footsteps running on our wooden floor and picture him sprinting into Mom's room.

"Who's that?" It's Mom's voice.

"It's Alayna! She's on the phone," says Martin.

"Oh really?" I hear noisy scratches on the other line before she answers. "Alayna?"

"Mom?"

"Oh, darling. We miss you already! Are you at the mansion?" she asks. I clasp my mouth, hearing her voice.

"Y-Yeah, Mom." I sob. "I miss you too."

"How is it? Are they nice to you?"

I'm not sure if Ms. Lennie was nice, but I shouldn't tell her that.

"I haven't met anyone, except for the head housemaid, but I'm sure they are." I sniff.

"Oh, honey. Are you crying?" If only Mom was beside me, she would have already wrapped me in her arms. I wipe my tears away.

"No. I just miss you all so much. I wanted to hear your voice."

"We're fine, Alayna. Your siblings love you," she says softly. "Do you want to talk to them?"

"I wanted to, but..." I laugh. "I only have an hour to

prepare, but I can still call you later."

"Sure, darling. Go ahead. I'm glad you called, but make sure to call me again, okay?"

"Okay," I promise.

"I love you, darling."

"I love you too."

I hang up. Not wanting to sink into homesickness, I remind myself why I'm here. I have twelve siblings, and Mom needs help paying for her neuromuscular scoliosis treatment and the debts she needs to settle. And this job is three times the salary of the last restaurant I worked in.

I continue setting my stuff out and go to the bathroom. It takes everything in me to avoid using the Jacuzzi, as it will make me forget the time.

After a regular shower, I step out of the bathroom. I choose denim pants and a shirt as an outfit, fix my hair into a bun, and don't bother to put on makeup, though I apply a small amount of lip tint for a glossy effect. I turn to gaze at my reflection in the full-length mirror.

Look who's ready!

I glance at my wristwatch, and I have ten minutes.

I come out of my room and double-check if I locked the door behind me. My limbs feel like they're not my own. I'm too nervous even to operate.

I blow out a sharp breath. I shouldn't be nervous. Ms. Lennie is an employee as well, and this mansion probably has more employees than I expected. But God, her stern face bothers me so much.

Reaching the end of the stairs, Ms. Lennie is already waiting.

"Miss Hart. You. Are. Late," she points out, word by word.

"*Late?* B-But you said—"

"Early is on time, on time is late."

"I'm sorry. I'll remember that."

"The first level has the living room, dining area, the main kitchen, and the staff's quarters," Ms. Lennie explains immediately. "The second level has the grand piano and the library. The third and fourth are for the Master's use. As the assistant chef, Alayna, you are allowed to enter his study on the third floor. I don't permit the housemaids to wander around the higher floors if they are not doing chores. But just like them, our curfew is at ten o'clock. No one can go upstairs unless it's an emergency."

"I understand, Ms. Lennie."

"Come, I'll show you the kitchen and introduce you to the chef."

I keep following Ms. Lennie until we stop in front of the central kitchen, and it is everything I ever dreamed of. It's polished with a gourmet marble island, professional-grade appliances, and ample food storage. There's also an informal eating area beside the windows from which I can glimpse a spectacular outdoor view.

"Mr. Katrakis," Ms. Lennie calls to the man in a white shirt and jeans standing in the prep area. I can only see his broad back.

A blond-haired man flashes out a wide grin the moment he turns. I can't believe how young and attractive he is, but what astonishes me more is he's who I expected.

"And who do we have here?" he asks, and God, his voice... It's deep, smooth, and manly.

"I want to introduce you to your new assistant chef," Ms. Lennie says. "This is Alayna Hart, and Alayna, you will address him as Mr.—"

"It's all right, Lennie," he interjects, finally extending a hand toward me. "Hello, Alayna. It's a pleasure to finally meet you. I'm Oliver Katrakis," he says politely, but it's as if he was anticipating my arrival. He has a very charming smile.

I shake his hand right away. There's a part of me that doesn't want to release his grip, but I do.

"It's a pleasure to meet you, Mr. Katrakis," I stammer in surprise. "I saw you in the articles. You're the CEO of Grethe and Elga Enterprises and Chairman Lucien's sole representative."

"Someone did some research," he remarks with a pleasant smile. "Technically, you are correct, Miss Hart. And yes, I'm also Brandon's cousin and his private chef as of the moment."

"Wow," is all I can say.

Well, that's new information. No one addresses Oliver Katrakis as the chairman's cousin in public records and news sites, but their relationship makes sense now.

"Alayna?" Ms. Lennie cuts in, her expression still passive.

"Yes, Ms. Lennie?"

"Mr. Katrakis will explain your job description. I'll leave you. I'll be in the living room."

Yes! I want to scream out loud in victory. The man seems more pleasant than her, despite being the CEO or the chef or whatever—no offense to her. I want to thank Ms. Lennie, but she's already excused herself and left.

"So, did you have a grand tour?" he asks with a genuine grin.

I smile back. "Yes, except for the higher floors."

"But you didn't see the outside?"

"Besides the dancing fountain and the eclectic porch?"

"Oh, you missed the good part, I see." His eyes gleam. "Why don't we take a walk?"

I shrug, then smile. "Yes, sure."

From the central kitchen, we stroll to the main hall and exit to a pathway toward a bridge to the left wing. Mr. Katrakis is taking me to a part of the house I haven't seen yet.

There's a terrace and an outdoor swimming pool on the second floor that overlook the city skyline.

"God! It's beautiful. I can come up here?" I say as I walk to the metal and glass barriers of the balcony to get a broader view of the city.

"Of course, you can," Mr. Katrakis assures me, stopping by my side.

"And I can use the pool?"

"No one will stop you." He smiles. "No one comes here except for me and Lennie, and now you."

"It's amazing..."

The landscape glows blue over the white clouds. He is right; I missed the best part of the mansion during the house tour. Here, I fantasize diving into the pool or probably spending my free day lying under the sun reading a new novel.

"Now, why don't we sit? Tell me more about yourself." Mr. Katrakis perches on the wooden bench, then offers the space across from him.

I blink. "What would you like to know?"

"Well, I already saw your resume..." He scratches his chin. "How about telling me something that's not on the paper?"

I hesitate. "I'm not sure if there's anything else."

He smiles. "Tell me more about your position in the Palazzo Franchetti. The head chef's food taster, right?"

"That's right," I say nervously.

"You must have an exquisite sense of taste. Interesting." He grins, amused. "That'll make you an exceptional chef too. But why did you come here? To a mansion, to serve a master you haven't even met yet when there are a lot of excellent restaurants out there where your talent is needed?"

"My previous position was my first job, and it didn't give me enough experience for being a chef. Though I assure you that I can—"

He cuts me off. "That's fine, Alayna. I understand what you mean, and as your new chef, I can teach you everything I know. Though I have to remind you that I'm very busy elsewhere, so you're going to have to serve Brandon alone with your cooking. He's the one who chose you for this job after all." Mr. Katrakis grins again.

Oh, of course. The faceless Chairman Brandon Lucien will be the one I'll serve, so he's got to be the one to choose.

I remember my interview with some secretary at Grethe and Elga Enterprises HQ. I was curiously the only applicant back then. He only asked me a few questions, and that was it. I got hired without even having to cook a few dishes. I couldn't believe it at first, thinking that it was peculiar. Then again, who would doubt the efficiency of a huge company like G&E Enterprises?

"That's reassuring," I say.

"And you grew up in Kansas?" he asks.

"Yes, in Lawrence, and I had never been anywhere else before I worked in Venice. I got my degree in culinary arts at The Culinary Center of Kansas City."

"I've only been there once. Does your family live there too?"

"Yes." I chuckle. "My mom and twelve adopted

siblings."

"Twelve!" He gasps in shock, then grins again. "Your parents must be good citizens in your town."

"They were, but then Dad passed away," I recall sadly. "How about you?"

"Me? What about me?" He stares; I'm not sure if he's offended or confused by my question.

"Is there anyone else in the family living in this house?"

"No, it's just me. They're all in Greece," he answers, simply and coolly.

I can't decide if Mr. Katrakis is easy to talk to or if I'm complicating things with all my questions. I still feel a bit of awkwardness, but he doesn't seem uptight. I decide to apologize anyway. "I'm sorry. You don't need to answer my questions."

He laughs. "It's fine. I'm just surprised. I rarely talk about myself here."

"Probably because no one dares to ask?"

Mr. Katrakis' expression brightens; he's amused. "You are so curious, aren't you? I was born in Greece—Athens, to be precise. But I spent most of my time in New York. Studying, exploring, building things—all that."

Oh, so he is Greek.

"That sounds productive," I say.

"It was."

"Then, how long have you been working for your cousin?"

"Ever since he's needed me." He sighs, his expression worried. "I can't remember, exactly."

"Oh." I take his answer as *no further questions, please.*

"All right." He clasps his hands together. "As for your job description, it's not very complicated, but Brandon is very picky. He has a particular appetite, so each day, I make

11

a menu for him to choose from. We must follow the menu and never improvise."

"I understand, sir." I used to work with the most ill-tempered head chef in the history of head chefs, sarcasm intended, when I was in Palazzo Franchetti. There, I was serving hundreds of customers a day and dealing with constant stress. So, I guess this is not so bad.

"Any more questions?"

I dare to ask about Brandon Lucien once more. "Will I ever meet him, then?"

He smiles. "It's not usual, but I believe you will."

Even if I don't exactly understand what he means, I believe him. "Thank you. I really appreciate this."

"You're welcome. I don't want to take away your first free day here. I'd better be going, Alayna." He stands up.

I grin. "No worries, sir."

"Sure. See you tomorrow then." Mr. Katrakis shakes my hand again, softly squeezing it before marching away. After a short stroll around the pool, I go back to the central kitchen.

Familiarizing myself with the workstation, I open every single drawer, explore the cold storage, and take a look at the stock of ingredients. I'm thrilled to find rare, very expensive, and special spices from different parts of the world—ones you cannot buy at most grocery stores. My thinking is, since I have signed a one-year contract, I might as well get used to the massive kitchen.

I go back to my room after thirty minutes of reading the recipes and ogling the ingredients. I now have less than fifteen hours for myself. There are questions in my brain and new information I need to process.

The conversation I had with Mr. Katrakis lingers in my mind, and I want to know more about his cousin. I sit down at the desk with the glowing MacBook. I hope that this isn't some sort of test and that I'm actually allowed to use the computer. I type "Oliver Katrakis" into Google—though I have already done this search a couple of times.

Hundreds of results pop up. I bite my lip, clicking the first link.

Oliver Katrakis is thirty–two and has been the CEO of Grethe and Elga Enterprises for five years. A Princeton graduate, double major, and award-winning entrepreneur. Besides his work, he has various interests and is gifted with many talents.

I exit the site and select the next.

G&E Technologies. One of the biggest firms owned by G&E Enterprises is now one of the leading IT companies in New York City.

Who is its faceless chairman, Brandon Lucien?
Who's behind the success of G&E Enterprises?

Still, nothing about the Master appeared. I close the tab and open a social media site. I type his name in the search bar, and numbers of similar names appear, but none relating to the chairman. I shut down the computer, then go to bed.

What did I expect? Of course, he wouldn't make a profile page on Facebook or something. He probably just wants his life to remain private. He wouldn't be the faceless chairman for no reason. But why does he have to be so enigmatic?

I stare at my high ceiling, and questions just won't stop flooding my head.

I woke up earlier than my alarm this morning. Heck, I barely even slept, with all these inexplicable emotions churning inside me.

Nonetheless, I can't decide if I'm excited or just nervous because I'm sure that work won't be easy for the next twelve months. I lazily swing my legs out of the bed and step into the bathroom.

After a shower, I put on a regular white chef's uniform and fix my hair. I hurry to the kitchen and arrive a few minutes earlier than Mr. Katrakis. I'm thankful for this, remembering Ms. Lennie's rules about being on time.

"Good morning, Alayna." He immediately puts on an apron when he walks in. "Are you ready?"

"Good morning, sir. Yes, I'm ready!" I reply heartily.

He draws out a sheet of paper from the wall and hands it to me. It's a copy of the meal schedule and the list of dishes he spoke about yesterday. It says breakfast is at seven, noon for lunch, and seven for dinner. Today is Tuesday, so for breakfast, *Elipsiomo* bread and *Kagianas*—a scrambled egg dish with tomatoes and topped with feta. I assist Mr. Katrakis in preparing the dish.

The dish is easy, and two or more other people working in the kitchen make it even easier.

"We might as well give Brandon a cup of English Breakfast. He likes tea very much," Mr. Katrakis tells me after we finish. He takes out a cup from the cupboard and pours brewed tea from the kettle. Then he transfers the food I cooked onto a plate and sets it with a garnish.

"Preparing Brandon's meal is like serving an important restaurant guest," he says, lifting the plates and setting them on a food trolley. "You're quite fast in the kitchen."

"Maybe because egg dishes are one of my specialties," I say proudly.

"Great, because he is fond of those." He grins. "One, in particular, is Eggs Benedict—which is his breakfast tomorrow."

All right, I guess this really isn't so hard after all. Not only was Mr. Katrakis quiet in the kitchen, but he was also kind. We were working well together; I could get used to this.

"Oh, I'll take note of that. So, um, I'll clean up here first, and I'll start to organize the ingredients for the Master's lunch?"

"Of course," he agrees. "But after that, I suggest you visit the library upstairs."

"I'm allowed?"

"Sure. I have a few recipe books there that you can borrow. And oh, there's fiction as well, if that's your style."

"That's perfect! Thank you, Mr. Katrakis."

"I'd better take this to Brandon, then I'll come to find you."

"You will?" I ask in surprise. I'm taken aback by my own words. "Sorry."

"Of course. I'll show you around. You can say that it's a part of your orientation from me," he says with a smile.

Honestly, I imagined Mr. Katrakis as a stern, intimidating CEO kind of person—if that's a thing. But he is so kind, and I can speak to him without formality, it seems.

I return the smile. "Thanks again, sir."

"You're very welcome. And, by the way, make sure Lennie doesn't see you go up there. It's not that you're forbidden to go. Brandon just uses it sometimes. If she does see you, let her know I gave you permission to use the library."

It sounds like a dangerous offer, but I would love to see the library, regardless. I watch Mr. Katrakis push the trolley outside.

After cleaning, I walk to the third floor and reach the

library. I turn the knob and grin when I find that it is open. I breathe in awe as thousands of books appear before my eyes. It's so beautiful! The library's floor is polished, and it has a granite fireplace and a comfortable, well-worn sitting arrangement.

I heave a sigh, relieved that Ms. Lennie isn't around to reprimand me.

I've always loved reading and collecting romance books at home, so seeing these shelves just makes my heart soar. I start my journey inside, searching for cookbooks.

Instead, I stumble upon a book placed in a glass cage in the middle of the classics section. I lean forward, touching the glass as I try to read the title. It's *Macbeth* and *Hamlet* by William Shakespeare. The air instantly abandons my lungs when I catch sight of the leather-bound cover. It's very old but still stunning.

"Wow," I whisper, but then I suddenly hear a snap behind me. I jerk in surprise.

I turn around and find Mr. Katrakis very close. I must admit, I've never seen someone as handsome as him. He's the kind of man who would sweep you off your feet with one look. His presence alone radiates charisma.

"Careful," he says softly. "That's a first edition."

I swear I can feel his breath on my neck. My eyes widen. "Do you mean this book is four hundred years old?"

"1663 to 1664, from the Third Folio. Do you want to see it?"

I shake my head firmly. "I don't think I can hold that book. That is very rare." I chuckle nervously. "But amazing. How did you get it?"

"Not without difficulty, and this is actually Brandon's," he mumbles with a frown. "One of his collections. Anyway,

I'll show you my shelves."

"Of course." I step aside.

I follow him as we stroll down the library's hall. It's huge. He points out each section from the classics, fiction, non-fiction to volumes of economy and business books. Honestly, I enjoy listening to his voice. He sounds so soothing.

We stop at one particularly tall shelf in the left-end corner.

"These books here are mine." He pokes a finger at a title and draws it from the shelf. The cover is new and glossy, and the size of a magazine. "This is called *Mastering the Art of Greek Cooking*. I wrote this book under the pen name of Oliver Youngwood." He gives me the book.

"And you write cookbooks too! What a surprise." I'm beginning to admire the man a lot. It's true what they said about him on the internet then. He's a man of many talents. "Just what else can you do aside from being a CEO and a chef?"

One side of his mouth curves into a grin. "I'll take that question as a compliment."

"What will I find here?" I ask as I open the first page and see pictures of unfamiliar dishes.

"You make good food, Alayna, but cooking isn't just following the recipe."

"It's the authenticity of the taste," I agree.

"Yes, and if you want to become Brandon's chef, you must study more. You know by now that he's Greek, and he's very fond of the traditional dishes, but he's into other cuisines as well. His mother used to cook for him as a child, and even if he was born and raised here, he never forgets where he came from."

Well, that's another glimpse of Brandon Lucien's

mysterious life. Had I known that he's Greek, I'd have probably taken the time to learn more about the country. But even his origin isn't in the public records. I have experience cooking several types of cuisine, even Middle Eastern and Asian—and I've always loved Mediterranean food, but my knowledge of Greek cuisine isn't as broad as my experience with Italian cuisine.

"And this isn't in the notes you gave me?"

"Those are just his favorites. You must learn more."

"Thank you. I always love exploring more in my field." Honestly, this makes me feel like I'm still a newbie, but this is a challenge I welcome.

"By the way, you don't have to call me Mr. Katrakis; Oliver will do."

I clear my throat. "But you're his cousin, and Ms. Lennie would think it's inappropriate—"

"I'm saying this so you don't feel awkward around me." He sends me another charming grin after cutting me short.

I blink. Am I being awkward? *"Fine. Oliver."* I laugh.

"Good." He beams. "Would you like to stay here a bit more?"

"I'd like to study this first. I can still come back here later, right?"

"Of course. Now, what would you like to know first?"

Back to the central kitchen, Oliver pretty much only speaks about Greece while we work. I learn that the country produces a range of fruits, nuts, beans, oil, and green vegetables, complemented by a selection of herbs. Those are the base of the traditional Greek diet. Seafood is also popular and a standard part of their regime, and during the holidays, they specifically use meat such as beef or lamb.

Knowing a little about them makes me want to visit the

place. Thinking of their festivals, I imagine a colorful life with people dancing in the streets, parades, men and women in costume, and probably fireworks, although maybe that doesn't take place in Athens as much as in the smaller cities. I want to explore more of their diet and traditions.

"One of my favorites is *souvlaki,*" Oliver says as we put the finishing touches on his cousin's lunch. "It's basically grilled meat on a skewer that can be anything from chicken, pork, lamb, or beef, or even vegetables—though I prefer chicken. And it usually comes with a side dish like pita bread or *tzatziki.*"

"Like a barbecue."

"Yes, like a barbecue." He chuckles softly. "But as I said, the flavor should be authentic for a Greek's taste buds."

I run my tongue over my bottom lip. Just the description makes me hungry. "I'd like to try that sometime."

"Of course. Sometime."

"I'm just kind of curious: You said you were born in Athens, but why did you come here? Your country sounds amazing... why would you want to leave?"

"Yes, it is." He smiles, not answering my question. "My family still lives there."

"Your parents?"

"Yes, my parents and my sister. Though you'll get to meet my brother soon. He just doesn't often come to the mansion." Oliver stands, walks over to the fridge, and grabs two bottles of beer after we finish our lunch. "Do you drink?"

I shrug. "Occasionally. Is it okay?"

He flashes a half-smile, sits across from me, and gives me the other bottle. "Technically speaking, I'm your direct superior, and I allow you."

"Thank you." I take the beer. "But I thought Ms. Lennie

was my *superior*."

"Well, she's in charge of the household, and her rules *somewhat* apply to you. Your position is as important as hers, but since I'm Brandon's right hand, she is also under my wing."

I nod, agreeing. Frankly, I prefer him to Ms. Lennie. She seems nice, but she's also so... *blank*.

"Is it bad that I'm more curious now?"

"About what?" Oliver chugs his first shot of the beer. "Tell me."

"Honestly, I don't mean to be nosy on such private matters, but I'm going to be living here now, so I'm curious about everything." I grip the bottle tightly, the condensation wetting my fingers. "It's not wrong to want to know more about him, right?"

"There are complicated explanations as to why we moved here, Alayna. I can't tell you about Brandon, but I can tell you some of mine."

I nod. "I'm listening."

"I only lived there until I was ten," he starts. "We moved here because we wanted to be free of the family circle."

"I thought your parents were still there?"

"They just moved back. I stayed here because America grew on me. If you are a member of the Katrakis family, you must follow all the rules. They honor it like it's some kind of legal thing."

"Rules?" I frown. "What kind of rules?"

"There are too many of them. You'll hurt your mind." He laughs. This man can really smile a lot! And that's probably why I like him.

I have my first gulp of the beer. Surprisingly, the sweet taste outweighs the bitterness. "Then tell me one important rule."

"I'll tell you something interesting. Women in the family should only marry a man from two of the few prominent families in Greece. The Stavros and Dragoumis. The same rules apply to them. They were the only clans in the 'alliances' of the Katrakis family. It's like living in the fourteenth century, right?"

"What is this? It sounds like there's going to be a war, for your family to need *alliances*." I chortle at my own joke. "And it only applies to women? Why?"

"I have no idea."

"That's totally unfair. What if I'm a Katrakis and I fall for someone from a different family. What would they do to me?"

"They'd kick you out."

My jaw drops. "As simple as that? Wow. I'm thankful I wasn't born in your family."

"You can say that. If only I could have chosen my family, I would've done it."

Chills run down my spine, and I grimace. "Oh my God. It's basically marrying a distant cousin. It's allowed now in the law, but I can't..." I shake my head in sheer disbelief. I feel suddenly ill. "You're right. I'm just going to hurt my brain."

"Stupid, isn't it? Why do you think we're here? Brandon despises the laws. *That* in particular."

"Yes, I figured." I'd probably just run away too.

His eyes gleam. "I like talking to you," he remarks frankly. "Your eagerness to learn things... It's what I like the most."

My cheeks redden. "Thanks." No one has ever spoken to me this straightforwardly, yet so sweetly.

"Now, would you like me to help you prepare for

Brandon's dinner?"

I look up at his handsome face. "Well, that's my job."

We begin sorting out the ingredients. Oliver assigns me to prepare the side dish while he takes care of the main dish as he continues to answer all my questions. But I'm careful not to ask too much. I don't want to cross any lines.

I find myself watching him move around the kitchen. I love how he exudes confidence, and I always find men who know their way around the kitchen sexy.

As I'm chopping vegetables, it suddenly strikes me odd that Master Brandon doesn't bear any of the mentioned family names. He's a Lucien.

CHAPTER TWO

BRANDON

Try not to make it too creepy... Try not to make it too creepy...

It's really simple. She'll just have to pick up the damn phone, and I'll ask her what I need. It's not like I'm going to show her my face.

It's very little information in exchange for a fortune I made sure she can't decline. I saw her profile, so I knew exactly what she would need.

Damn it. But how am I supposed to talk to her if I'm this anxious?

I have not spoken to anyone besides my closest relatives for a long time. But this is the *first* time I think I'm close to reaching my objectives, and Oliver assured me that we finally found the right person.

That's what I hope, at least.

"Brandon?"

I swivel my chair around and meet Oliver's curious face. "Have you spoken to your new assistant? What is she like?" I ask.

"My new assistant or your new *informant*?" Oliver jokes and laughs. He pulls a chair in front of my desk and sits with his ankle resting on his knee.

I roll my eyes. "Oh, please."

"She's a little nervous and very curious, but I'm certain she's talented. Though I also think she's quite easy on the eyes." A smirk plays on the side of his mouth.

I throw a crumpled paper at him. "I don't care what she looks like! I need to know if she's cooperative enough so we can move forward with our plans. How about you speak to her instead of me?"

His eyes squint at me. "You know that you have to be the one to speak to her."

"You know my situation. I'll only creep her out," I retort. I pick up my stress ball and grip it to relieve my agitation.

"Don't be so hard on yourself. We can give it a little more time before moving forward, yes?" he says.

"I've waited long enough, don't you think?"

"She'll be around. Besides..." Oliver stands up and stretches out his arms. "I really need an assistant or someone I can trust with your meals. You have to get used to other people's cooking other than Lennie's and mine, and you know exactly what I mean," he says frankly, and he has every right to say those words to me. I can't depend on him my whole life like I've done in the past decade.

I'm well aware that Oliver has a life of his own. Nevertheless, I honestly can't imagine myself going through all this without him.

"And Lennie's not going to be here forever," he adds.

I gaze up at Oliver. "Neither can she," I say, referring to his new assistant.

"You're thinking too much. Relax, man. The future is uncertain," he implies and grins. "Anyway, I have to get your dinner ready."

ALAYNA

Over the past month, everything has been the same with Oliver and me. He is still funny, helpful, and I like being with him. I would've been so lonely if he weren't in the house. I feel like we can be good friends.

However, I've been busier than ever for the past few days. Oliver has been working long hours in the office and often comes home late. He's still the company's CEO, after all. Considering how much he does around the house, I'd almost forgotten.

We have not had many talks since then, as he is so busy. Similarly, Ms. Lennie will only come to my station when the food is ready to serve our boss in Oliver's absence.

I'm getting used to my job. I love making good food, and I've always dreamt of becoming a professional chef and owning a restaurant someday. Well, being an assistant chef means a lot more to me than being a food taster. Cooking has been my passion since my dad taught me how to move around the kitchen. He also used to tell me that good food is the way to reach people's hearts. And I believed him. It reached mine as well.

My profession has been my escape from my greatest nightmares. I just wish he were still here to see me and my achievements.

Today is my lucky day because lunch is beef stroganoff. This is the dish I feel I've already perfected; my mentor back in Venice would always praise me whenever I cooked it for her. I switch my mp3 music on, putting in my earphones before I start cooking.

I finish preparing the meal at eleven-thirty. I take out a bottle of Merlot from the mini wine cellar and place it on the marble island with a glass. I find a notepad and write a note on it.

"I made you a topping sauce. It's my own recipe. I hope you like it - Alayna."

I leave the condiments to mix together and close the lid. An hour later, Ms. Lennie finds me in the kitchen, bringing back empty dishware. I rejoice at the sign of a clean plate.

"Ms. Lennie." I greet her with a smile.

"Miss Hart," she says. I can tell by her tone she is about to reprimand me, and my smile fades. "Master Brandon likes the meal, but he said it's better if you don't leave notes and clear the tray, or he'll just throw it away. Didn't Mr. Katrakis tell you not to improvise?"

My mouth parted. She's talking about the condiments I don't see on the tray anymore. I couldn't understand what was wrong. He liked the meal, and he ate all of it. Why were they both upset?

"But I only did that because—"

She doesn't give me a chance to speak and leaves.

"Thanks, Ms. Lennie!" I shout to the door, unsure if she even heard me or not.

Of course, I remember the improvisation rule, but I am also a chef. Oliver always told me that written recipes are not everything. He entrusted me with his cousin's meal, and

I know that food should not be taken lightly.

At dinner, I make him *moussaka* and serve it with a parsley and mint salad and crusty bread. Deliberately, I take out my stick-on notes, writing another.

"I'm glad to hear that you like the food, but those condiments were needed. Also, I added an egg soup. Kalí óreksi!"

Ms. Lennie delivers empty dish wares to the kitchen a couple of minutes later and disappears. I guess our boss didn't complain this time, but then I notice a note on the pepper mill.

You make good food, Miss Hart, I give you that, but I don't think you need to add notes every time.

Oh my God! Did he just reply?

I smile in victory and laugh out loud. He has beautiful handwriting too.

Five days later, Oliver still isn't working in the kitchen, though I'm pretty much enjoying my job as the days go by.

Ever since I started writing notes to the elusive Brandon Lucien, I'm beginning to feel his presence—like I'm actually cooking for a person. He isn't so invisible anymore. He's actually, and peculiarly, responding to my notes.

For today's lunch, I heartily make him a marinated and smoked chicken with *tzatziki* sauce. This time, I make him brownies for dessert.

I write him a note again.

"Try the food with a glass of champagne. It tastes better."

Ms. Lennie doesn't seem to mind me anymore, but she always tastes the food before serving it to our boss. As usual, I never expect a reaction from her. When she returns, I find another note from him, and this time he provides a note clipper.

However, the brownie box went back untouched.

I read his note.

You're right. A glass of champagne does make it taste better. But weren't you told not to improvise? I don't eat brownies.

I laugh at his answer. I'd already started improvising, and he was eating it anyway.

"Someone's happy." Oliver's soothing voice snaps me out of my thoughts. He is leaning on the doorframe with arms crossed over his chest, looking regal in his bespoke three-piece gray suit. I don't usually see him in very formal business attire.

"Hi," I greet him. "I'm making a savory pie."

His eyes gleam. "Oh, wow. Would you give me some?"

"Sure. Let this cool for a second." I briefly stop mincing the garlic and move over the crockery to grab a plate. I put two slices on the plate and carefully set it in front of him.

"Thank you." He picks up a slice and takes a bite. "So, how's your day?"

"It's getting better." I grin. "How are you?"

"The crucial days in the office are over," he says. "I can work here again, but as I can see, you're getting used to it." Oliver flashes a smile and looks at me meaningfully.

"We're talking now," I say proudly and smile back.

"Yes, I heard about the notes." He takes another slice of pie. "But how did you manage to pull that one, hmm?"

"I guess he's telling you about it. I don't know." I shrug. "I just tried to write to him, but I didn't expect that he would respond."

"That's progress, and since Lennie is already up to her neck with house chores, I really needed someone I could count on whenever I'm absent. Like you."

"Right, but Ms. Lennie is still someone you can count on. She's just a bit busier than everyone," I comment. "I'm glad to work with you."

"Are you?" he teases, and he's got a playful smile on his lips again.

"You've been a good friend too."

His smile widens. "I wish to be friends with you too, Alayna." He puts down the fork on the side of the empty plate. "Thank you for this. I enjoyed the food."

"You're most welcome."

"I'll cook Brandon's dinner tonight," he offers and glances at the fish fillets on the prep area, then back at me. "You've been busy for the past few weeks. Why don't you go to my shelf now and grab my booklet?"

"Is it all right?"

"Yes, so we can start your next lesson. I have dishes I want to share with you."

I grin. "Thank you."

"I'll be right here."

I wash my hands thoroughly and take off my apron. Eager to see another one of Oliver's recipe collections, I hurry out of the kitchen and head to the library.

I only want to take the booklet, but the library is so tempting to explore, I decide to stroll around. I go to the library's second floor to check for more books, but the section is all about computers, systems, information technology—which isn't my thing. However, it makes sense since Grethe and Elga Enterprises is a leading technology company in New York.

I wander some more and find another door. I open it, thinking it could be the library's extension. But to my surprise, I stumble into another room with a king-sized bed. It isn't the library's extension at all! I'm in someone's room.

However, there's no sign of life inside, so I calm down, step back and find another door. Wanting to get out, I open the door, only to find out it isn't the exit I'm expecting.

A sound of running water coming from a shower catches my attention. My eyes widen in shock to find the broad, ripped back of a tall man. He has a slim waist, and his back has defined muscle cuts. I stagger back, but my eyes trail down to the most perfect, round butt I've ever seen in my life.

Every hair on the back of my neck stands at the sight of him. It isn't my first time seeing a man's butt—I've seen plenty, actually—but this man's ass is undeniably different from any I have seen before. He's incredibly sexy.

Oh my! Is that him?

I turn quickly, realizing I'm trespassing on someone else's privacy.

"Who's there?"

This is asked in an angry shout. I swiftly run out of the room until I miraculously find the door where I came from and escape through it. The stairway toward the mansion's left wing catches my view, and Ms. Lennie is waiting at the bottom. I'm even more nervous now. She is glaring at me, her arms crossed over her chest. When did she get there?

"Miss Hart." Her voice is tight. "Are you clueless, or can you simply not follow directions?" This is the first time in weeks that I'm getting the stern tone from her.

"I was in the library, and then—" I try to explain. "I got lost. I'm sorry." I stop and catch my breath.

"It's been a little more than a month, and you're already making trouble. I understand that this house is huge, bigger than you can imagine. What's unacceptable is your disobedience of my number one rule."

"What did I do?"

"The Master called me. He said someone was in his room."

Oh, gosh. Of course, it's him. Who else could it have been?

"You are the newbie here, so I believe it was you," she continues. "Mr. Katrakis had high hopes of you and he's never wrong, but I guess there's a first time for everything."

"I understand..." I answer humbly.

God, I don't want to disappoint Oliver now. Our working relationship is doing so well. What would he think about me now? He even entrusted me access to the library; surely, none of the employees could go there freely.

"I admit it, but like I said, I got lost! I will never deny my mistake, but I was hoping you would understand."

"I don't like the way you answered me. Follow me," she says with caution. She doesn't seem to like anything I do. Maybe she doesn't even like the fact that I'm breathing.

"Um, where are we going?"

"He wants to talk to the person who invaded his room. It's also the first time an employee gets fired on her first month."

"What? What do you mean, fired? This is crazy! I didn't mean to go into his room," I insist guiltily while walking fast behind her. My thoughts hover to millions of ways to convince her not to take me to the Master. I have a bad feeling about this. I'm not actually ready to see him yet.

But being ready wouldn't matter to him. And, well, I've already seen him. Not all of him, just his back. Unfortunately, I didn't get the chance to see his face.

However, the scene keeps playing in my mind. He is tall, with broad shoulders. His arms were spread wide, which made his triceps flex. He has ample legs that make me wonder how it would feel to be wrapped around them—

I shut my eyes. I have completely lost my mind.

"Miss Hart, it's time that you finally meet him." She spins around and finally faces me. "And just so you know, you don't need to see him to be able to talk to him."

Uh, what?

I quietly follow Ms. Lennie as we stroll through a corridor I haven't seen before. I can't help but overthink my situation. I suddenly want to speak with Oliver to apologize and probably ask him to help me with his cousin. I don't want to lose the job.

But how do I get away with this? How is it possible that I don't have to see him to be able to talk to him? What's the point of talking to me if he will fire me, anyway? Though I remember that he has every reason to. In the past weeks, I tried improvising dishes and sending him notes. Maybe he's already fed up with me.

We stop by another sculptured wooden door.

"The Master shall speak with you inside. You don't need to knock. You'll find a white door upon getting in. Open the door and sit in the chair provided." Her face is stone-cold. She is looking at the space behind me, avoiding my eyes. The way she explains it makes me feel like I'm visiting a prisoner.

I do what I'm told. There might be a chance I won't get fired if I obey quietly.

Ms. Lennie's stolid face vanishes slowly when she closes the door.

I'm surprised that the entrance looks sunny as I find the white door Ms. Lennie is referring to. It's probably the simplest door inside the mansion. It's flat white without any carvings or designs, with only a silver doorknob. I open it with my already sweaty palm.

I gasp at the sight inside. Another medium-sized, empty room appears in front of me. There is nothing on the walls, and everything is painted in white, except for a computer and a telephone placed on a glass table.

The entire room is giving me chills. It's like an interrogation room for criminals. I knew he was a bit eccentric, but this confirms my suspicions that he isn't normal at all. He's a weirdo.

Why would he put something like this in his house? Then I remember what Oliver told me before. He asked me not to freak out. Is this what he meant?

The telephone on the desk abruptly rings.

"Oh my God!" I yelp in surprise. I touch my chest, for my heart is pounding abnormally. All I can think about is running for my life. How could anyone expect me not to get freaked out by this?

"Answer the phone and sit," a cold, stern voice suddenly says loudly. I look up and find a large, implanted speaker in the gray ceiling.

God. This is creepy. I swallow. If I could only chew my nervousness like a delicious meal, I'd have a happy stomach.

"I believe I told you to sit," he says again, and honestly, his voice doesn't sound eerie at all. It even sounds... *melodious.*

But the realization hits me. How does he know I'm not

sitting?

Oh, no. He can see me. He can see how nervous and afraid I am.

I slowly walk toward the chair and sit down. I blow out a deep breath.

"Now, place the telephone to your ear so I can hear you speak," he instructs.

Hesitantly, I reach for the white wireless telephone, then place it to my ear. "Hello?"

"Good girl." The voice is still coming from the speakers and not through the telephone. This is getting more and more strange.

Is this man the famous billionaire, Chairman Brandon Lucien? I'm beginning to doubt it. What if he is really some psychotic man who murders—

No, no. He can't be that. I'm sure I entered the right house. Oliver Katrakis, the CEO of Grethe and Elga Enterprises, is definitely the man with whom I've worked the past month—which means this man over the phone is indeed the faceless chairman everyone speaks about. The man who answered my notes. I probably watched too many horror films.

"So, Alayna. Why did you come to my room?"

Okay, that was straightforward. "I was lost," I answer, not sure where I'm supposed to look.

"Yes, but no matter how significant your reason was, you still broke the number one rule in my house."

"I know," I whisper. "I'm sorry. It's just an accident—"

"I understand, but I'm afraid I can't accept your reason. It's a pity. I find you talented," he admits with a hint of disappointment in his voice.

"You do?" I burst out but cover my mouth instantly.

"Sorry." I lower my eyes in embarrassment.

"Yes. Honestly, you make my mealtime fun, and I'm getting used to your little notes. I like the food you make, but I'm afraid I have to fire you."

"I'm sorry. If you would at least give me a chance—"

"But I am so eager to fire you right now, Miss Hart," he says, cutting me off. "One thing I despise the most are absent-minded people." There is a long pause on his end. "But I need something only you can provide, so of course, I'm giving you a chance if you cooperate with me."

"What?" My voice rises. "What do you need from me?" What else can someone like me give to someone as wealthy as Brandon Lucien?

"I meant to speak to you. I'm sure Oliver already told you about that."

"Y-Yes... he did."

"I am giving you one week, a good compensation amount, but that's if you give me what I need. That is your only chance, Miss Hart, and then you are free to leave my house. You have nothing to lose."

My chin drops. Nothing to lose? He's firing me after a week! This job is everything to me now. Here I can cook to my heart's content, and I have a boss who helps me learn so much about my profession. Everything was working so great. Just why did I have to screw this up?

But then he said he would give me good compensation. Maybe I could try to negotiate.

I clear my throat. "What is it that you need from me, sir?"

"The *reason* why you are in my house."

Were there other reasons than working here?

I remember all the hints Oliver has been giving me. He meant it when he said I was chosen. He meant it when he said I will soon know why. Still, I don't fully understand.

My thoughts are interrupted when the computer on the desk suddenly turns on. An image of me and a middle-aged woman pops up on the screen.

Lucia Moretti. One of the best chefs I know. I met her at the culinary training center in Venice after graduating from the institute in Kansas. I enrolled in a six-month training course to broaden my knowledge of Italian cuisine, and she was my mentor.

"What do you want from her?" I ask.

"Good. Judging by your question, I believe you remember her. This is what I need from you. I want you to tell me where she is," he demands, like it is so easy. Like I'd just know exactly where she is at this moment.

Did he hire me for this?

"What? I don't think I can do that."

"Why not?"

"Because it's been a long time. I can't know exactly where she is right now or if she's still there..." I half-lie. I *do* know where she is. I've spoken to her after I left the training school, and she's pretty much open to me with things about herself. But I couldn't just give a stranger such information.

What if this man is some sort of thug? No normal person would speak only on a telephone when he could ask me himself.

"As I said, you will receive better compensation if you cooperate."

"This is what you meant? First thing, providing information like that to a stranger is illegal. Lucia can sue me for invading her privacy."

And did he really think I could be bought with money?

"Lucia?" he repeats, sounding confused.

"Yes, her name. Lucia... Moretti."

"I guess she goes by another name now," he says in a low tone but a little exasperated. "Did she tell you that's her name?"

I frown. "Why would she lie about it?"

"Her name... Her real name is Annette Teller. She's *Italian* now, I see," he says sarcastically.

Oh crap. I gave him more information than he already had. "What? I'm not sure what you're talking about."

"Is she still in Italy? When was the last time you've heard from her?"

"I told you I don't know." I look down.

"Why do I think you're not telling me everything?" He exhales. "Miss Hart, if you can just tell me everything, you will be compensated. That is a promise."

His proposal instantly makes me ponder. It would absolutely change my family's life. I'm sure the compensation he mentioned isn't just a few dollars. I suddenly imagine living in a mansion like this with my twelve siblings and seeing my mother healthy and strong again because I would finally be able to get her scoliosis treated.

However, something so easy must hide a risk. One thing I learned from my mother; money shouldn't be treated lightly. It should be hard-earned.

I hold my breath and answer firmly, "I don't know where she is."

"Miss Hart. Doesn't your mother need medical attention? Neuromuscular scoliosis, am I correct?"

My cheeks flare. "How did you know that?" I almost squeal angrily. "That's an invasion of privacy!"

"You're not the only one who can do research, Miss

Hart," he points out.

"But not up to this point—"

"Just answer the question."

I gulp hard. "Yes, s-she does."

"And has a debt of twenty thousand to the bank."

I feel my blood drain from my face. Those debts were because of my mother's medication too. I shut my eyes briefly and exhale a breath.

"Fine, that's enough."

"Good, because I strongly believe you can gain something from this if you'd just tell me something useful. I'll pay for your mother's medication, settle your debts for you, and you will be rewarded with a prize you've never touched in your life."

His first words sounded as sweet as heaven, but this man is certainly so full of himself.

"Are you belittling me?" I ask.

"I'm just stating the facts."

Wow. I'm almost out of words. "Why are you telling me this just now? Why not when I started working here? It doesn't make sense. I feel like this is the only reason why I'm here."

"And now you're belittling yourself. I did say you have a talent."

"But you were going to fire me. I can't help you with that, Mr. Lucien—I mean, Master..."

"Then this conversation is useless," he says. "You are right, Miss Hart. You're fired."

CHAPTER THREE

Is he going to fire me over some information? I couldn't lose this job. I have debts, and I have no place to stay in this foreign city. I can't just go back home, bringing nothing but failure to my family. Well, of course, I still need money, but this job was way more ethical than receiving unlabored cash.

"Wait..." I give up. He's firing me anyway, so why not talk back? "First of all, you signed me up to a one-year contract. You can't just fire people just because you want to. That's against the law. My job description is an assistant chef, and what you are asking now isn't written in the contract. Second, what you are asking for is very private. I can't just give such information away to strangers, especially to a stranger like you. Why do you want it anyway? I at least want an explanation. Lastly, in all honesty, I can't trust someone who would speak with me this way. I can't even *see* you."

"I hired you, Miss Hart. What makes you think I don't have the right to fire you? And in all honesty, too, I enjoy firing stubborn people, especially those who don't seem to know when to zip their mouth," he adds, not hiding the unpleasant tone in his voice.

"I beg your pardon?"

"I think you're forgetting something here. You went into my room, and you watched me while I was in the shower. If that isn't *unlawful* enough, then I don't know what is. But you've made your point, and for your information, I'm not just a stranger."

"What are you to her then? A child she doesn't know about?" I mock.

"No, but she was acquainted with my father. Then I found out you were the last person she interacted with in Venice."

Another picture appears on the screen—a picture of Lucia and me walking in Campo San Rocco two years ago.

"Bastardo," I mumble in Italian. "Why do you have this?"

"You see, I'm not supposed to tell you this; I've been looking for her for a very long time, but she's gone. I can't find her anywhere in Italy anymore."

For someone who doesn't socialize, this man can talk a lot. However, I feel my face blanch with guilt. He does sound a bit desperate.

If he is so eager, I'd better make a deal. Mom's medication and payments for my debts should be enough, but this job is important too. I can't leave this house and lose the opportunity because I opened a wrong goddamn door in the library. I might as well try to offer him my terms.

I think about the situation thoroughly. I won't be able to tell him where he can find Lucia or Annettewhatever he prefers—because Lucia told me she was moving to teach at the University of West London. I asked for her email address because I didn't want to lose the connection. We exchanged emails in the first few months, but one day she stopped answering.

"I knew her for six months when I was in Venice," I begin. "She was my teacher, but she's not in Venice or anywhere in Italy right now. So no, you won't find her there."

There is a long pause on his end. I wonder if he collapsed or just decided to cut our conversation.

"Where is she now?"

I jerk when I hear him talk. I thought he'd dismissed me already. "Fine. I will tell you. Let's make a deal."

"This should be worth it."

I shrug. "Apart from your offer earlier, you're not going to fire me."

"Miss Hart, aren't you listening to me? I don't need people like you in my house."

I roll my eyes. That remark hits me hard, but I won't bend just because his voice is so commanding. "Please, if you'd just listen to me."

He doesn't answer.

"First, I'm really sorry. I wish you'd believe that what happened today was an accident. This job means a lot to me—"

"Quit the introduction and tell me your terms," he snaps.

"All right. I will accept the support for my mother's medication, the settlement of my debts, but I won't accept the additional cash compensation. I want another employment contract. Make it two years," I demand.

"Done. Anything else?"

Whoa! That escalated quickly. He even sounded bored.

"Tell me, why are you looking for Lucia if she's related to your father? You could just ask him and—"

"That's a private matter, and it doesn't concern you," he interjects.

"Fine. I'm sorry."

I knew to stop prodding the issue. I have to fight for my rights and my job, but there is no need to bring up intimately personal matters.

"What else it is that you want, Miss Hart?"

"I need the contract first, and then I'll give you her location."

"I'll have it ready," he declares. "Oliver will give you another contract."

"Do it privately, if you please." I'm not sure if this was going to work, but I have to try. "This might be too much to ask, but let's just say I need to trust you. What you want from me isn't simple. I should at least see the person I'll be giving the information to."

"I—" he pauses. "I cannot do that, Miss Hart."

"Let's do the contract signing privately. That or I'll leave. Your chance to know where Lucia is will be gone forever."

I don't know where I got the courage to say those words because I'm just as afraid that he'll say no, and I'll really lose my job. But in all honesty, it's not just because of what Oliver said. I can't make a deal with a person who can't even show himself.

"Who do you think you are to tell me what to do?"

Seems like my proposition wouldn't work. "Goodbye. I'm packing my things right now because finally I've found a reason to." I stand up and put the phone down. I start counting my steps mentally as I turn.

One... two... three...

"Hey!"

I knew you'd do that! I smile. Lucia seems like a great deal to him. She can't be his lover because Lucia was already forty-five years old when I met her.

I walk back, then place the phone to my ear.

"Yes?" I answer confidently.

"I don't meet people just like that."

"Yes, but I need to see you sign the contract in front of me. I need to make sure you won't fire me after you get what you want. Let's just say that I have trust issues. What's so hard about that?"

"How did I ever stumble across a woman like you?" he remarks irritably. I know if he had a choice, he would have me dragged out of his house.

"And what are you afraid of?" I dare to ask.

"You better be careful with your words, Miss Hart."

What I said to him made me feel guilty right away, but I tense up. "Do it privately or throw me out of your creepy dungeon," I say with a flat tone and put the phone down. *I have to go,* I murmur, but I was sure he didn't hear me.

"Get back here!" His voice echoes throughout the whole room, and the phone rings once again. "Pick up the damn phone!"

I rush out of the room. Ms. Lennie is still at the door when I come out, standing like a statue and wearing her expressionless face like an expert. The people in this house don't have any sense of humor at all—except for Oliver, of course.

"He didn't fire me."

"I know. He just called."

Really? That was fast.

"I don't know what you did to our master, but I'm bothered," she comments. "I've known him since he was a kid, and I raised him until he reached eighteen. He closed his life to everyone outside this door, and I can't believe you actually asked him to come out," she says, trying to avoid my gaze.

"I didn't do anything. But he needed something important, and no one in this world could give that to him, except me," I said truthfully and proudly.

Her mouth twitches. "If you're done talking, then follow me now."

My shoulders fall. "Where are we going?"

"To your workstation. You're going to work now as his private chef."

"His what?" I squeal but cover my mouth immediately. "But that's Mr. Katrakis' position."

She stops. "Are you following me or not?"

"Oh." I mirror her pace and follow her to the central kitchen, but instead of stopping, we turn left to another door—like an extension.

Ms. Lennie opens the door. It's a kitchen I haven't seen before, but a smaller one. All equipment provided in the central kitchen is all here—only compacted in less space, but it looks terrific. I will be able to move around here comfortably.

"Another kitchen? Why? I'm fine with the central kitchen."

"This kitchen belonged to someone before, and don't bother asking who. Master Brandon wants you to use it. Treat this place carefully."

I nod obediently. "Am I the only one who's going to work here?" I ask instead, still feeling astonished.

"Yes, and thanks to you, Mr. Katrakis doesn't have to make the Master's meal anymore. I'm going to leave you here. Treat this kitchen as your own."

"Thanks."

I can't figure out if her statement is sarcastic or not. Her tone is monotonous. I never even asked the boss for another job position, and I didn't mean to take over Oliver's place. Guilt suddenly floods over me.

BRANDON

I've never been closer to finding one of the persons who could be the reason for my family's demise before. Finding those murderers has become my life's purpose. They ruined my life enough.

Annette Teller, my father's fucking mistress. Oliver and I have been looking for her for a long time, and this very intriguing chef is bearing the information in her hands.

For some reason, this Alayna Hart has triggered something in me—something inexplicable. I'm very meticulous with the food I consume, as it is one of the few things that can bring me joy in this very boring life. Oliver knows I won't eat something my tongue would despise. But Alayna makes every meal special, despite not following the rules about improvising. Her little handwritten notes, I admit, are entertaining.

Strangely, the person who can bring delight to my meals is also the person who could end my agony. I craved and longed for justice in this life, and I'm finally close to that reality. That way, I may finally get my redemption.

Ten years ago, I was there when they died. I saw Elga's lifeless, ruined body with my own eyes and how my mother cried my name with her last breath. But I couldn't do anything. I was too weak to even save myself. I was just a guy who only knew how to fuck up his life—someone who only lived for himself and left his family in darkness.

I can never bring them back, but I should at least give them the justice they deserve.

However, Miss Hart demanded to see me. It's one of the things I fear the most. And for the first time in a very long time, I'm stuck behind a wall I created.

CHAPTER FOUR

ALAYNA

I heard what you did," Oliver says the next morning when I see him. He's not in his usual chef uniform but his gym clothes. He steps into my kitchen.

I instantly feel apologetic. "I'm sorry. I didn't mean to take your position."

"Nah. I should be thanking you. You've proven you can do the job alone, and you're saving me, after all." He slides his hands in his pocket, smiling. "You've given me more time to focus on other important things."

"Um... I asked him to come out." I shrug.

His eyebrows knit together. "Yeah? How did it go?" He leans on the sink.

"I didn't mean to ask him to come out immediately; I just got carried away in the situation, and I remembered what you said. Besides, I can't think of any way to make him come out unless there's a valid reason. And I'm sure you know the reason."

"Hmm." He crosses his arms and scratches his chin. "Yes, I do."

"And why has no one told me the real reason I'm here?" I ask nicely, although I'm sure all the decisions are up to his cousin.

"Okay, if you feel like I've hidden this from you, I'm sorry. But we can't afford to lose you."

"I'm not going to leave. I need this job." I look up at him. "But another reason why I wanted to see him is that the information he wants is confidential. It's more on the trust side. I need to know if I can trust him."

He listens to me intently and nods. "I understand. You are entitled to your rights."

"Though I have to apologize. I was pretty reckless back there. If I could turn back time, I wouldn't be that insensitive. But when I was talking to him in that room, it was strange. How does he live like this?"

"It's been difficult, Alayna. It was his choice."

"I'd be lying if I told you that I didn't want to know his reasons. It's not my place to meddle with your business, but somehow I did," I say with guilt. I stare back at the spices I'm mixing and pick up the ladle.

"Let's just say your way is a bit different, but this is why I think you are the person most capable of helping him. He will tell you about the thing he needs from you anyway, despite the little incident. But did you really see him?"

I shake my head. "No. At least... not his face."

"Nice timing," Oliver continues in a teasing voice.

I flush. "What bugs me right now was my proposition. I asked him to come out! I don't know where I got all the nerve to demand that."

"You're torturing yourself." Oliver moves in front of me and holds my shoulders. "Calm down. He might be, you know, weird, but he's a good man. He's considerate. He even let you stay, remember?"

"Because he needs something," I answer, then roll my eyes. "I'm not this kind of person."

"I know. You don't have to worry about that. You must've forgotten that I'm still here to help you. So, what's on his menu today? I don't always memorize everything."

"I prepared a *courgette* and *Kostopoulos* lemon."

"Well, I will bring this to him now."

"Wait!" I halt and add the additional spices I made for the chicken. Oliver then picks up the plates and places them on the food trolley.

At dinner, Oliver still isn't home, so Ms. Lennie takes our boss's meal to his room. This time she asks me to follow her. I don't know why, but I do as I'm told. We stop at his room, and she knocks three times. Not waiting for someone to answer, she opens and unlocks the door.

"Stay here," she demands sharply.

"Oliver doesn't usually ask me to come. Why am I here?"

"The Master has something he wishes to say to you."

I nod in silence. The supposed contract signing will be tomorrow. I tap my feet and bite my lower lip as I watch Ms. Lennie continue inside.

Ms. Lennie comes back a few moments later with the empty dishware. Undoubtedly, he likes what I made for him again.

"What did he say?"

"He did not complain about the meal," she informs me with a blank expression.

I smile in victory. "But did he say something about my contract? Is he going to privately see me?"

"Master Brandon said he wanted to talk to you," she repeats firmly, her expression blank as usual. "You can't just force him like that. He is a very busy man. Isn't it enough that Mr. Katrakis believed your scheme? You had to involve him in your plan?"

Scheme? Plan? This woman surely thinks I'm such a gold digger. This is why I like talking to Oliver more than her. Her strict character bothers me. She is so overprotective; she can be insensitive with her judgment. And why does she have to be hard on me all the time?

"Sorry, I just needed assurance. I didn't mean to look like I'm only taking advantage of the situation. I'm going to speak to him now."

I don't wait for her to speak about something else again and march toward the white room. I open the door and sit in the chair inside. I pick up the telephone.

"Hello?"

No answer.

"Anybody here?"

Nothing again.

I sigh, shaking my head. "Hello?"

I jerk in surprise when the speaker produces ear-shattering whistles, and I hear his voice again. "Good evening, Miss Hart."

"G-Good evening. Why did you ask me here?" I ask, trying to calm myself.

"I need some time," he says, and I sense the tension in his voice. "I'm going to have to arrange the contract first and speak to my lawyer. Why would you want to see me in the first place?" No hint of anger in his very masculine voice anymore.

"I was just... you are..." I breathe. "I don't know what the hell's going on with me anymore," I confess truthfully. "But I need to trust you, and I can only do that if you show yourself to me." I also don't want to end up like Ms. Lennie, who became humorless.

"I am a monster, Miss Hart," he states gruffly. "You wouldn't want to see me... if you only knew."

"Knew what?"

"This conversation is over." He drops the call and disappears from the line.

What the heck was that?

My head throbs in pain. Everything is more complicated now. I walk out of the room and decide to go to the central kitchen, wishing to speak to a normal human being. Perhaps Oliver. Fortunately, he's there, in a designer suit. He's having a sandwich. I can't help but chuckle.

"Alayna, join me. I made sandwiches."

I look at the food on the island, and my stomach rumbles. It looks delicious. "Hey, thanks. I'd love to. When did you arrive?"

"About thirty minutes ago."

I approach him and pick a slice. He watches me as I take a bite. "Hmm." I gaze at him in surprise and swallow the food. "*Porchetta*."

He grins. "Right? I knew you'd like it. You're fond of Italian cuisine."

"And the bread... It's *ciabatta*." I eat another bite, bigger this time. "Hmm. It's delicious. You know what actually confuses me?"

"What?" He munches on his sandwich as well.

"How you two are cousins. You're crazy if you don't notice the huge difference between you."

He cocks his head. "What do you mean?"

"I spoke to him again. In the creepy white room."

"Oh." His expression brightens. "Tell me more."

"He said he'll give me the contract, but I have to wait."

"But that's a start, right? It's progress."

"I don't know. He is so enigmatic, and there's... never mind. He's odd."

"You'll get along with him soon," he states, so sure of himself. "He's not always like that." He munches on his food again.

"I don't know about that. But I hope you're right. He's my boss, after all. I mean, the higher boss." I shrug and chuckle. "Thank you, by the way."

"For what?"

"For being normal."

He chuckles back. "You're welcome. Good night, Alayna."

"Good night, Oliver."

I can see half of his face through a shaft of light that slips from somewhere in the room. I want to step back, but I'm pinned to the wall with his hands on my wrist, pushing me a little harder. His breathing rapid, his chiseled mouth almost touching mine. A familiar smell of aftershave tickles my nose.

"Alayna Hart!"

"Oh God—" I look around me as the sharp sound of bells ring.

Ms. Lennie glares at me. She is holding a small bell, enough to wake a girl who had an intimidating dream. Next to her are two maids who look precisely alike, and they are staring at me. Obviously, they are trying their hardest not to laugh. Their small, marble eyes betray their fake expressionless look. I feel my face burning with shame.

What are they doing here?

"The Master will see you in ten minutes. He expects you to be early," Ms. Lennie says.

"What? He's—he's what? Why?" I ask in a panic. "What did I do wrong now?"

"For your information, young lady, you forced the Master hand with your conditions. I want you out of your bed now and stop complaining. He sent these clothes for you to wear to your breakfast with him," she explains. My eyes travel to what they are holding. A white-silk bulky dress and white flat shoes patterned with sequins.

I frown. *"Breakfast?"* He's really—never mind! I rush out of bed, grabbing the shoes and the dress.

The twins jerk, shocked by my sudden move.

"We're supposed to help you with that, miss—"

I hold up my hand, signaling them to stop. They eye each other, then settle their gaze back on mine.

"I can do this all by myself, thank you," I say and waltz toward the bathroom.

I gargle mouthwash and search for dry shampoo. "Moisturizer, hair mask, shower gel—no. Where is it? There! Dove!" I've certainly formed a habit of talking to myself in private. I open the cap and spray the shampoo on my hair.

I didn't know working in a mansion could be such torture. How am I supposed to get ready within the ten-minute lag he gave me? Ms. Lennie just woke me up!

I quickly put on the dress, but I notice it has too many ties.

Ties? Ties don't zip. Zipper zips, not ties. How am I going to tie this up all by myself?

I go out of the bathroom, almost tripping. Ms. Lennie and the twins are still in my room. I heave a sigh of relief.

"Turn around and swallow your pride. You can't tie that dress in a perfect knot alone," Ms. Lennie scolds. I lazily turn my back on the twins. "Don't you have any sense of fashion in you?" she questions. "Take off your bra."

The maids secretly laugh.

Wait. Take my bra off?

"Are you kidding? I'm going to have breakfast with him and not wear a bra? Isn't that a little inappropriate? I should be presentable!"

"Yes, you should be. And this bra could slip out of that dress. Didn't you notice the padding?"

I place both my hands in front of the dress and squeeze it a little. *The padding.* Yeah, there is padding. But no, I had not, in my entire life, tried to go out of my room without wearing a brassiere.

"No!"

"The Master isn't going to strip you, young lady! I can't even believe he'll actually show himself after all these years."

"It's uncomfortable. God, I'm only going to eat breakfast with him. Why is everyone overreacting?"

She doesn't answer the question. She unhooks my bra and grabs it out. "You'll feel comfortable soon enough. You'll feel the padding doing its job."

I roll my eyes. "You are curious too, aren't you?" I ask, raising both my arms so the dress perfectly fits my body.

"I know his family. I've been working for them for a long time." She tightens the knot on the dress. "To be honest with you, I want to know how this meeting will go. I am expecting you to tell me how he is in front of someone else." Her voice softens. It is surprising to see this side of her.

I smile a little. I can see that she cares for him. "Sure."

"Come, now. I'll take you to the dining room."

"To the dining room? He's going to show himself to everyone?"

"No. It's just you and the Master."

I blow out a sharp breath. "I'm ready."

Ms. Lennie takes me to the mansion's dining room. We stop at the entrance, and the maids gather around her.

"This is how far I can take you. Mr. Katrakis will serve breakfast in about an hour, and that will give you and Master Brandon enough time to talk. You are late, as usual. He might be inside when you go in."

"Thank you, Ms. Lennie. I've been looking forward to this day."

She doesn't smile, but her expression is pleasant. "Good luck, and you don't have to knock."

I never bother knocking. When I get in, I expect him to be sitting, waiting impatiently at the long table, but he isn't. He is standing in front of a beautiful painting of a young girl in a yellow dress. It's as if the girl is staring at him. I beam when I realize he really is the man from the bathroom. He has the same features of the man who stands in front of me, the same perfect back covered in a black bespoke designer suit that impeccably hugs his body.

I clear my throat, loudly enough to catch his attention. "Hi..."

"I know you are there, Miss Hart," he says icily, yet the melodious sound is there. He is still looking at the painting.

"I'm sorry I had to do this."

"Sit down, Miss Hart."

I tug at the chair on the other side of the long dining table and sit quietly.

The world seems to have stopped, then slows down as he turns to show himself to me. His face. Half of this face has precisely the same features of the handsome young man in the painting in the living room. I'd stared at it every day for the last month, so I was sure of this. But he doesn't show me his entire face. He's wearing a mask.

A white mask on the right side of his face.

He settles across from me. He places a black folder in front of him and taps it three times.

"This is your contract. I want you to watch me sign this using my own hand"—he lifts his fist, showing me his thumb—"as you have asked for."

I don't fully understand what he's just said. I'm too distracted looking at his exquisite male beauty. Even showing only half of his face, it is undeniable.

Intense gray eyes, dark, wavy hair that falls right at the back of his neck. His bone structure is defined, and he is savagely breathtaking. His undershirt and suit are both black, but his tie is a dark gray that matches his mysterious eyes.

There is no single trace of Oliver's genes in his features. While Oliver is golden and charming, his cousin's presence alone radiates power and dominance. The natural reaction of a typical person is to be creeped out, given the mask on his face. But I find myself captivated.

"Miss Hart?"

"Hi. Yes?"

"Did you hear what I just said?"

"Yes." My eyes are still glued to the unmasked side of his face.

He looks away, but my gaze follows his movement. "Don't stare at me."

"Please, don't look away." I don't know where my words came from.

"Don't what?"

"Don't look away," I repeat softly.

He clears his throat. "Let's proceed, Alayna."

"Say that again."

"Alayna, please..."

"Mister Lucien, I mean, Master Brandon. I—you—um, you are wearing a mask."

His jaw ripples and he almost crumples the paper he's holding. "Does it bother you?"

"No, no. I'm just wondering why."

"It has nothing to do with our deal." He finally faces me. I almost fall out of my seat. All those times I looked at the painting... I never expected that the portrait would really turn out to be him.

"You're the young man in the painting."

He peers at me. "How do you know?"

"I just know. It's you."

He lets out an exasperated breath. "If you still want your contract, I don't want you to say anything that doesn't have to do with our deal."

"I'm sorry. I'm just surprised. But you're here, physically, and I'm glad you showed up." I smile.

"You're not going to say anything to Lennie. If you do, I won't hesitate to terminate this contract. Do you understand?"

Why? She is so worried about him. "Sure."

"And stop looking at me like that."

"I'm sorry, you're just so—so beautiful." My eyes widen in shock when the words hang in the air. I cover my mouth and look down at my lap.

Silence fills the room for a couple of seconds. I'm thinking of a reason to divert his attention.

"The painting!" I cry. "Uh... the girl in the painting, she's beautiful. Who is she?" I ask, then swallow hard, praying he won't remember what I've just said.

How can I be so stupid? One doesn't make comments expressing admiration for such a dangerous person. How could I even say those words so quickly? All I wanted was to know why he was hiding from the world when he had nothing to be ashamed of.

His expression is annoyed. He stares at me with a questioning look, then takes a deep breath.

"I could fire you right away for being too nosy. You'd better be thankful that the information you have won't make you a jobless newbie."

Wow! I exclaim mentally. Am I supposed to thank him then? It was he who made such fuss about it after telling me he was still going to fire me. I only protected my rights.

"Yes, and unfortunately, I still have that information," I retaliate. His sex appeal shouldn't outwit me.

I must admit, I'm enchanted with him. I don't know how or why since he is so mysterious. Oliver is also attractive, but a burning force and intense magnetism just radiate from his cousin.

This man... Damn! I can't help but admire his physique. It's a shame he doesn't have a good character.

"You are one intriguing woman," he says. "Let's get this done. I can't stand being here for too long."

I clear my throat. "Of course, but this is your home. Could you at least stay until breakfast? I heard from Ms. Lennie that we're going to—"

"Could you please stop your machine-gun mouth and give this room a bit of silence?" He shuts his eyes briefly, then stares back at me dangerously. His lack of interaction with people has changed him into some caveman.

Calm down, tactless lioness, I remind myself.

"I'm sorry. I know it's none of my business. I'm just curious."

"Curiosity kills the cat; ever heard of that? Now, let's proceed to the signing of the contract."

My lips twitch in guilt. "Of course."

"In the file placed in front of you is a copy of the contract. I want you to read the contents carefully. Any questions and objections shall be entertained after you read everything. Until then, please try to stay quiet," he adds brusquely.

I look down at the folder lying on the table in front of me. I open the first page, then read the content.

Employment Contract dated this 11th Day of October 2020

Between

Mr. Brandon Katrakis Lucien

Chairman

Grethe and Elga Enterprises

And

Miss Alayna G. Hart

Private Chef

Miss Alayna Hart shall be employed full-time as a Private Chef to Brandon Andre Lucien, from the 11th day of October 2020 to the 10th day of September 2022.

1. Miss Hart shall provide all the information about Annette Teller as a part of this contract, as and where permitted by Law.

2. Miss Hart must complete two (2) years of employment beginning with the commencement date to the end date, as and where allowed by Law.

3. Miss Hart will be paid her wages twice a month. She will have her rightful benefits and bonuses twice a year.

4. Miss Hart is entitled to paid annual leave (sickness, vacation, and maternity leave ranging from 15 to 30 days and 150 days for maternity leave).

5. Miss Hart is entitled to sickness allowance.

6. Mr. Lucien shall provide medical assistance to Mrs. Elizabeth Hart and settle all Miss Alayna Hart's debts from her creditors.

7. Mr. Lucien shall end the employment with no prior notice and compensation other than wages for hours of work already completed, as permitted by law, if the employee violates rules and regulations.

Signed by:

Brandon Katrakis Lucien

Chairman, Grethe and Elga Enterprises

I nod slowly, trying to think of something to demand. I fail, as expected.

"It seems fair enough. I have no questions," I mumble as I try to hide my delight.

It is more than fair! He is unexpectedly generous. What more could I ask? He's providing me bonuses and benefits. It's more than the average benefit an employee can have working in a different company.

"Good." He clears his throat. "Before I sign this, Miss Hart, let me remind you of our deal. Are you one hundred percent sure of Annette's whereabouts?"

"Absolutely one hundred percent. I promise." I hold up a hand. "After we parted, we were exchanging emails. In the bottom email is her work information. You'll be able to find her that way, I guess. I can write it down for you, but I have to check my email first. Do you want me to get it for you?"

"We'll take care of that later. Now I will sign everything, and I'll give you time to review your copy. You can bring it to me after."

"I—uh, I could just ask Oliver to bring it to you too."

"Let's not pretend like you aren't involved in my private life. You asked for this, and I don't think letting you in my room will make a difference," he answers as he presses his thumb on the ink pad in front of him.

"You can't possibly call that a private life. You never even answered any of my questions." Including showing himself to me in an odd way—wearing a mask and all. God! I'm beginning to have a habit of retaliating now.

He stops, then looks straight at me. "Besides being nosy, you are certainly overreacting," he comments. "I'm not done signing the contract. I'm thinking of changing my mind."

"Fine." I give up. "I won't say anything. Please sign my contract."

He finally presses his thumbprint on the contract and adds his signature. The dining room begins to feel humid. My dress doesn't feel comfortable anymore.

"Now, always remember I can and will terminate this contract if you are lying," he warns coldly.

Chills run down my spine. *Act cool, lady, act cool.*

I abruptly feel a pang of pain in my stomach. I'm starving.

He checks his wristwatch. "Oliver will be here in a moment."

I nod, smiling slightly. "Oh, right. He's allowed to see you."

"Yes. He's the only family I trust."

"He's your cousin, after all."

"I noticed you've been very close to Oliver," he observes.

My forehead furrows in confusion.

Oh, of course, he knows! Oliver probably opened up to him about me, and even if he didn't, I noticed that the house is fully installed with CCTVs. For the sake of privacy, the employees' rooms are an exception, of course.

"I guess so. He's helping me out," I answer, trying to make myself comfortable.

"Good morning, Brandon, Alayna." Oliver's cozy voice suddenly fills the room. "Am I interrupting something?" he adds as he walks toward us, carrying a tray stuffed with our breakfast.

"Just in time, Ollie. We're done with the contract signing," Brandon answers.

Mr. Katrakis places the plates in front of me. It's a full French breakfast with salmon fillets, eggs, crème Fraiche, brioche bread, and a cup of du lait chocolate.

"Thank you," I acknowledge, smiling.

"You're welcome," Oliver answers, then grins sweetly. He waltzes toward his cousin then puts the same plate of breakfast in front of him.

"Bon appétit," he says when he's done. "Call me if you need anything."

Master utters his thanks, and his cousin exits the room. His forehead furrows, but the corner of his lip twitches in what seems to be a smile.

My stomach once again demands food. I swallow as I stare down at my food.

"Getting really dreamy, huh?" he remarks, eating a portion of his food.

"What do you mean?"

"You like Oliver."

I shrug. "Well, what's not to like? He's very accommodating."

His face turns serious. "It's written all over your face." His gaze is piercing yet delicate. He puts down the fork and knife on either side of his plate. "Anyway, I'm going back to my room. Enjoy your breakfast."

CHAPTER FIVE

y jaw drops. What the hell was that?

I watch him swiftly wipe his lips with the napkin provided. Is it something I said? Something I did? Is it the food? I take a bite of the brioche, then pop it in my mouth. No, of course, it's not the food. It's delicious.

He stands up and takes several steps away from me, but my feet seem to have a mind of their own. I follow him in a flash, just in time to stop him from opening the door.

"Wait!" I yell as I grab his arm.

"Don't touch me!" he shouts, pulling his arm back. His voice is like the Beast's—Belle's Beast. My heart skips a beat.

His masked face looks down on me; he is glaring and breathing heavily. I stagger back.

"Rule number two. I hate being touched."

I shudder at the sound of his voice. I feel ashamed for only grabbing his arm. Is this another reason he hates going out of his room other than his hiding-from-the-whole-world game? He hates being touched?

I back away, feeling embarrassed. "I'm so sorry, I was wrong. It won't happen again." I breathe a sigh of sadness, realizing that I crossed the line. I shouldn't have asked him to come out.

He says through gritted teeth, "If hating you can be a rule, I'd be happy putting it as number one. You are very brazen and presumptuous. You need to behave." He steps forward and lowers himself to my height. He is too tall compared to my five-foot-three. He leans over to my ear, then breathes on my neck. I'm not able to answer. I almost stumble. "Someone should teach you, Miss Hart. It's a shame I can't."

Electricity flares all over my body through his words alone. I gasp at how my body reacts to him. He didn't even touch me. I didn't know such a feeling was possible. Unless, of course, he is using a black-magic spell on me.

My inner self chuckles at my thoughts. What's up with me, thinking that a billionaire would use black magic to make my knees tremble if he can do it effortlessly?

He pulls back, then turns around. "Don't forget the address. Bring it to me at dinner."

He walks away, leaving me breathless and unsettled.

It is afternoon when Ms. Lennie comes to my kitchen while I'm preparing dinner for the almighty Master.

I have been ill at ease for the last few hours. I'm bothered by his earlier actions. He was too dark. He's unfathomable. And he was wearing a mask. Yet I'm still enthralled.

"You seem troubled," Ms. Lennie observes.

"I just spoke with a person who has hidden from the world all his life. Maybe I just can't get over it," I answer while stirring the corn and kernel cheese soup I'm making.

"How did it go?" she asks icily.

"He signed the contract and we spoke of a few things before breakfast, but his mood changed so suddenly. He walked out on me."

"Is that all?" she asks. "Did you do something odd again that angered him?"

"Nothing, believe me."

"Well, your talent in cooking is unquestionable, but you are rather clumsy at times," she remarks in a flat tone.

Is she scolding me now or something?

"This time, I don't think I did anything." I stop and turn off the stove. I pick up the pot and transfer the soup to the bowl.

"That smells nice," she says.

"Thank you." I lift the bowl and move it to the island to prepare it with the rest of the dish. "You know... I didn't like how he didn't even eat his breakfast," I continue, unsure why I'm suddenly talking to her. "I dressed up for it, and I felt insulted. I couldn't help but get mad. I had a reason, then he told me I needed to behave? I think that applies best to him."

She tenses. "It's been a long time since the Master locked himself away from the world. You are the first person who made him come out after a decade. What does he look like?"

"He's tall and—" I pause. Oh, no! I remembered I wasn't supposed to say anything to Ms. Lennie. I promised to keep my mouth shut. Unfortunately, I just told her half of everything. *What's holding you back?*

"He's fine," I add.

"He's fine? Are you blind, young lady? He is good-looking, isn't he?"

I glance at her in surprise. I didn't expect those words from her.

But yes, he is. I thought the unmasked side half of his face was beautiful, but I decide not to tell her our boss was wearing a mask.

"Don't say that aloud," I hiss. "He might hear you. It might get into his head." I shake my head in disbelief. Besides, I shouldn't care what he looks like.

"Your reaction showed enough attraction," she points, crossing her arms over her chest.

"I don't feel it. His character doesn't even allow me to consider his physical traits."

"But I hope this will make you realize that our master isn't cruel. He won't bother himself this much just for a piece of information."

"I understand." I slip my hand in my pocket and feel the paper in my palm—the piece of paper he needs. I wrote Lucia's whereabouts on it.

"I should go now, Miss Hart. I still have things to do. Hurry with that soup."

"Yes, Ms. Lennie."

I go to the boss's room at precisely seven in the evening. It is his usual dinner time. Tonight, I cooked Greek tangerine beef and a bowl of soup. I bring the signed documents of our contract with me as well.

I knock three times. "Master, your dinner is here," I call loudly.

I don't bother waiting for an answer. I push the door open and drag the food trolley in. The room is surprisingly bright when I enter. I didn't notice that his private space was so vast and spotless before. It looks like a house inside another house. He even has his own living room.

"Hello?" I call, but he doesn't answer. The silence is deafening. "The soup will get cold." I stroll toward the bedroom, but there's just an empty bed. My shoulders fall. "Ugh, God. I really need a massage. My shoulders are killing me," I complain as I knead my shoulder.

"You should get one." I jump in surprise upon hearing his husky voice behind me. When did he come in? I spin around to see him. He is wiping his wet hair with a white towel wrapped around his waist, but I still can't see his face because he covers it with another towel.

But what startles me the most is...

Is that a scar on his right chest? Man, of course, I notice how sexy he is. I always have, but I just can't seem to ignore it. I immediately look away, but the image of it has already been imprinted in my mind.

It's a keloid scar, slightly pink, thick, spread across his shoulder blade.

What happened to him? It doesn't look like a scar you get from an accident. It seems somewhat like burn scars that were made... on purpose.

"I'll give you a pass to the spa I own near my office building. Do you know where my company is?"

"Yes, I know where it is."

"I'll give you gift cards."

Carefully, I lift my head but avoid looking at his face. "Thank you for your generosity." I force a smile.

"Is that how you thank people? What's wrong?"

"Nothing."

"By *nothing,* did you mean my scar? I need you to get out of my bedroom," he instructs. "Unless you want to watch me put my pants on. Wait for me in my living room."

I wonder what it's like to see him nude all over again. Now, it won't be just his sexy back. I'd love to run my fingers over his stomach...

Stop, Alayna! What did I just think? When did I become so aggressive? I groan inwardly and decide to just leave.

Thankfully, it didn't take him long to get out of his room. He sits on the couch in front of me. He looks normal, but not too normal—just a barefoot man in his black shirt, gray sweatpants, and a mask.

Does he possibly have a scar on his face too? Is that why he keeps on wearing a mask?

"Here." He hands me gold cards with the logo of Grethe and Elga Enterprises on it.

"Thank you." I look up and smile. "Do you mind if I ask you something?"

"Just do your usual." He walks to the couch and sits, then he grabs the book from the side table. I follow him and slump in the lounge next to him.

"What are Grethe and Elga?"

"It's not what. It's who," he corrects.

"Who are they then?"

"Hungry for information, Miss Hart?"

"No. It's okay if you don't want to answer."

"They are my mother's and my sister's names. Well, they *were.*"

"Oh, no. What happened?"

"They died ten years ago," he says curtly.

Ten years. Oliver said that it was a decade ago when he started hiding from the world. Is it possible that his family's death is the reason?

I feel all the blood rush to my face. I know how hard it is to lose someone. When my father died, I felt like my world fell apart. I thought I wasn't going to survive. "I'm so sorry. Really. It must be so hard for you. But how about your father?"

His brows furrow. "I don't talk about him."

"My father died too," I mumble against my will.

But surprisingly, he sounds apologetic. "I'm sorry."

"It's okay. I have twelve siblings to take care of at home."

He nods. "And you're the breadwinner."

"Since my father died." I shut my eyes; my breath quickens. "I'm sorry I'm talking too much." I don't know why I've suddenly opened up. Maybe it's because I can see the sadness in his eyes. We aren't too different in this, after all.

His gaze softens. "It's all right."

"Oh, before I forget..." I slip my hand in my pocket, then grab the folded piece of paper. "I have Lucia's information." He hasn't explained why he's looking for her, yet I'm willing to give the information away. Well, he wouldn't bother if it's not important to him.

"Wait."

My hand automatically pushes the paper back into my pocket. "Yes?"

"Keep it, or maybe give it to Oliver instead. I don't think I'm ready. *Yet*."

I don't completely understand what he meant. He even offered a price for this and signed a contract. "I thought you needed this?"

"Ollie will take a look at it. Where's the contract?"

I guess that's when I should stop any further questions, though I'm inquisitive.

"*Oh*. Here." I pick it up from the food trolley and give it to him.

He nods, doesn't bother to check the content, and puts the folder on the side table.

I hold the handlebar of the trolley in an attempt to leave him alone, but he stops me again.

"Wait."

"Yes?"

"You don't mind, right? Joining me for dinner?" he asks, his tone holding a doubt.

I smile but am slightly astonished. "Not if you're going to walk out on me." I shrug.

"I won't. I promise."

The awkwardness is undeniable. The world takes its time spinning, and everything seems to be in slow motion.

I clear my throat. I want to ask him why he wanted me to have dinner with him. He doesn't socialize with other people, but he can actually eat with someone comfortably. This might be the first time he shares tables with somebody.

"Stop staring," he says softly.

"Oh, I'm sorry." I look away quickly. "But if you don't mind me asking—"

"I was wondering when your next barrage of questions was coming." He continues to eat, apparently with pleasure.

I can't help but notice how gorgeous he is, even if it's only half of his face. It's just too bad he's wearing a mask.

I search for any mark or scar that might have slipped out a little, but I see nothing. Maybe he has hidden it well. Or perhaps not. I'm not even sure if he really has a scar there.

"I told you to stop staring." He meets my gaze this time, jolting me back to reality.

"I was wondering why you asked me to eat with you," I say swiftly, then close my eyes.

"Why do you ask?"

"It's just... You don't go outside your room and never meet with other people, but you can comfortably eat with someone."

He laughs as if I just said something hilarious. "I'm not sure if it's funny or insulting that you're basically describing the life of a beast. To satisfy your curiosity, I eat with Oliver every single night, Miss Hart."

"Of course. How thoughtless of me." I give a small laugh. "I'm really sorry, Mr. Lucien—I mean, Master. It's really hard to call you Master."

"You can call me whatever you like."

I'm slightly stunned at his reaction and how surprisingly calm he is about it. "Thank you, but I'd rather call you that. Ms. Lennie might hear me calling you *whatever I like*."

"The dinner was great." He puts down his empty plate and wipes his lips with a napkin. "Thank you, Miss Hart."

"You're welcome. So..." I clear my throat. "If you need anything, you can just call me." I'm done with mine as well, so I finally stand and start clearing the table.

"You're leaving?" he asked, sounding confused.

"Yes, thank you for letting me share the meal with you, and I'm sorry again about your mom and sister."

He nods and springs up as well, walking to the couch.

Lying on my back that night, I stare at the ceiling of my room, feeling delighted. Deep inside, I know and feel that he has a good and generous heart, but he makes me think about him too much.

I roll to the side, resting my head on my arm. I still have too many unanswered questions about him. What is he hiding beneath the mask? Are there scars? Did someone hurt him? How did his family die?

I exhale in frustration. It's not that I even care. I've known him for a very short time. I've barely talked to him, but he is kind to me. I finally doze off, picturing him taking his mask off as the lights dim.

"Alayna, I didn't expect you to be this early."
Oliver waltzes into my station in his running outfit the next morning. A white towel is hanging on his shoulder, and one bud of his earphones is still in his ear. Judging by his outfit, he's probably going for a run.

"Good morning, Oliver. Going for a jog?"

"Yes, my morning routine." He glances at the small bowl I'm holding. "Oh, you're making crêpes."

"Yep, and I made a syrup. My own recipe," I brag, smiling. "Strawberry this time." I lift the spoon and circle my tongue around it as I savor the sweet taste of honey and strawberry. My favorite flavor. "I think this is good."

I put three layers of crêpes on a plate, then pour the strawberry syrup on top. Oliver is watching me as I place bacon and eggs on another plate.

"Let me help you." Oliver transfers the plates to the trolley, opens the fridge, and takes a pitcher of water and lemon. He slices the lemon into thin strips and drops the slices in the water. "And since you're officially his private chef, and this is not listed on the schedule, give him this every Monday, Wednesday, and Friday. He works out after breakfast, and today is Friday."

"Work out?" I frown, confused. "Oh, of course. He has his gym in this house. I'm so silly."

"Yes." He smiles. "All done! Off you go."

"Thank you."

"Alayna, I've noticed you haven't been outside since you came here."

I look up at him with a frown. "Oh, yeah. I haven't, right?"

"You know you should go out sometime and see the city. I thought you said you've never been to New York before."

"I actually haven't thought of going out. But you're right, I've always wanted to see the city. Your cousin actually gave me a gift card to one of the spas nearby. I might use it."

Oliver's forehead wrinkles. "He gave you a pass to the spa?"

"I was a little surprised too, but who am I to refuse?"

"What did I tell you? He's a good man."

I shrug. "I think so now."

"Maybe I'll drop you off at the spa," Oliver offers. "I'm going to the city tomorrow anyway. But only if you'd like."

"You would do that?"

"Of course." He beams.

"Yeah, sure. I'd love to."

"Oh, take that to him now." His hand motions toward the food trolley. "He's probably done with his exercise."

"Right. Thanks for the tips, as always."

He chuckles softly. "Don't mention it."

I push the trolley outside and carefully walk through the hallways. It is very early, and the silence in the house is deafening.

Again, I knock on Brandon's door three times and don't hear an answer, so I step inside. The dim light in the room adds to my creepy feeling, tempting me to light a fire and settle on the couch by the fireplace with a cup of coffee. I even imagine myself sitting with him. The thought alone makes me giddy.

I find the remote control for the air-conditioner on the table, and I lower the temperature so the food won't cool down. Then I set his breakfast on the table by the window.

"Alayna?"

My head shoots up, jolting a little when I hear my name said in his deep voice. I love it when he says my name. I finally see him before another door.

His top half is bare, and his chest is glistening with beads of sweat. His face is still covered by the mask, and he is wearing gray sweatpants that follow the shape of his thighs. A white towel hangs on his shoulder. My throat dries up at the sight of him. His muscles are ripped, hard, and I instantly ache to run my fingers over his chiseled abs. He is simply breathtaking.

I try to speak nonchalantly. "I brought you your breakfast."

He is panting heavily, and his gray eyes are looking directly into mine. "Mm, thank you." He paces toward me and checks the food. "You can leave now, Miss Hart."

"If I may, could I take a short break tomorrow? It's Saturday."

"It's fine. I won't call you on your rest day."

Of course, no *reasonable* employer should call you during your rest day. I smile, satisfied with his answer. "Thank you. Oliver actually offered to drop me off at the spa."

His brows furrow. "Oliver offered?"

"Yes, since he said he's going to the city tomorrow anyway." I feel like I have to explain. I don't want him to get the wrong idea. "Is this all right?"

"Why wouldn't it be?"

I grin in victory. "Thank you!" I clasp my hands together. "Oh, you should eat your breakfast while it's still hot. I'm sorry I was late. Oliver told me that you work out after breakfast."

"I don't work out after breakfast. I work out *before*." He opens the lid and slightly sniffs the food. I think I see him smile a little.

And I still can't stop grinning, too excited for tomorrow. "Maybe he just misspoke."

I watch him settle on the seat and pick up the utensils, but he still doesn't touch the food. "You may leave, Alayna. You can get the dishes later," he says in a glacial tone.

Quietly, I leave his room again. But something inside me doesn't want to.

CHAPTER SIX

At precisely nine o'clock in the morning on Saturday, Oliver pulls up in his black Aston Martin. The window of his car glides down and reveals his smiling face.

"Hey, Alayna. Did you wait long?"

"Hey, you're just in time."

"Come on in," he invites, cocking his head. I open the passenger door and step inside.

Ollie said he's going to briefly meet someone today, but I did not bother asking him where he's going. He promised he'll fetch me after the spa so we can go home together.

The receptionist at the G&E Spa acknowledges Oliver right away and assists us. I watch how he makes the receptionist blush with his captivating smile, which makes me realize Oliver is naturally kind to everyone. He introduces me to her. She tells me her name's Sarah and calls over another young woman. I follow her to the back of the spa. Oliver waves at us and leaves the building.

Moving through the entrance is like entering another world. Every arched doorway is framed by pearl-colored silk, while ornamented pillows brighten elegant armchairs and chaise lounges.

There are small, decorative bamboo fountains, and soft instrumental music is playing through hidden speakers. The air smells of floral fragrances that warm my senses, making me feel like I've escaped into some kind of sophisticated garden.

The G&E Spa, owned by none other than Brandon Lucien, is luxurious, a generous treat for those who can afford it, and now I'm going to enjoy it for free. The attendant gives me a menu of treatments. The spa has individual suites for a sauna, manicure and pedicure salon, facials, a mustard foot soak to help with body aches and pains, and some skincare treatment packs.

She told me my gold certificate covers six thousand dollars' worth of treatments—making me want to faint but also think I'm probably the luckiest of customers for getting such a card. I think thoroughly about what I need: a waxing, a specialty massage, and just general pampering. For once, I'm able to afford all three, and I couldn't be more excited.

I take a deep breath and relax as the massage therapist's expert hands move over my body.

After the lovely hours at the spa, Oliver is waiting for me in the lobby, reading a magazine. I clear my throat to get his attention, and he tenses up when he sees me.

"How did it go?"

I giggle. "I've never felt so light in my life. I feel amazing."

He nods. "And I'm glad you enjoyed it. Come, I'll take us somewhere we can eat for late lunch. Do you mind Mexican?"

"Mexican? Sure, I'd love to."

The restaurant we go to is a casual outdoor place located in Hell's Kitchen, on the West Side of Manhattan. I didn't expect Oliver to take me here. Nonetheless, I don't really mind.

We settle at a table, and my eyes widen at the menu. There are so many options—and they're all so expensive. I wonder if I should take advantage of Oliver's generosity or ask him to take us somewhere cheaper. A few minutes later, plates of quesadillas, taquitos, the restaurant's famous chicken enchiladas, and two glasses of horchata arrive at our table. Eagerly, I pick up a piece of enchilada and take my first bite. I hum in delight, closing my eyes as I taste the food.

"I haven't had Mexican food in such a long time."

Oliver laughs at my reaction. He picks up a piece for himself. "This restaurant is one of my favorites. I know the chef."

I look around us; almost all the tables are occupied. "It's pretty popular, I see. Maybe we can try these dishes at home."

"The kitchen's yours, Alayna. I've seen how you got Brandon to try your own recipes even when you were told not to improvise," he teases.

"Oh. I'm sorry about that." I wipe my mouth with a napkin. "I'm just flexible when it comes to food."

"It's fine. Brandon likes it anyway." He drinks his horchata with pleasure. "A real chef always brings out a masterpiece. An artist in the kitchen..."

❧

It's already past seven when we return home. My legs and feet already feel sore, so I soak my body in the Jacuzzi, adding some bath salts I got from the spa to the water. I choose some relaxing instrumental music and plug in my earbuds.

After the bath, I put on a very comfy silk robe and lie on my bed. I grab my phone and call Mom.

"How did your therapy go today?" I ask.

"I feel great, Alayna. The numbness in my left hand and fingertips has decreased. It's amazing."

"That's so great to hear."

It's the first session of her therapy today, but I didn't completely tell Mom why I suddenly have the means to send her to exclusive sessions. I wasn't able to provide for her complete care before because the treatment is beyond our budget. But last week, Mom received a call from the best private orthopedic hospital in Lawrence, Kansas, and "I" was the one who admitted her as their new patient.

"Thank you, but you still didn't tell me how you managed to get me these treatments. I know hospitals like that with famous doctors who appear on TV are expensive."

"I have a great signing bonus with my new employer," I half-lie, though it is indeed what Brandon promised me. I just omitted the other details. "Besides, you've been suffering from it for years now. You and the kids are my priority."

She sighs through the line. "But you still have to save for yourself."

"Don't worry, Mom. I can manage. I'm living the dream here. I finally get to see New York."

"Oh, how is it there, honey?" she asks excitedly.

"I went for a walk around Manhattan today. I went to a relaxing spa and enjoyed a very delicious treat at a Mexican restaurant. Then I thought about you. I wish you were all here."

"One day, darling. We can all be together again." I feel her smile. "Just always remember: be good to your colleagues. It's easier to work that way."

"Don't worry. My superiors are very kind and generous," I say.

"I'm glad everything is going great with you. I know I shouldn't worry about you, but I can't help it."

I chuckle. "There's nothing to worry about. I promise."

The rest of the weekend was full of relaxation. The pain in the muscles of my hands, arms, and back is gone. For the rest of Sunday, I spend all my time reading a new book and watching cooking shows on the internet.

On Monday morning, I deliver the food to the Master, and even if he doesn't ask me how my weekend went, I thank him for the spa.

"It's been so relaxing. Thank you."

He nods casually and lifts the lid of his food. "You're welcome, Miss Hart." He sits at the table while I serve him and stops when he notices something else on his plate. "What is this?"

"It's quesadillas. I know it's not on your schedule, but Oliver and I went to a Mexican restaurant and had this. I just thought of making some for you. It's really delicious."

He raises an eyebrow and exhales.

"Is there something wrong? I can just take that away—"

"No, it's fine." He looks up at me. "But why is it that everything you do is against the rules?"

I couldn't answer for a moment. He's right, I've broken some rules, but he permitted it. I've added private touches in his meals, but he ate them anyway. He let me see him, allowed me to speak to him like this, while the others can only speak to him in that white room.

"I'm sorry if I've been so nosy. Maybe this is just the way I am. I mean, I'm not justifying it, I was wrong and—"

"Do you understand what's happening here, Miss Hart?" he cuts me off, gazing up at me with his shrewd, penetrating eyes.

Semi-dazed by his question, I hold his gaze. I can't get over how beautiful he is. "I'm sorry if I'm making you uncomfortable."

"But you don't." His scowl darkens and his expression becomes confused. "It's strange that you don't."

His words make my cheeks flare. "Sorry."

"You keep saying sorry, but you still do whatever you want," he states. "I might as well give you permission to do everything here."

"What? You don't have to do that."

"But I have. In the future, you'll have to tell me first before you want to add something to my meal before serving it to me."

I finally smile in delight. "Of course, I will," I say breathlessly.

"And I assume you know where these doors lead?" he asks, referring to the doors in his space. I nod. "Two doors on the right side lead to the library and the one on the left is to the gym."

"Yes."

"Except, of course, the door beside my bed—that's my bathroom."

"Yes, um, that too." I briefly shut my eyes, remembering my first encounter with him. "Why are you giving me permission now, if I may ask?"

"You are like a storm, Miss Hart. With your very nosy character, anything could happen."

What?

"Now you can leave," he instructs and picks up the quesadilla first, which adds to my joy.

I decide to just come back later to get the plates. I've disturbed him enough with my presumptuous actions. I might as well let the man eat peacefully.

I walk toward the door slowly, still all ears in case he has any comments about the food. I keep walking. As I'm about to walk out the door, he finally speaks.

"Alayna..."

I stop, still facing the door.

"Oliver is a good man," he says unexpectedly. I turn around in surprise.

"Yes?" I ask, my forehead furrowed.

"But I don't like to share."

It is bad enough that talking to Brandon makes me feel anxious. It doesn't help that every time I leave his room, I feel as though I'm battling against unfamiliar feelings.

But I don't like to share...

His voice echoes inside my head while I try to understand what he meant. He is not sharing *something* with anyone. What does he mean by that?

I must've been walking so absorbedly that I don't notice anyone or anything on the way.

"Alayna!"

I jerk as I hear my name. Ms. Lennie is only a foot away, looking at me with a frown.

"Are you okay?" Ms. Lennie asks, moving closer in my direction.

"Yes, of course, Ms. Lennie. I'm sorry, I was just trying to think of what to do for my rest day." If there's something I've gotten pretty good at since I arrived here, it's making excuses and explaining away my behavior.

She nods, looking unconvinced. "Mr. Katrakis is waiting for you in your kitchen."

"I've got to go, Ms. Lennie. Sorry," I say in a hurry.

"Alayna? Alayna!" I can hear her calling me as I march away, fast. I all but run to my kitchen and find Oliver at my station. He springs up from his seat as soon as he sees me.

"Alayna? What's wrong?" he asks curiously. God, how I wish there were no hidden cameras in my kitchen! Of course, that's just wishful thinking. I'm still glad these cameras don't record sound.

"I'm fine. I ran because Ms. Lennie said that you were here. Do you need anything?"

His left eyebrow shoots up. "I don't think you're running because of me." He smirks and crosses his arms across his chest. "Spill the beans."

I puff. "Nothing."

I shouldn't bother Oliver about it. Maybe what he said is he doesn't like sharing me with another employer? Wait. Or maybe he doesn't want his cousin lingering around me in my workplace since I'm his private chef now? Or maybe he doesn't want me sharing the workload with his cousin anymore?

"You seem preoccupied," he observes.

"I'm just amazed that he finally allowed me to go into his room without getting mad."

His expression brightens. "Oh, I keep telling you he's a good man. I guess he's getting used to having you around. He's starting to trust someone again."

I answer with a smile, though inside, I'm slightly stunned by Oliver's openness. Of course, he's always been open, but what he just said has made me think of some other reason why his cousin might not be coming out of his room. He may just have a strange way of coping with his heartbreaking past.

My work routine goes on without incident in the next couple of days, and I've not spoken to Brandon since our last conversation. He doesn't speak to me whenever I enter his room to bring his food. There are also times Oliver wants to deliver it so I can have some extra rest. He's always considerate.

In the kitchen, when I'm finished cooking the boss's meal, I try out new recipes from Oliver's booklet. There are other dishes here that I find hard to recreate because I can't seem to get the exact authentic taste.

In university, I needed a full week of concentration before getting a dish perfect, especially if it involved meats. I remember being in a school camp in the Wisconsin mountains, where bear meat was popular. It was difficult to cook. Luckily, the list of dishes isn't as hard as the dishes in my culinary classes back then.

From what I've learned from Oliver about Greek cuisine, dishes with feta and oregano aren't always *Greek*, just as

Parmesan isn't always Italian. It is important to refrain from experimenting with Greek recipes. I can experiment as much as I want to with other dishes, but I'm extra careful to leave the recipes close to my boss's heart alone.

Right now, I'm making *tempeh gyros* and roasted *saganaki*. There are rarely any leftovers after these experimental dishes; I either eat all of it myself or, if it's really good, I'll share it with Oliver.

Speaking of Ollie, he finds me in the afternoon at my station. It's usually the time when he comes from the office.

"Hey, that looks good." He stares at the platters in front of me.

"I'd like you to try this," I say, offering him a bite.

He picks a piece of the roasted cheese, then nods. "It's good, but something's missing."

I blink. "What do you think it is?"

He looks at me. "Lemon."

"Oh, of course. The final touch." I'm supposed to put it on before putting it in the oven. "I'm making this again."

"Alayna, can I ask you a small favor?" Ollie asks me suddenly.

"Of course." I grin at him. "What is it?"

"You know some Nihongo too, right? I finally saw your profile and you speak four foreign languages."

I smile. "Sure! What can I help you with?"

"My fiancée's mother is coming next week from Tokyo, and she texted me in Japanese characters about planning a birthday surprise for my girl. I ran the text through a translation app, but she's not very good at English, so I don't know how to reply," he explains.

I'm stunned at what he is saying for a moment. "Wait. You're engaged?"

He laughs. "I guess I never mentioned it. Yes, I am, Alayna; but we wish to keep it private for now."

"Wow!" I beam. "Congratulations, Ollie. How long have you been engaged?"

"Betty and I have been in a relationship for a year. I proposed to her two months ago. Brandon doesn't know yet, but I will tell him eventually."

"I'd be glad to help you reply to your future mother-in-law. Can you show me the text?"

"Oh." He slips his hand into his pocket. "Of course."

I continue to make another dish with the ingredients in the prep area while Oliver is scrolling through his inbox. Then he shows me a message from a person called Mrs. Davis about the upcoming birthday of her daughter Beatrice in two weeks. He says that his fiancée is half-American, half-Japanese, and she grew up in Tokyo before her family moved to New York a few years ago.

Oliver wants to take them to the theater because Betty is fond of classical music and theatrical plays. He hands me his phone so I can type a message on the screen.

I type what Oliver is saying but in Japanese characters, acting as his interpreter. I remind him that I'm not very fluent in Nihongo, so there might be typos in my texts. He assures me not to worry and tells me that I've actually helped him a lot.

"But don't you think she'll know that it isn't you who texted this?" I ask.

He scratches his head again shyly. "I'll tell her a friend helped me."

I give him his phone back. "Let me know if she replies or if you need help responding again."

He smiles. "Thank you, Alayna. I know I can count on you."

"You've helped me a lot around here." I smile back encouragingly. "I'm just returning the kindness."

To my surprise, Oliver gently touches the top of my head—a simple gesture that only my father ever did whenever he was praising me. My heart aches a little at that memory, but I feel delighted at the same time; I'm reminded again of that feeling.

In the evening, I'm alone again in the kitchen preparing for dinner, and after I'm done, I go into his room.

"Master, I'm coming in." I step inside. I push the trolley to the table and find him fast asleep on the couch in front of the unlit fireplace with a laptop on his chest. Poor man, even in his sleep, he still wears the mask.

Not wanting to make any noise, I carefully place the food on the center table, but he must have felt my presence. He groans and emphatically opens his eyes.

"Alayna," he says and sits up. "How long have you been here?"

"I just got in. I'm sorry if I woke you up."

"It's all right. I was expecting you."

I smile a little at his remark and continue setting the table.

I'm about to get the pitcher of water when he abruptly grabs my hand and pulls me, dragging me to his side.

I gasp in surprise. "What are you—"

He slides his arm over my waist and pulls me close. My heartbeat quickens, and my breath comes with a hitch. I can feel his breath on my ears, and that instantly makes me shiver.

I try to jerk away, but he pulls me back against him. My hands land on his lap, I unintentionally touch him. And, damn... He's hard.

I squirm against his thighs. "Oh my God!"

"I can make an exception," he whispers in my ear. Tiny bolts of electricity flow from my head down to my core. "Don't move," he orders.

"W-What exception?" I try not to breathe in his scent, but it is no use. He smells so good... so manly. It warms up my senses.

"Exception to take the shit out of you for flirting with Oliver."

"I am not flirting with Oliver!" I retort. What is he talking about? "We've done nothing but talk since I got here."

"But I notice you're getting closer to him. I told you I don't share."

I gasp. "What's that supposed to mean?"

"*I want you.*"

Every hair on my body rises. I'm not sure if I'm hearing things now or am just delusional. "Let me go, please. This is wrong!"

His eyes gleam. "It feels right to me."

"W-What do you want?"

"I said I want you. Are those words not clear?"

"I thought you hate being touched," I say breathlessly. "Why are you doing this now?"

He chuckles. God, his smile. I almost want to faint.

"Is that what you think of me?" he asks.

"What do you want from me?" I continue to wriggle. "Please, let me go. I can't feel my hands anymore."

Brandon lifts me, then lays me on the couch, clasping my wrists and pinning my hands above me. "Better? Am I making you uncomfortable?"

I squirm against him again, but he is keeping his grasp tight.

"If this is about Oliver, you should not—"

"This is about you and me," his voice thickens. "Do you like him so much that you think this is about him?"

"You should stop. He's been friendly to me, always."

His eyes study me. "Let's say he is. You didn't answer my question."

I look away from his intense gaze. I jerk my arms from his grip and shove at his chest, then sit up.

"No, I don't, and even if I liked him..." I lift my chin. "What are you going to do about it? Am I not allowed to like someone in the house?"

Someone like you? Someone so mysterious and with too many issues?

He lets out a humorless laugh and slumps back on the couch. His eyes turn icy. "I was right all along." His jaw twitches. "You like my cousin. And to answer your question, I won't allow you to like someone in my house."

I agree. *I can't like you.*

"I told you I don't like Oliver." I grit my teeth. His mistaken statement and ideas are starting to piss me off. "Oliver is the only person in this house I can be friends with, and I don't understand what the hell you meant about not sharing. You don't own me. No one owns me."

He looks away from me, stands up, and walks off. "Please leave, Alayna. I guess I can't talk to you like this."

What the heck? He just told me he wanted me, and now he's asking me to leave? What a mercurial man!

"You know that you can't possibly shake me like this, then just make me leave. Fine," I snap. He's confusing me about everything...

I stand up and head toward the door.

He is so unpredictable and hard to please. He is a huge mess that I need not pay attention to, or I'll just get myself hurt in the end. I'm about to open the door when he speaks.

"Because you make me feel alive again," he suddenly confesses, and there is a note of defeat in his voice. His footsteps approach me. "I've been dead for so long, and Oliver is the only person who stayed for the last decade of my pathetic existence. And you like him, Alayna. It's too complicated."

"You made yourself into this person," I say, still facing the door. "People in the house care about you, but you just can't see it."

He is now behind me, and gently he turns me around. "You don't know me," he hisses, then points to his mask. "You don't know the nightmare beneath this thing."

"I don't judge you, really. And do you think that *thing* defines your life?"

He lets go of my hand and sighs. "Where have you been all this time?"

"Do you really want me to leave?"

He lifts his hand and cups my face. My heart rate rises as I feel his thumb brush my cheek. He steps even closer. He's never been closer to me than he is now.

"If you don't go..." he whispers. "I can't stay away from you anymore." His mouth is an inch from mine. We are close enough that we could kiss.

How can a simple yet gentle touch like his make my whole body shiver? This is different. *He* is different.

I've been in a painful relationship before, and I tried to close myself off to unwanted feelings that would trigger my nightmares. I feel safe doing that. Falling in love for me is always out of the picture, but no one has ever made me feel this way. The excitement, the desire, the urges... He isn't even doing anything.

I stare up at his face—masked or unmasked, I don't care anymore.

"I saw how Oliver looked at you," he murmurs. "I can't want someone my cousin likes."

This man really has no idea.

"Stop jumping to conclusions," I tell him. "You don't know anything about your cousin. You should try to understand the people living in your house. You should start to see the world."

If what he said is true—if he really likes me—then maybe I could use this chance to make him come out of his room.

"But I can't."

"It's been a long time. You've been here for ten years. You can't stay in here forever."

"Do you know how much I wanted to get justice for my family's death?" Suddenly, he is opening up. "Do you know why I can't grasp this opportunity, even when I'm so close to finding them?"

"Why?"

"I'm not capable of going out. It's all useless."

I raise my hand and try to touch him, but I stop myself. I remember he didn't want to be touched.

"I'm sorry," I say, but he catches my wrist.

"It's fine," he whispers, searching my eyes.

"You don't mind if I touch you?"

He shakes his head.

I smile a little and touch his hand again. Willingly, he entwines his fingers around mine. My heart melts at the sweet gesture.

"I don't know what's going on with your life, and I'm not going to ask. But this should end. You have to start living. Maybe take a stroll around your house."

He shakes his head again. "Too many people. I can't."

"Well, you can try when there's no one around. The staff sleeps at ten-thirty."

He lets out a forced laugh. "Do you think I didn't know that? Oliver and I set those rules."

I grin. "Shall I walk with you if you do, then?"

"What if they see me?"

"What are you afraid of?"

He grits his teeth. "I'm not stupid. I know that it's strange for people to see someone wearing a mask."

"You're shaking."

"I'm fine."

I attempt to touch his arm, using my other hand. "You feel amazing."

"Do I?" A playful smile curls at the corners of his lips. He is so beautiful.

"It makes me feel that you're real. Not a distant stranger." I meet his gaze. "Do you understand what I'm saying?"

"If only you knew the monster in me, you'd be trembling in fear."

"Everyone has a monster, even me. But life must go on, I guess. We can't always get whatever we want."

He stops holding me. "You may be right, but I can't protect you if I'm like this, Alayna."

"Why would I need protection?" I ask in confusion.

"You don't need to understand. I'm already saying too much, and too much isn't good—at least for us. Let's talk about this some other time, Alayna. I want to rest." He is dismissing me; he is just too erratic.

I groan inwardly because I don't want to leave him yet, but the man needs his space. I steal a simple touch of his arm and finally manage to go.

CHAPTER SEVEN

BRANDON

God, no. What have I done?

There is nothing else I could do but send her away. I'm only trying to bear the anguish I feel in my chest the moment she is close to me. I like the feeling of her skin, her warmth, the look on her face when she smiles...

But damn it, it all burns me. I still can't bear it. I thought I was getting better, but it is still there.

I'm wrong. I'm only getting worse.

I clench my fists over my chest. "Fuck! Not again," I groan. It is burning, and it is too damned painful.

Where is Oliver?

"Ollie..."

It hurts. My chest, my head, my face. God, it all hurts.

I fall on my knees. I can't feel anything but the scorching in my chest. I force myself to stand and grope the phone with all my remaining strength, pressing the speed dial.

Oliver answers at the first ring. "Brandon?"

"Where are you?" I ask, catching my breath.

"Brandon, what's wrong?"

"I need you right now," I grunt. "Please, brother..."

"I'm on my way."

It is the last word I hear from him, and everything goes dark.

⤋

There are familiar voices, whispers—I can hear them talking about me. One of the voices is Oliver's, and the other is someone I don't wish to hear again. I know that voice well.

Ah! My doctor. Oliver's younger brother. The other person I used to trust. I haven't heard from him in a while—almost a year. Almost a year since my last episode. It's funny to hear him again. It means I will never get better.

I want to move or open my eyes, but I can't. I also can't speak. Maybe they shot the medication into me again—the one they use to calm me.

"I know. I thought it was an opportunity, Cassius. He finally had a chance to get out of his comfort zone." It's Oliver's voice.

"It is good for him, Ollie, yes. It is a good sign that he can actually let anyone in again."

"Her name's Alayna. She's amazing. I'm in awe of her actions and strength. She's an undeniably talented chef. Brandon told me he's intrigued by her. I'll introduce you to her later."

"Ollie, don't engage yourself too much with her," Cassius warns. "Your eyes do not lie. I can see that she's appealing to you."

What? No. No way!

"No, of course. You know me, brother. Besides, you know my current status, which I still haven't mentioned to him."

Status? What is it that he didn't tell me?

Cassius clicks his tongue. "Tell him right away, Ollie. It's not good for Brandon if you are hiding something from him. You know what I mean."

What the—what the hell was that about? Hiding what from me? Damn it.

"He'll understand. He's more understanding than all of us," Oliver states, almost certain. "I'm glad that part of him remains, but I thought his illness wasn't going to bother him again. I thought he was healed."

"His scars and the injuries, especially the one on his chest, are all healed, Ollie. What he is suffering from isn't physical. It's all in his mind. His body remembers the pain. I don't know when it will stop. It depends on him."

"I don't know what happened exactly. Brandon was shouting for help, but he was already unconscious when I found him. It was after Alayna left," Ollie explains. "Do you think something happened?"

Yes, she touched me, and I wanted her to. I thought I was fine. Everything felt right.

"Maybe she touched him," Cassius guesses. "Do you remember what happened last year? It caused his last episode, and now..."

Ollie sighs, and silence follows.

"That's also possible," he concludes. "It happened before when you tried to calm him down."

"I know, and it was my fault back then. I'm not going to give up on him—even if it takes a lifetime." Cassius's voice is low and full of guilt. "But thank you for calling me. I'm just worried he might not want to see me again."

"You know Brandon. He would be glad to see you again. You needed to do what you had to."

"How about you?" Cassius asks abruptly. "How are you? You don't come home anymore. Mom is worried. You almost give your whole life and your freedom to this setup—his company, his life. When are you going to stop stressing yourself if you can get our help? I can help you, Ollie. You don't have to tell him. Grethe and Elga Enterprises is a burden already heavy enough to bear. Do you still sleep?"

"Don't worry about me. This is only temporary. You have a job. Take care of Mother. She needs you more. I just hope that someday Brandon will come out and finally face everything. He's already done it once because of Alayna."

Is that how much of a burden I put on Oliver? On everyone? I sounded pathetic in Cassius's words, and I knew it was true. They should give up on me. There's no more hope for someone like me.

"Anyway, I'll still be in Manhattan until next week. We should grab a drink sometime," Cassius adds.

"Of course. I was actually planning to go out this weekend with Betty, before her birthday," Oliver says. "But yes, a night out sounds good since you're already here. What do you think?"

Betty? I've never heard that name before.

"With Alayna?" Cassius asks curiously.

"I can't see why not? She has to go out of the mansion and have fun sometimes."

"Just make sure that doesn't mean anything. Your fiancée might misunderstand." He laughs.

"She's beautiful, yes," Ollie admits. "But no, Cassius. She's off-limits. I think you know why, and that's why I'm asking you to come."

I can almost hear Cassius's smirk. "Do you think Brandon likes her?"

"That's a high possibility. He's different with her." Ollie chuckles. "But I should warn you too. She's not a woman you see every day in Athens."

"Mm. No wonder Brandon is so infatuated."

"Hey, stay for dinner."

"Of course. I have no reason to decline."

Abruptly, their voices and footsteps fade away. The last thing I hear is the sound of a door shutting. Funny, I still can't move.

ALAYNA

"Alayna, do you have a minute?" Oliver asks when he and another young and very attractive man who resembles him come into my kitchen in the morning. I've just finished preparing breakfast and am about to take it to Brandon.

"Of course, Oliver." I look from him to the other guy, whose eyebrow is raised at me. There's an amused smile on his lips.

"I'd like to introduce you to my younger brother," Oliver says. "This is Cassius. He's the brother I told you about before, and he's also Brandon's doctor."

Oh, I remember. Oliver told me about a brother who also lives in Manhattan.

My lips part at the sight of Cassius. He looks very stylish in his casual turtleneck and brown Hermès coat, and I must admit this man is breathtaking. His features are clean cut, his mouth firm, and he is also blond and tall, like his older brother, with a pair of deep sapphire eyes. And he smells sinfully good: of mild soap and spicy wood perfume.

Finally, he steps forward and reaches out a hand to me.

"I've heard so much about you," he says in a baritone.

I shake his hand, and I instantly feel the warmth of his skin. His hand is a bit rough—and strangely, there is electricity running between our palms. I look up at him and study his face intently. He is much more handsome up close. He flashes out a playful smile, showing his perfect white teeth, and two dimples appear on his cheeks.

I smile back. "I hope you heard only good things. I'm Alayna."

"Oh, you're taking that to Brandon?" Oliver asks, referring to the food on the trolley.

"Yes, I was about to."

"I'm afraid the food has to wait. He hasn't woken up yet."

"Oh." I blink. Brandon usually wakes up early, so I wonder why he's still sleeping. But then I realize it's not usual for a doctor to be here early in the morning. "Did something happen?"

Oliver clears his throat in hesitation. "Brandon lost consciousness last night. I looked after him until this morning, before Cassius came. Alayna, we actually wanted to ask you what went on before you left."

My eyes widen. "What happened?"

"That's what we wanted to know," he says. "Did something happen before you left his room?"

"We just talked," I say—which is partly true, but we kind of had a moment, well... *ish*. Though I'm sure, I could say anything to Oliver, not with his younger brother around. Cassius's presence intimidates me for no reason. I have to admit, I find him very, very attractive. I can't help it.

"What did you talk about?" Cassius asks smoothly, slightly startling me. I wonder if he can sense the effect he's having on me. It's making me uncomfortable.

"It was nothing important."

"Are you sure?" Oliver asks again. "Because you are the last person he spoke with. By the way, I'm not implying anything. I just really wanted to ask you."

"I know. Nothing's going on between us, and besides, he was fine when I left. Really, nothing important happened." I laugh nervously. "After we talked, he sent me away."

He sent me away suddenly after a somewhat heated conversation. After he told me he wanted me...

Is he sick? Did I perhaps cook something that hurt his stomach?

"All right. I'm sure he's fine." Oliver nods and smiles again. "Anyway, I'll take care of this," he volunteers, holding the handle of the trolley. "Why don't you prepare something for the three of us? Let's have breakfast together when I get back."

I nod. "Sure. I'll get started right away."

"Oliver, I'll go with you," Cassius says. "I need to check on Brandon while I'm still here. See you in a bit, Alayna."

Cassius leaves with Oliver.

CHAPTER EIGHT

Cassius appears in the dining room a few minutes later and walks toward me. "That looks good," he says, looking at the food on the table.

"Thanks." I smile. "Where's Ollie?"

"He's still with Brandon."

"Is Brandon going to be okay? Is he unwell? Did he ask for something? I can prepare it for him and—"

Cassius cuts me off and chuckles. "Relax. He's fine, and he's eating the breakfast you prepared. He's doing great, so don't worry," he assures with a small smile.

The thorn in my chest finally stops pricking. I sigh in relief. Last night, he didn't seem very well when he asked me to leave him right away. "Thank you. I was so worried."

"He'll be fine." He grins once again and looks back at the food on the table. "Can I have a taste of this?" he says, pointing to the sweet side dish I made of mascarpone cream cheese laced with vanilla.

I chuckle. "Of course, you can." I offer him a fork, then he slices off a small portion, tasting the food.

He hums in approval. "Wow, tiramisu crepes?"

"Yes."

"This tastes terrifically good, Alayna," he says as he chews. "I remember now that I had this for breakfast a few times in Italy." He scoops another dollop and chews it slowly.

I watch him as he runs his tongue over his lower lip...

Oh no! I quickly look away. How can I think like a starving monster, let alone about this man? I just met him two hours ago! I suddenly feel like I am betraying Brandon, which I'm not, since we aren't even together. But it feels wrong.

Well—it isn't wrong to become attracted to someone when I'm single, right?

"Uh, thank you."

"Alayna studied culinary arts, and she worked at a restaurant in Venice," Oliver says. I hadn't noticed him coming in. "And fortunately, there's never been a time when Brandon has complained about his meal."

My cheeks flush as I prepare the plates for us. I laugh. "You're being too nice."

"Really? Because I swear, this is what an authentic tiramisu tastes like," Cassius insists.

"Brandon wouldn't hire her if she weren't talented," Oliver remarks.

The two brothers sit next to each other while I serve them breakfast. Besides the crepes, I also prepared apricot-pancetta strata and a pitcher of fresh cucumber-lemon juice.

While we eat, the Katrakis siblings speak mostly about their home. The reason Cassius hasn't visited is that their father wanted him to go to Athens. I never bother joining their conversation because listening to them makes me want to know more about their family.

Apparently, they have a sister who is also coming to New York to continue her culinary degree, and she cannot wait to see her cousin again. I immediately assume they are referring to Brandon.

Their father, Aegeus Katrakis, is a general surgeon and runs a hospital in Athens. He specifically summoned his younger son to Greece because he needed to perform surgery on another cousin. Besides being a surgeon, Cassius seems able to act like a general practitioner since he is Brandon's doctor. He also mentions that he works in the Rutherford Hospital, and he has patients here in Manhattan waiting for him, so he couldn't stay long in Athens.

I wanted to ask him why he is working here when his family owns a hospital, but I keep the curiosity to myself.

While the two brothers continue to talk, a loud ring abruptly interrupts them.

"Hold on a sec." Oliver raises a hand and draws out the phone from his pocket. He glances at the screen. "It's my assistant. I have to answer this."

"Go on," Cassius says. "Must be important."

"It is. Please, excuse me." Oliver stands up and quickly exits, leaving his brother and me alone.

An awkward silence falls in the dining room. I savor my breakfast slowly, conscious of Cassius's presence next to me. I watch him from the side of my eye as he slices the crepe with a fork and takes another bite.

"So," he begins, breaking the silence. "I heard Brandon has a thing for you..." His voice echoes in my ear, "And something happened before you left his room. I'm sure of that."

"What do you mean?"

"Did you touch him?" he asks straightforwardly.

The air abandons my lungs. "W-Why would I do that?"

"Simply because you like him." He grins meaningfully. "What happened between you and Brandon?"

I'm not sure if I like where this is going. Just what happened to him when I left last night? I'm sure I didn't do anything that might have pissed him off this time, apart from our very strange conversation about him wanting me. Is there anything else I missed? Did he perhaps tell his cousins about it?

My blood races to my cheeks at the thought. I shake my head. "I still don't understand what you mean. Nothing happened—"

"Sorry about that." Oliver suddenly reappears, startling me. He frowns at us. "Whoa, what's the sudden change of air?"

Cassius looks up at his older brother. "I'm asking Alayna if something happened before she left Brandon's room."

My mouth opens. Okay, he is attractive, I must admit, but this guy sounds so self-absorbed. God, I thought he was nice. How is that his business? How can he tell Oliver that?

My voice rises. "I said nothing, okay?"

"Come on, bro. Don't scare Alayna." Oliver sits back in his chair. "But I have to admit that I'm curious as well. You just didn't ask the right question, Cass."

I bite my lower lip nervously. Could they detect something? Whatever was happening between Brandon and me was supposed to be our business alone, right?

"We just talked," I almost whisper, avoiding their eyes.

"We know Brandon's condition very well," Cassius inserts, "and he's not going to end up like *that* if nothing happened. You touched him; we know for sure. Unless someone else was in his room, which is not the case, I guess."

Why is touching their cousin such a big deal? What is going on? I am starting to get offended by their accusation. I did not expect these questions to come from Oliver.

"We won't hold it against you, Alayna," Oliver says softly, "we just need to know."

"If you think I *harmed* him in any way, I didn't. I swear. If you don't want to believe me, I'm fine with that," I say tersely.

The brothers exchange a surprised look.

"It's not like that, Alayna," Oliver says. "Of course, I trust you. You're just not getting the whole picture, I guess, or where we're coming from, but I hope we didn't offend you."

"I'm sorry, but it's too late for that."

"Okay, I guess I need to apologize to you too. I'm sorry if my questions were insensitive," Cassius says sincerely. "It's just hard to explain for now."

I don't answer.

"Brandon is actually asking for you, Alayna," Oliver says.

My heart lifts. "He is?"

He grins. "Yes, he'll be waiting for you."

As much as this excites me, I don't want to leave the table without emptying my plate.

⚜

I stand in front of Brandon's room, expecting Oliver's signal. He and Cassius follow me when we finish our meal and ask me to wait before coming in.

In another couple of minutes, the siblings walk out. Oliver approaches me first.

"Alayna, you can come in now."

I proceed to the room without speaking. Honestly, I feel like it's the first time I'm meeting Brandon.

When I step into his living room, Brandon is standing by the window. His room is still as dim as before. He is bare-chested, wearing only black sweatpants, and barefoot. As always, he is beautiful.

"Oliver said you wanted to talk to me," I begin.

"I don't think I can let you walk around my room anymore." He doesn't bother facing me.

His statement and cold voice confuse me. "What? I thought we were fine like this. We were starting to get comfortable in each other's company, right?"

"Yes, I thought I'd be okay. Having you around has been the highlight of my whole ten years of hiding. I thought I could carry on, but I'm no good for you."

He finally turns, exposing the scar on his chest. It looks inflamed as if it were fresh. It's painful to look at. His cousins still haven't told me what happened, but I choose not to ask any questions.

"You deserve better," he whispers. "You should not be with a man like me."

"Stop." I shake my head in disbelief. "Don't say anything. Is this what you want? Is this what you want to be like for the rest of your life?"

"Of course not." His eyes darken. "Do you think I want this? Don't you see this scar? Until this thing goes away, I won't be able to live how I want to."

"Yes, I can see that." I swallow dryly. "But what you said doesn't make sense... after what you just told me... You don't want me to touch you? Fine, I won't, if that's the issue here. But you're sending me away right after you told me you wanted me?"

There, I said it. The words slipped out of my mouth bravely. I can't keep pretending his confession doesn't affect me.

"Alayna..." He takes a step closer, reaching out to me.

"Don't come any closer." I wipe my tears away. My voice tightens. "If this is about me touching you, I can work with that."

"Do you think this is all about that?" he snaps. "How many times have you tried to touch me, and it didn't matter? I didn't care about that. Something went on between us, but I am not capable of making it into something more."

"Why?"

His face expresses an inexplicable emotion. "I won't be able to protect you. I won't be able to give you the life that you want."

He's acting like we're over before we ever really began... before he ever even tried.

"Then come out and face the world," I tell him. "You can talk to me and tell me what's wrong. You can tell me everything. Let's try, Brandon."

His brows furrow. "What did you just call me?"

"Master?"

"No, you called me..." He swallows. "Say it again."

"Brandon..."

A laugh escapes his lips but doesn't reach his eyes. "I haven't heard that name in a long time." He pauses. "Except from Oliver."

"I'm sorry, I just got carried away."

I look up at him. His mouth is only an inch away from mine.

"Do you think this will work?" he asks softly.

"*We* will make it work."

His mouth covers mine instantly, and I drape my arms around his neck, his muscular arms wrapping around my waist. I tangle my fingers in his hair and arch my back toward his rock-hard torso. He groans at my response and deepens the kiss with his tongue, seeking an entrance. I open my mouth and give him access—my stomach flutters with pleasure, excitement, and bewilderment, all at the same time.

For a couple of minutes, we are in the same position, but then he carries me to the couch and lays me down. I curl my legs around his waist, pressing him against me, my hands messing up his hair. We kiss, nip, and lick each other's mouths, learning more about how to taste and feel each other.

Moments later, he pulls away and kisses my cheek.

"Alayna, if we are going to choose this path, it's going to be difficult," he whispers in my ear.

"I know, but it doesn't matter now."

I've never wanted anyone as much as I desire him. I never wanted to kiss anyone like this in my life. I lean into him, so I can taste more of him, but he shifts his face away.

He frowns. "But if I don't send you away, you won't have the life you deserve."

I ignore him and cup the unmasked side of his face, and he doesn't seem to mind. I feel his warmth and the cold, metallic touch beneath my skin. No, he is burning... feverish.

"You couldn't know that."

Brandon shuts his eyes as if in pain. He grits his teeth, and his face turns bright red. Unexpectedly, he stands and holds his chest, suddenly panting.

"Hey, are you all right? Oh my God!" I exclaim as he brusquely collapses on the floor. I instantly run to his side. "Brandon, what's wrong?" I try to touch him, but his hand stops me.

I back away, but he grasps my wrist and looks at me instead.

"Alayna," he whispers hoarsely. "I don't want you to see me like this. I'm sorry, but you have to leave now."

I touch my mouth, preventing my tears from falling.

"See you like what? Are you hurt somewhere? Do you need help? I could help you to—"

His grip tightens on my wrist, and he shakes his head. "Call Oliver, please..."

"All right," I nod, panicking. "I... I'm going to call him."

I don't understand what's going on with him anymore. Hurriedly, I stand and sprint out of the room, fortunately finding Oliver and Cassius outside the door. I trip, almost losing my balance.

Oliver catches me and holds my arm to steady me. "Alayna? What's wrong? What happened?"

"I think he's in pain," I say, still dumbfounded. "I don't know what happened."

"What did you do to him?" Cassius asks, his tone accusatory.

I shake my head. "I don't know! I didn't do anything."

"Did you touch him or not?" he insists.

"Yes!" I exclaim. "But he allowed me to."

Oliver shuts his eyes and squeezes his temple. Cassius mutters a curse. Now I am utterly confused.

"Ollie, could you check Brandon? My briefcase is still inside. Give him the pill. He needs to sleep first before I give him the medicine," Cassius instructs.

Oliver scowls. "Are you sure? He's been sleeping all day."

"I don't have a choice. Go on, I'll be after you. I need a word with Alayna here."

Oliver briefly shoots me a glance and eventually nods, then walks into Brandon's room. We watch him until he's out of sight, and Cassius starts speaking.

"If you'd just told me the truth earlier, this wouldn't have happened."

"I don't know what is going on, and no one is telling me anything. How could I possibly tell you, of all people, whether I touched him or not? That's supposed to be a private matter," I point out, my voice rising.

"Not to me," he answers. "Look, it's not my place to stop you or question whatever Brandon's going to do with his life. But this has happened before, and I don't want it to happen again. It almost killed him—"

"What do you mean it almost killed him?"

Isn't that too much of an exaggeration? Who could die at a simple touch?

Cassius heaves a sigh and rests his hands on his waist. "This is much more complicated than I thought."

"Can you just tell me what's going on with him?"

"Brandon is ill, Alayna, and I'm not supposed to tell you this."

"Ill?" I frown in surprise. "He seemed fine to me. He has scars, but those are just scars, right?"

"His sickness is not physical. It's in here," he explains, pointing out his temple. "It's in his brain. He has a *psychalgia*."

I let out a frustrated breath. A what? "That's the first time I've ever heard of that."

Cassius tenses up. I can sense his hesitation, but eventually, he goes on. "It's a psychological disorder caused by traumatic physical injury. His case is acute. It rarely happens, only affecting him when it's triggered. As you can see, it has affected his way of living. This illness caused him to lock himself away from everything around him. He is traumatized, depressed, and grieving. Did you see the scar on his chest?"

"I did, yes. Accidentally."

"That scar is only a scar. He doesn't have any internal damage. But his body remembers the pain. If his brain tells him that it hurts, it is going to manifest as physical pain, and the pain is real."

"A psychogenic pain," I conclude.

"Something like that."

I almost want to fall on my knees; my head is suddenly spinning. I know that he is suffering because he wouldn't lock himself away if he were okay, but I didn't expect *this*. Not only is he in agony, but he is suffering mentally as well.

"I want to know what happened to cause his scar," I say.

"I'm sorry, Alayna, but in that case, I think you should ask Brandon. I cannot say anything more than I've already told you."

My heart twitches and my breath quickens as I try to find the right words. "Who... who do you think hurt him?"

"No one knows what happened that night, Alayna. Only him."

My throat dries up. Brandon probably doesn't want to tell anyone because he doesn't want to remember it. I guess I understand him. I was like this too, when my father passed away.

"Anyway, don't take it too far if you're leaving here anyway," he continues. His statement sounds more like a piece of advice.

"What do you mean?"

"Brandon won't make it a second time." He looks at me with sincerity this time. "Alayna, I can see that you are a good person. However, this whole setup isn't normal—for you or him. If you choose this path, you can never turn your back and do what you want. Are you ready for that kind of life?"

Turn back from the life that I want?

What do I want?

I only want to pluck my family out of poverty. I want to be a world-class chef, build my own restaurant, and see my mother healthy again. Those are my dreams. Those, and... probably start moving on from the horrors of my past. Since I arrived here, I've been too preoccupied with things to think about... *that.*

Have I already forgotten about it?

I hate to admit, but Cassius is right. I can't be so selfish as to turn my back on the reason I am here. I shouldn't sacrifice everything just because I like someone. Maybe I just got carried away with the situation; maybe I'm too enchanted with Brandon and confused myself.

My life is not in this house. I didn't expect that a short while in this mansion could change me so much.

"I've only known him for weeks!" I laugh mirthlessly. "And I don't know if I'm able to stop."

"Hey..." Cassius calls out softly, reaching out to me, and gently pats my shoulder. "I'm sorry. I didn't tell you to stop. I just told you the possibilities, but it's all on you. Brandon needs someone like you beside him. That's also another possibility." He smiles faintly.

I shake my head. "I don't know what to do anymore."

"I believe my brother already spoke to you about this. There's another way. You can still help him come out."

"I already did." A cold, stern voice abruptly thunders behind us. I jolt in shock when I find Brandon out of his room, still bare-chested and barefooted. His eyes glower at his cousin and me. The pain is still in his eyes as if he is barely able to withstand it. Oliver is just a step behind him.

"Brandon." Cassius moves away from me.

"What the fuck are you telling Alayna?"

"I'm just explaining the situation."

"And who gave you the right to say anything?"

"But it's the truth, Brandon. Don't you think she has the right to know?" Cassius's voice remains calm.

"What to do you fucking know about the truth?" Brandon barks, but his piercing gray eyes dart to me.

"Brandon, you can do this later." Oliver interrupts in front of us. "Go back to your room for now. It's not good for you to be here. You're still feverish and—"

"Isn't this what everyone wants for me, Oliver? To come out of my fucking cave?" Brandon marches toward me, grabs my hand, and shoves me aside. Then he faces Cassius. "You just came back, and you think you know everything? Ah, it's not even twenty-four hours, and you're putting your nose where it doesn't belong."

"It's not like that, Brandon." Cassius remains composed.

"I told you that being my doctor is the only thing you can do for me after what you did last year. So why do you keep getting in the way?" Brandon asks angrily.

"Why don't you give people a chance?" Cassius says. "You don't give anything a chance. I told you I was wrong, and I'm sorry. I left this house because I thought you would do better without me but look at you now."

"I was willing to welcome you back!" Brandon's eyes are wide. "But you just fucking blew it up when you started to open your mouth."

"I can't believe you are still this immature." Cassius pauses and glances at me. "Until when are you going to keep her here?"

Brandon seethes under his breath. "It's none of your fucking business."

"Face reality, Brandon. Everyone here around you has a life."

Oliver doesn't say anything, but he hurls out a deep breath.

"Lennie gave up her freedom just to stay with you," Cassius continues. "You can't expect everyone to stay with you forever, doing nothing but keeping their mouth shut. Don't you think that Lennie deserves a life that's more than this? We deserve to know why we're doing this so we can help you. How about Oliver? Did you ever ask him what he wanted in his life? He's always been with you, ever since your—"

"Are you done?" Brandon cuts him off with a shout. "Do you think I didn't know any of that? Did I ask all of you to do that for me? I didn't ask you—"

"No, you didn't." Cassius smirks. "We did this to ourselves. Is that what you are trying to say here? Can't you see how selfish you've become? Now there's Alayna. She's not Oliver or me. I know that it's not my place, but someone should tell her what she's dealing with."

"Cassius, no," Oliver interjects, grabbing his brother by the shoulder. "That's enough."

He jerks away. "No, Ollie. I wanted to tell him this so he will stop treating everyone as his servants."

"Excuse me, can I just say something?" I finally interrupt after listening to their quarrel. "Everyone here has a point, but this conversation doesn't if everyone is angry, don't you all think? Do not let this lead to something worse."

None of them answer.

"It's past twelve, and I think all of us should take a rest," I then say.

CHAPTER NINE

It's been three weeks since I last saw Brandon's face, and Oliver told me he will be taking the food to him instead of me for now. After the night his illness struck, I gave him space. It was also Oliver's advice since his cousin needs to heal again. I have no idea how this illness can affect people; I'm afraid that I might hurt him again, so I keep my distance.

I told Brandon that I wasn't bothered by any of the things I was told, but after learning about his situation, I have to be more careful around him. Any skin-to-skin contact with him can trigger pain. That is the reason he doesn't want to be touched.

But unwilling to cut our connection, we were sending each other notes about his meal or how our day had gone. I sometimes went to his now-less-creepy white room so I could hear his voice, his laughter... until he stopped answering me. No more notes and he doesn't answer my calls anymore in the white room.

It's bothering me now, wondering what happened to him, and all I can do is wait. But my heart aches for him. At the same time, I can't help but get mad. He should've at least told me he doesn't want me anymore if that's what's going on.

Tonight, I am preparing a Greek-style lobster pasta and will side it with *horiatiki* salad. Knowing that he is eating the food I'm cooking for him relieves me somehow. This way, I know that we are still connected.

Then I remember why he hired me for this job. Aside from being his private chef, he hasn't asked for Lucia's information until now. How's he going to look for her when he can't come out of his room?

A knock on the door interrupts my thoughts. It's Oliver.

"Hi." He greets me with a smile.

"Oh, hi!" I smile back. "You can take this to Brandon now."

"Of course. By the way, Alayna, it's Friday now, and I'm planning a night out with Cassius. Would you like to come? I know a place."

My mouth parts. Oliver might have noticed that I've been lurking in my kitchen and my room for the last two weeks. I only go outside when I'm looking for special ingredients.

"Is that okay?"

"Yeah." He beams. "Come on, join us. It's going to be fun."

I blink rapidly, slightly surprised.

"Alayna?"

"O-Okay." I exhale a soft breath. "I guess I'll go with you. I should probably get dressed now."

"Sure. I'll wait for you outside."

Oliver is leaning on a white sports car when I come out of the mansion, and he looks very stylish now in his black leather jacket, ripped jeans, and combat boots. He is casually dressed while still managing to look expensive.

I look down at myself, and I am definitely looking plain. There is no sense of fashion in my outfit. I put on a royal blue, haltered, knee-length dress that is not very classy. I never felt the need to buy flashy clothes. Nonetheless, I remember I'm not trying to impress anyone anyway.

"Hi," I say to get his attention. He's currently frowning at his smartphone.

Oliver looks up at me. "Oh, hey." He swiftly puts away his phone and attentively opens the door on the passenger side of the car. "Hop in."

"Thanks!" I step inside, and Oliver gets in the driver's seat.

"Buckle up," he says.

He grins and guns the car engine to life.

Oliver brings me to a nightclub, but the place is nothing like I've ever pictured. I've been to one before with my colleagues back in Venice, but unlike that very smoky and compact club, this place is luxurious.

Dancing inside the club feels more like dancing under the Northern Lights. Under the dry ice, smoke spins in an array of neon greens, blues, hot pinks, and yellow golds. The DJ adds the excitement with a LANY remix song playing over the dance floor. I love the atmosphere!

Oliver and I go upstairs, which is for the VIPs. Of course, he won't go anywhere if there isn't a place for a VIP like him.

"Do you usually come here?" I ask.

"Yes, are you surprised?"

"Well, not really." I shrug. "Maybe just a little bit."

"Come, my usual place is out there. Cassius said he's already here."

"Hey, Oliver!" An attractive blonde lady in a red dress walks toward us. She waves her hand.

"Jenny, hi! How are you?" They kiss each other's cheeks.

"I'm good. It's a great night. Have a nice time!" she says with a gentle touch to his shoulder before she leaves.

As we walk through, another man in a russet jacket appears at his side. "Oliver, what's up!"

"Hans. I thought you were in Singapore?"

"Yes, I came back yesterday. Oh, let's catch up. My girlfriend is downstairs."

"I'll catch up with you later. I have company."

Hans glances at me. "I see, but it's good to see you."

"It's good to see you too." He pats Hans's shoulder.

We settle by the VIP floor and slump on the couch near the end corner, where it isn't too loud. Oliver takes off the jacket he's wearing over a white shirt. Honestly, I am always surprised to see such different sides of him. He's usually a very composed man, yet he seems to know how to have fun outside Brandon's world.

"I'm shocked," I admit.

"At what?"

"At you. This different you."

"A man has a right to have fun. I'm a regular here. This is where I come whenever I want to chill."

"I see that you've got a lot in your hands. Being Brandon's CEO, right-hand man, and everything else. I'm just not used to seeing you so carefree."

"I'm more of a friend than family to Brandon," he corrects.

I look away. "Sorry. I didn't mean to bring up work."

He chuckles. "It's okay. Do you want anything to eat or drink?"

"Do they have orange juice here?" I joke, then laugh. "Can I have a blackberry gin & tonic, please?"

"Of course, I'll get you some. Wait for me here."

"And oh! I'd like to have strawberries too."

"No problem." He winks at me and starts walking away.

Fifteen minutes later, he still hasn't come back. I watch the people passing by, and the ambiance is starting to get dreary. I'm also beginning to worry.

Did he get stuck on the dance floor? Did someone spill juice on his shirt? Or is he in the restroom?

I stand in my seat to look for Oliver, but Cassius appears instead.

"Cassius..."

He is gorgeous, more so than the first time I saw him. I notice that his fashion taste is similar to his older brother's. He's wearing a black coat and a black shirt, unbuttoned on the chest to expose his smooth pectorals.

I quickly look away. What the hell am I thinking?

I notice a small grin playing on his lips. He places a glass of blackberry gin and tonic and a plate of sliced strawberries in front of me.

"Why are you bringing this instead of Oliver?" I try to sound flat.

He shrugs and sits next to me. A breath of relief rushes out of his mouth as he sits.

"Probably having fun on the dance floor with his future wife," he says. He's holding a glass of drink in his hand.

I frown. "Betty came?" Ollie didn't say she was coming.

"Yes, he's occupied, so he asked me to join you." He flashes out a sexy grin.

"Oh, I thought—"

"Disappointed?"

"No, of course, not. Though I wouldn't have come if I knew."

"Jealous?" He drinks the glass of his liquor straight, watching me askance.

"Why would I be? I'm not even interested in him. I don't need to explain to you."

"Relax, I'm just kidding." Cassius puts down his glass, picks up a strawberry, and pops it in his mouth.

I roll my eyes. "Well, it's not funny."

"How are you doing?" he asks out of the blue. "I heard you stopped seeing Brandon." He looks at me and munches another piece of strawberry.

I face him. "It's more like he stopped seeing me. He doesn't talk to me anymore. I don't know what happened to him now."

"Oh, you'll be fine."

"I am fine." I shrug. "I managed before I met him; I'll manage it now. I am better than fine."

He lets out a delighted laugh. He should stop using his charms on me. Or maybe he just isn't aware that he's doing it? Damn me.

"Okay, this night was supposed to be about having fun. Do you want to dance?"

"Are you asking me to dance?" I ask.

"I think I am. Come on!"

Cassius stands and grabs my hand to take me to the dance floor. He begins to move his body to the beat. The song "One Kiss" by Calvin Harris and Dua Lipa is now playing.

"May I?" He stretches his palm, seeking permission.

I nod, and carefully he slips his arms around my waist. I slightly start at the gesture. The electrifying heat instantly radiates out of him again, and I can feel his breath on my cheek. The warmth between us as he sways with me grows more intense by the second. My heart is beating abnormally fast. His scent, his face, his touch...

"Are you okay?" he whispers. His hand drops; he starts swaying his hips.

I move my hips to his rhythm.

This is something I cannot do with Brandon. Something I won't ever experience with him, my brain shouts.

"This is probably the most sinful thing I have ever done in my life," he whispers.

His statement confuses me. "Why?"

"I think you are attracted to me; I'm not dumb," he points out.

My brows arch at his confidence. "You're unbelievable."

His face slightly grimaces. "And yet, you are still Brandon's girl."

"We never got to that point," I say honestly. "I don't even know what he thinks about me now."

"I can see that you are still his. Can you say you don't have feelings for him?"

I avoid his eyes. "I don't have to answer that."

"Come on." He flashes a half-smile. "There's no need to hide, Alayna."

"Yes, I guess I do," I snap. "But can you just stop talking and at least finish one full dance?"

He laughs softly then spins me around so my back is against his chest. "Brandon wouldn't like this very much. You, dancing with me."

"Stop provoking me," I warn. "It's just a dance. It means *nothing*."

Again he laughs at my statement, but then he presses me against his body, and this time his mouth is very near mine.

"I'm sorry," he breathes. "I won't mention it again."

"Good. Then let's dance, and don't say anything more."

When we return to our table, there's still no sight of Oliver. We can't find him anywhere in the VIP area or on the dance floor. He's probably with his fiancée, or he went home without me.

"Things got heated up with Ollie and Betty earlier," Cassius says.

I frown. "What happened to them?"

"I don't know. I guess they've already left. I'll take you home," Cassius says as if reading my thoughts.

"Are you sure?"

"Don't worry, I won't come in. Brandon would be furious if he sees me with you."

My shoulders fall. I guess I have no choice. "I'm so sorry, Cassius. I hate to make you take me home... I just don't know much about the city."

"Even if you knew the city well, I wouldn't let you go home alone."

"Thank you, by the way. It was fun."

"You're welcome." He smiles. "Can we do this again?"

"Of course. Saturday is my free day."

"Saturday, then. I will take you somewhere else. I don't know why Oliver brought you here. This is his usual place, but it isn't for a girl like you."

"Why not? Am I not allowed to have fun?" I cross my arms.

"It's not what I meant. You can come here as much as you want, but never come alone."

"Why not? This place looks fine."

"Yes, but there are nasty guys in here. You wouldn't want to encounter one. And since it's getting late, I'll take you home now."

"Of course. I'll just use the restroom first."

He nods. "I'll wait for you here."

I hurriedly come out of the restroom after freshening up, surprised that even in clubs such as this, the line is still a bit long. I don't want Cassius to wait, so I am heading to the stairs when I suddenly bump into someone.

"Ouch!" I touch my forehead and try to look up at the person who abruptly stops in front of me.

"Going somewhere?" asks the most melodious voice I've ever heard in my whole life. It's the voice I've missed the past few weeks. I thought I was only dreaming, but it's real. He's here.

Brandon.

BRANDON

Why the fuck is she still out at this hour?

I emptied a bottle of whiskey, but I still feel nothing. The alcohol won't affect me. I frown at my wristwatch to check the time, and it's already past two o'clock in the morning.

What else can I do? Is this the life Alayna's hoping for? Going out, dancing in a club with someone else? Is this the price of everything I can't do for her? Has she already chosen this path? I almost died by fighting against myself. Is everything I fought for the past month for nothing?

A knock on the door interrupts my thoughts. I open it immediately, hoping to see Alayna.

"Brandon?" It's Oliver, but he's alone. He steps inside and closes the door.

"Where is Alayna? Is she in her room?"

He doesn't answer right away. "She's with Cassius," he breathes. "I'm sorry, Brandon. I had a small misunderstanding with my girlfriend."

I frown hard. "When did you get a girlfriend?" I start to ask, but that isn't important. "She's still there? Why did you leave her with him?" My voice is rising.

Oliver scratches his head. "It was unavoidable. I'm sorry, but she'll be fine with him. He'll drive her home safely."

"But that's the problem, Ollie!" I snap. "I don't trust Cassius."

His eyes are apologetic. "Are we going to argue about this?"

"Bring her here, or I will. Right now, Oliver," I demand.

"Will you calm down? Cassius won't do anything to her."

"Do you think I'm just going to sit back and leave her alone while Cassius is grinding his dick on her?" I hiss, pointing out the door.

"It isn't like that, Brandon. You don't understand. I was in a tight situation earlier. I told you my girlfriend came... and we kind of—"

"I can't believe I am hearing this!" I cut him off. "I'm going out. I'm getting her back." I snatch the car key from his hand and stomp out of my room.

"Brandon, no!" he shouts.

"Not this time, Ollie," I growl.

"Wait!" he calls out again, now coming after me.

I grit my teeth and stop, then face him. "What do you fucking want me to do?"

"Are you trying to kill yourself?" He grabs my shoulders. "You won't even manage two miles. The club is in the middle of the city. Cassius will take care of Alayna. He'll bring her here."

"How do you know? He's different than you, and I don't give a fuck if the club is at the end of the earth!"

Ollie runs his fingers through his hair and heaves a sigh. "Okay. I'll take you there. I'll drive."

CHAPTER TEN

A few weeks ago

I never thought I'd be setting foot in this place again. I look up at the clear morning sky for the first time in ten years. The children's park where I used to play is still here, but a lot has changed.

The slow creaks of the rusty swings and the sweep of the wind send shivers down my spine. The park is now barely visible as the moss and vines covered the surroundings. All memories of my childhood come flooding back.

This has been a place of joy, peace, and contentment. This is where we played, ran, fought. The once silver slide has bronzed. Now this place could serve as the set for some horror film.

"Are you really sure about this? There's no turning back now," Oliver says.

"We are already out of the house, so let's get started."

Oliver smiles. "See? What did I tell you? You can do things if you just put your mind to it. Look at you now. I should've searched for Alayna long ago and brought her to you."

"I'm not just doing this for her. I'm doing this for myself," I remind him.

"But, Brandon, you can walk around the house, and you managed to come out. I see that you don't have a problem in getting out at all," he stated.

"It's not that I can finally come out, Ollie. I'm still struggling. I don't want people to see me. I don't want to encounter them. I can't even look at myself in the mirror because all I see is a dead man's reflection. This is my insecurity." I touch the covered part of my face.

"It's not as ugly as you think. The world is even uglier, and yours is just skin."

"I don't want to see the world that killed my family."

"But you found yourself again," he says. "How else are you going to find justice? This is the answer, and you are finally getting there."

"I know where I can find Annette now," I inform him.

"You do? Does Alayna really know where she is?"

"Yes, but I cannot face her if I'm like this. You are right. I need to get better. You know that there's no one I could ask but you."

"I never turned my back on you." Oliver steps aside and holds the whistle. "Take off your mask, Brandon. It's a distraction."

Gently, I pull the rubber tie around my ear and take off the mask, letting it fall on the ground. I shudder as the cold wind blows against my bare face and cover it with my hand.

"You don't have to hide your face from me," Oliver says kindly.

I tense up and slowly meet the world in front of me.

"Now, can you see that tree over there? That's about half a mile. I need you to run there and get back here. Don't stop until you can't run anymore. We need to work on how far you can go when you run. I don't know if this is going to work, but we will still try. Even if it's hard, I don't want to hear *'No'* or *'I give up.'* Do you understand?"

I nod while holding my breath. As long as people don't touch me, I can do this.

"Are you ready, Brandon?"

"Y-Yes..."

"I said, are you ready?"

"Yes, sir!" I answer as loudly as I can.

"On my mark. Three... Two... One..."

I begin running as I hear the whistle blow.

ALAYNA

"Going somewhere?"

I look up at the man blocking the way. It is that mask, the same gray eyes, and melodious baritone voice. I'm still not sure if I'm dreaming or if the alcohol has already affected me.

How is this possible?

"Brandon," I say, still unsure. "No... It's impossible."

A deep groan vibrates in his throat, and his chest tenses up. He grabs my wrist, his thumb pressing on my pulse. I can feel the warmth of his palm on my skin.

"Do you not know when to stop or when to come home?" he asks, sounding furious.

I shake my head. "This must be a dream," I murmur. "I must be dreaming. You seem so real!"

His jaw clenches. "Because I am!"

I gawk at him, still astounded. It's him. He's really here.

"Wait!" I jerk my hand away, but his grip tightens. "How are you here?"

"Is that important?"

I manage to pull my hand back and glare at him. "Why are you touching me? I thought you hated it so much."

He leans closer and shuts his eyes as he moves away. "Come on now. Let's get you home."

"It's been a week since you last talked to me. Besides, I still want to stay here." I cross my arms. No way is he getting away with being so moody.

"No, you're coming with me," he insists. He grasps my hand again and drags me out of the restroom, heading to the exit.

"Hey, let me go right now! Hey!" I scream. People look our way, but they don't seem to care. "How could you come all the way here just to tell me what to do after ignoring my calls and notes? You didn't even say hi."

"Hi," he says but doesn't look at me.

"You know, you can't just disappear like that and appear when you want to!"

Brandon stops and finally faces me. "I can appear anywhere if I want to. So please, come with me while I'm still being nice."

"I'm going to call security if you try to force me."

His eyes peer at me a little more closely. "Do you know how things work around here, Alayna? I might fire the security first if they try to touch me. Everything you see here is *mine*. Do you understand?"

I scowl. "You own the club?"

"Yes."

I roll my eyes. "I really don't stand a chance, do I?"

"I don't want to do this, but you're leaving me no choice."

Brandon wraps his arms around my waist, and as if I were a sheet of paper, he carries me on his shoulder. My eyes widen as the world spins, turning me upside down.

"No! Put me down, Brandon! Put me down, please, please... I'm coming with you, okay? Just put me down," I cry out, but he doesn't listen and heads to the exit.

Two security guards get in the way, but Oliver appears out of nowhere and stops them. They acknowledge him and step back.

Brandon sets me down as soon as we are outside. I suddenly feel sick to my stomach.

"How could you do that to me?" I say, panting hard. "What are you doing here anyway?"

"Let's do this at home. Shall we?" He waltzes toward the black Jaguar and opens the door.

"What about Cassius? He's still inside."

He grimaces. "What about him?"

"Don't worry, Alayna," Oliver interjects. "I'll talk to my brother. Get in the car and go home with Brandon."

"Fine." I exhale a breath of frustration. I turn to the other side and settle into the driver's seat. I pull the door closed, but Brandon stops me.

"What are you doing?" He scowls. "Move aside."

"All right, all right!" I move to the passenger seat. Brandon steps in. "Wait. Can you drive?"

I mean, he locked himself in his room forever, right? There's no way he knows how to drive this thing. I suddenly feel terrified for both of us.

"I wasn't born three hundred years ago. Of course, I can drive."

He buckles his seatbelt, then guns the car, pulling out of the place like an expert.

I wake up with a gentle squeeze on my shoulder. I groan as I feel the discomfort at the back of my neck. I massage the painful part lightly and gaze up at the window. It's still dark. We are already on the mansion's front porch.

"We... home?"

I shift my head toward Brandon, and his icy eyes are watching me. "About thirty minutes ago," he responds hoarsely.

"What time is it?"

"Three in the morning."

"Oh." I look away from his eyes. I'm already melting. "So, should we... should we get inside now?"

"Yes, but you and I need to talk." He steps out of the car first. I follow him and head to the mansion.

The only light in the hallways come from the warm fixtures on the walls, and it's very quiet, apart from Brandon's light footsteps and the clacking of my heels as we move to the twin staircase.

Brandon abruptly stops and looks over his shoulder.

"You are going to wake up everyone in here."

"Sorry. I'll take them off."

"Hey," he hisses, "I didn't tell you to—"

I bend down and pick up my heels.

He exhales. "I said you didn't have to."

We stop in front of his rooms, and he lets me go in first. He walks straight to his bedroom and takes his jacket off, leaving only a black T-shirt. I notice that he is more muscular than when I last saw him. He sits on the bed.

"Sit." He taps the space beside him.

I slowly step closer and sit quietly. I can't say anything.

"Are you just going to sit there?" he begins to ask. "Speak."

I look up at him. He is already gazing at me.

"I didn't expect this," I say. I can't exactly complain. I admit that I miss him, but I am unprepared for this. We haven't talked for a week, and now he is expecting me to say something.

"I know you have a lot of questions. Now is your time to ask."

"Well"—I cleared my throat—"how did you manage to go outside?"

"Oliver helped me. I wasn't supposed to come out until..." He pauses.

"Until?"

He tenses up. "What's with you and Cassius?"

"Didn't Oliver tell you? He was *occupied*." I try to avoid his eyes.

"I know when someone is lying to me, Alayna," he says softly. "Do you like him?" His tone is calm but dejected.

"No, it was nothing." I shrug. "Look, there's still a lot of things I don't understand about you. You lift me up one moment, and then you bring me down the next. I am not ready for that kind of relationship. Cassius was there. He is *available* and—"

"Available?" He laughs without mirth. "Interesting."

I sigh hard and shut my eyes. "I meant he was there to dance with me—to talk, and I had fun. Something I know that you don't do."

"Ah, and what else is there that I cannot do? Touch you? Go out to the nightclub with you?" He shakes his head, a pinch of disappointment in his eyes. "And to summarize it all—you like him, am I wrong?"

"I don't like him," I assert firmly. "He was just there, that's all!"

Brandon reaches out, tucking a strand of hair behind my ear. I jerk away. His fingers brought tingles of electricity all over me.

"You suddenly didn't want to see me. Why?" I ask.

He backs away and stares blankly at the ceiling. "My world is dark. Cassius was probably right. You deserve better, someone like him. It's not even a surprise."

"No, you're wrong. I like *you*," I say, tears already building in my eyes. "I've liked you since the first time I saw you. You are strange, and you are far from normal. Everything about you is a mystery, but I can't help it. I don't know why or how... I just like you the way you are."

His expression softens. "I'm sorry, Alayna. It's not that I don't want to see you. I do. But there are just things I need to do."

"Then... I'm glad to hear that."

"And I like you, too." He gazes at me. "Everything about you."

"You do?"

"I'm willing to give it a try. You don't belong to my world, so let me belong to yours."

Brandon stands, his eyes not leaving mine. Then he pulls off his black shirt over his head, exposing the scar on his chest. The scar covers almost half of his left chest. The dry, yellowish, dead skin around it is almost painful to see, but I don't look away. I can't. Instead, I stare at his imperfection.

"Touch me, Alayna," he says tenderly; it's almost a whisper.

I swallow hard. "Are you sure?"

He doesn't respond, but I lift my hand and begin tracing his oblique muscle with my finger. I slowly move to his rock-hard abdominals. I finally stand; my hands are still on the flatness of his stomach.

Brandon lets out a hitched breath. I stop.

"Are you okay?"

He nods. "Don't stop."

He holds my hands and brings my palms to his chest. I can slightly feel the texture of his scar against my fingertips.

Gently, I trace the scar. The skin is oddly soft, but the surface feels thick. I shut my eyes and stop. I'm not sure anymore if I can carry on. He's panting, and I can see that he's trying to bear the unbearable.

"Go on. I want this. Don't stop, please," he pleads.

"What if I hurt you again like the last time?"

"This time you won't," he murmurs. We stare at one another and he presses a kiss to my forehead. "I'm not supposed to do this. If I kiss you now, I won't be able to stop. Oliver's hard work will be for nothing."

"What do you mean?"

"I'm not done with fixing myself."

"But you seem fine now. You can come out now, and you even drove a sports car!"

"No. You'll know if I'm completely healed. Besides, I may not know how to handle you like this." He flashes a meaningful smile.

"What? Are you telling me that you are a virgin, and you don't know how to kiss?"

He let out a delighted laugh. "No, I'm not a virgin."

"Okay, so you are not a virgin, but you lack experience?" I ask without trying to sound offensive.

He leans into my ear and whispers, "Alayna, I haven't had a woman for the last ten years, but it doesn't mean I don't know how to satisfy one, especially in bed."

"Oh." I clear my throat. "I see."

"If I put you in my bed right now, you won't be able to stand up for a day because you won't feel your legs. I can be very gentle, but I can also be very rough. So, if you are not ready with this tiny body of yours, refrain from whatever you're going to say." He moves away, but the millions of tiny sparks his words provoked remain and excite my senses.

"All right, you've made your point. So..." I slip my arms around his neck. "Will I see you again tomorrow?"

"No, but you will soon. Just give me some time. It won't take another month. I promise." He kisses my nose. "It will kill me if I don't see your face again."

I smile. "I can't wait. It would kill me too. I'm sorry, by the way. I didn't mean to—"

Brandon cuts me off, his thumb brushing on my lip, causing my mouth to gape open. With a low groan, he leans toward me; his mouth descends to my neck, and his lips carve a sensuous path to my ear. They continue to move across my throat, to my chin, and finally claim my mouth in a kiss.

It feels like a dream—so erotic, doing this with the most beautiful and enigmatic man in the world. His kiss drowns me, and he is hungry. He thrusts his tongue into my mouth, greedily devouring mine. All I can hear is the sound of our kiss. I feel dizzy from the demanding possessiveness of his mouth. I don't realize his hand is already on top of my breast. He gives it a gentle squeeze.

"Ahh..."

"Shh... Your reactions are going to be the death of me."

I blush. My insides are tingling, a pressure building in my core. He's the only one who can make me feel this way. I'm already getting addicted to this.

Brandon pulls away first.

"It's getting late. You need to rest."

Oh, God. How could he leave me so turned on like this?

CHAPTER ELEVEN

I t is Sunday the next day, and I can probably rest longer in my room. I stretch my arms and legs and step out of the bed.

Butterflies flutter in my stomach as I suddenly remember the steamy kiss I shared with Brandon. I touch my lips and smile. I want to see and kiss him again. Last night was perfect. Well, he was perfect.

My thoughts are abruptly interrupted when I hear my phone beep. I sigh and lazily pick it up from the bedside table.

I scowl at the screen. I have four missed calls and three messages from an unknown number.

I check the time logs, and the last call was thirty minutes ago. I don't usually answer unsaved phone numbers, but given the fact the caller bombarded my phone, it must be urgent. Or maybe it was from home.

I try to call back the number.

"Hello?" someone answers right away. It's a man's voice.

"Hello, may I know who's calling?"

"Alayna," I hear him clear his throat. "It's me."

"Who's 'me'"—I pause; the voice sounds quite familiar. *"Cassius?"*

"Yep," he answers and chuckles. "You left without saying goodbye. How are you?"

"I'm fine," I answer simply. "What's up?"

"Good. I just wanted to know if you're okay."

"How did you get my number?"

"Hmm," he hums. "I asked Ollie. He had to babysit me because I was already getting furious."

"Furious, why?"

God, what am I doing right now? Brandon doesn't want me talking to him.

"Because I'm attracted to someone who's already taken," he confesses and forces a laugh.

I remain silent, unsure of what to say.

"Anyway, I heard it worked," he continues. "Brandon came out of the house officially after a decade. But I'm sorry I ruined it last night. I didn't mean to get in the picture."

What worked? Get in the picture? "Hold on. Don't make me solve a riddle here."

"I'm not supposed to tell you a patient's condition."

"But it's Brandon. I know what is going on with him now, so what is holding you back?"

"I wasn't supposed to tell you that before either, but I had to know what went on the last time he had an episode. Anyway, I'm finding a way that could help his condition... help him get better, especially now that we have seen hope. You are his hope."

I shake my head. "I don't like being called such a thing, Cassius."

"But you are. I knew that when Brandon found out you were with me, he'd have no choice but to come out and get you. Fortunately, he responded positively."

"Wait," I interrupt him. "Are you saying you plotted all that?"

"Is that bad?"

"No, I just..." I pause. "Cassius, Brandon came out because of *you,* while he thought it was because of Oliver's help."

He pauses a little. "Uh, yes. Brandon didn't want to see me, so I had to ask Ollie." There's melancholy in his voice.

"But even if you do this, Brandon will still—"

"Hate me?" he presses. "I don't mind. I have a debt to pay."

Debt? What kind of debt? I want to ask him, but I keep the thought in my mind.

"Why are you telling me this?"

"So you won't misunderstand me. I want to clear my intentions. I am a very honest person, Alayna, but I just really wanted to help Oliver. He's in a tight situation right now. You know what I mean."

Instantly, I thought of Ollie being engaged. On the other hand, I still didn't understand why Brandon doubted him. There must be something more to it. Something he hasn't told me. Brandon wouldn't hate or distrust his cousin for no reason. He clearly said that he doesn't trust him, but Cassius is obviously doing everything he can to make it up to him.

"The next few weeks are going to be tough for Brandon," he goes on. "He might not be able to see you for a while."

"I know." I sigh. "He just told me, but he said it's not going to take another month."

"Brandon didn't know that it was going to be difficult this time. It's going to be very painful."

"Does he know now?"

"How could we possibly tell him that? This could be his second death." He pauses. "I mean, not literally, but he needs to be strong to make it work this time. He's not completely healed."

The mask. He still has the mask.

"When are you going to tell him, then? He'll eventually find out."

"Brandon needs time. You've seen the scar on his chest, but you haven't seen his face, and you will never wish to see it. It's his biggest insecurity. I want to help him make it go away, but he's just too afraid of my hands."

"What is it like?" I snap. "His face... What is he hiding under the mask? Is it anything like the scar on his chest?"

"Look, I can't disclose something private, but at this moment, you are the only person he listens to—more than Oliver. Have patience with him, Alayna. I have a feeling he will open up to you soon."

My heart rises. "I hope for that too. Thanks, Cassius."

"Anytime. Oh, I have to go. I'm flying to Athens tonight, but I'll be back next week. I'll keep in touch."

"Sure."

"Alayna." He hangs up.

Sometimes, I wonder what it would be like if I didn't know any of them. I imagine myself in a restaurant cooking to my heart's content. But how empty it would be if I never got to know Brandon. Right now, even if the path I've chosen is hard, I can't see my future without him in it.

❧

I feel a bit refreshed after a cold bath, but my head is still throbbing. It's my rest day, but I want to check my supplies. Ms. Lennie is in charge of Brandon's meals on the weekend. I find her at my station with a new girl.

She looks so young and charming. She has wavy, dark brown hair, pouty red lips, and curvy hips. She is wearing a similar uniform as a cook, only simpler. I can't help but wonder: Did they hire new kitchen staff? If so, why is she at my station?

"Good morning, Ms. Lennie," I greet her. "I'm just going to check the supplies so I can ask the grocer for refills." My attention wanders to the brunette beauty next to her. She's slicing the salmon into thin strips.

"Good morning, Alayna. No need, dear. I already asked someone to fill up the supplies," she says. "And Alayna?"

"Yes?"

"I'd like you to meet Casey. She's going to be your assistant, and she's only in charge of cooking on the weekends. Oliver decided to leave the kitchen to you, and Casey will deliver the food to our master."

Wait. What? If I heard her right, she clearly said this Casey will deliver food to Brandon.

Who is she exactly? Jealousy strikes me. I'm afraid Brandon allowed someone else other than me to enter his room.

I lean toward Ms. Lennie's ear and whisper, making sure my voice is almost inaudible. "I need a further explanation. Did Brandon hire someone else? I thought I was his private chef now, and—"

"Casey will be delivering the food to his study." She interrupts me with a faint smile. "She is also Oliver and Cassius's sister. She's the youngest."

Sister! I didn't think of that.

"Oh, Casey? Come here, dear," Ms. Lennie calls her.

When she raises her face, it's the most beautiful I've seen in my life, but there's no hint of the Katrakis brothers' genes on her. I'm instantly star-struck by her dark hair, small nose, and plump pink lips. And her mesmerizing gray eyes; they're just like... Brandon's.

"Lennie." She smiles sweetly.

"Casey, this is Alayna. She's the Master's private chef. She's going to help you with everything that you want to know. You've probably heard of her from your brothers."

She waves her hand. "Hi, Alayna."

"Casey is a new culinary transferee at the Institute of Culinary Arts in Manhattan. She's only a sophomore, so she still needs your supervision. She's going to be staying here with her brother until she graduates. Also, she's your age."

"It's nice to meet you, Casey." I smile as I reach out a hand; she takes it with a light squeeze.

"You too, Alayna."

"Well then, I still have chores to do. I'll leave you two for a moment." Ms. Lennie excuses herself and leaves.

Casey continues slicing the salmon into bite-sized pieces. It's probably best if I don't disturb her. I still don't know how I'm going to approach her. She also seems different from her brothers, and the atmosphere suddenly feels awkward.

"Um, I'll probably see you tomorrow. It's my–uh–rest day today," I announce.

"You are beautiful," she says unexpectedly without bothering to glance at me.

I flush. "Oh, thank you."

"No wonder my brothers were so smitten with you." Now Casey stops and looks up at me. "I wondered what you looked like. Now that I've seen you, I finally understand what's going on."

"What do you mean?"

"My *brothers* like you, Alayna."

I blink, confused. "Well, I don't think Oliver likes me since he's engaged."

"No, he likes you. He's engaged to Betty, but it doesn't mean he can't like you. He's just too gentlemanly to say it. On the other hand, Cassius might've made the first move already?" she says meaningfully, as if certain.

"I... I have nothing to say to that."

Her eyes gleam. "But Brandon is the one you like?"

I frown. "How did you know about all of that?"

"My brothers talk about you and Brandon. I happen to know everything, and when I say I know everything, I mean it."

"I don't know how to put this, but I certainly don't want them speaking about me."

She blinks her long eyelashes. "Okay, how about we talk later? I'd really, really like to get to know you, Alayna."

I laugh softly. Honestly, there is something pleasant about her. I don't know if it's her smile or her sweet soothing voice. It would be nice to speak with someone else in the house other than Oliver.

"There's nothing I could tell you."

"I'm sure there's probably a lot to know." She speaks even more very softly. "But I don't mean to intimidate you. It's okay if you're busy. I don't want to take your free time."

This might be quite burdensome, but I'd like to know more about the family as well—or probably know more about Brandon.

"No, no. It's okay. I'd love to talk a bit later."

She smiles again. "Really? Honestly, I know that you are curious about a lot of things, and I'm quite inquisitive. I want to know what's going on in this house."

I smile. "I'll see you later."

"I'll come by your room. See you, Alayna."

A knock on my door interrupts my browsing. I open it to find Casey carrying a tray of potato chips, French fries, and two bottles of orange juice.

"May I come in?" she asks with a grin.

"Sure." I step aside to let her in.

"Whoa, you have a nice room!" She walks toward my study desk and places the tray down. Casey settles in front of my computer, picks up a potato chip, and pops it into her mouth. "We used to visit this mansion when we were little. This was our grandmother's before it became Brandon's. I kind of missed it, but don't you think it's too lonely now?"

"A little, but really?" It's the first time I've heard that. "I thought this was—"

"Brandon's house? Sure is, but this house was only given to him when he turned eighteen. But oh, I'm sure you already know what's going on with his life."

"Not anything... besides his condition. Brandon isn't very open." I slump at the edge of my bed, and Casey swivels the chair around and rocks forward. She offers me a snack.

"Would you like some?"

"Thank you." I slide my hand into the chip bag and grab a couple.

"I don't know many things as well," she continues. "But there's something."

"All right, so tell me why you want to speak with me."

"Hmm. *That.* I want us to get along first. I want us to properly introduce ourselves. Is that fine with you?"

Talking about myself isn't always a good idea. There are details I'd like to remain undisclosed. I am just a simple girl from Kansas with a mother and twelve siblings to people. "I think you already know about me, so I'll skip mine. Tell me more about you? Oliver did mention a sister."

"They are nice, my brothers, aren't they?" She grins.

I agree. "Well, they are."

"Yes, even though I'm adopted, I feel like I'm a princess."

Whoa, what an introduction! I blink, unable to speak.

"I know that it's not something to brag about," she continues. "Mom always wanted to have a daughter after she gave birth to Cassius, but she wasn't able to bear another child. She almost died giving birth to him. They adopted me when I was three."

"Then, that's probably why you're not blonde?" I mumble unintentionally. I didn't mean to sound nosy.

"You noticed?" She touches her wavy chocolate-brown hair. "I always wanted to dye my hair blonde, but it would be fake, no?"

"I think your hair is beautiful as it is," I say in all honesty. It matched her ash-colored eyes.

"Thanks."

"And at what age did you learn that you're adopted?"

"I knew my whole life. But I didn't get along with them at first. I remember Ollie and I didn't get along very well when we were kids. He was kind of hard-headed when he was young."

I couldn't help but laugh. "Oliver was like that?"

"Yeah!" She chortled. "Cassius, on the other hand, was very thoughtful. We were close, and he's very kind. I'm sure you find him charming too." She winks.

I force a smile. "I guess."

She puts the bag of potato chips aside and grabs the bottle of juice. "But you're in love with Brandon," she concludes.

My head shoots up. My chin almost drops at her frankness. "I don't want to put it like that for now. I mean, that's strong speculation. I like him, but I'm still figuring myself out... and things about him."

"It's because you are confused." She smiles kindly. "But don't worry, I actually understand you. Brandon is very complicated."

"I'm trying to understand him, but I'm not giving up."

"That's the spirit." She chugs the bottle of orange juice straight and heaves a sigh of relief.

"So... are you close to Brandon?" I ask.

"Very. We all used to hang out together. My brothers and Elga as well."

"I hadn't heard that before."

"Brandon and his family always lived here in Manhattan. They used to have a small house in Queens, and we moved there too for a brief time. But then we all moved back to

Athens when Aunt Grethe and Elga passed away. Since Brandon needed someone at his side, Oliver and Cassius stayed with him here. Then he inherited this mansion."

I nod. "Is it all right if I ask you something else?"

"Shoot."

"I heard of this rule, that women in the family should only marry someone from these other two families—I've forgotten the names."

She nodded. "Stavros and Dragoumis. I'm surprised you know this. That could be my fate too, even though I'm adopted. What about them, anyway?"

"Did Brandon's mother marry someone else?"

"You are very perceptive, Alayna. Well, yes, our family has always been complicated. Our grandfather cut his ties with Aunt Grethe when she married Brandon's dad. She was exiled from the family, and they moved away and lived a modest life."

"That rule is bullshit, to be honest," I say.

"Yeah, right? Who wants to marry a distant relative? Gross." She grimaces. "My father hates that too. However, when Aunt Grethe gave birth to three children, our grandfather miraculously changed. He didn't care about those rules anymore. He was willing to welcome them back, except, of course, for Brandon's dad. Aunt Grethe was his favorite, after all, but she didn't want to leave her husband."

I shake my head in slight disappointment. "But Brandon's dad did abandon them for his mistress."

"And much worse, Brandon's dad is a son of a servant— one of the Katrakis' oldest servants who also has a drop of French blood. So much for the movie-like drama, right?"

I didn't think that dumping your own family because of rules was right, but in this case, I couldn't blame their grandfather. Brandon's mother married an irresponsible man. His son was suffering here alone, and the grandfather was his only family left but still chose to abandon Brandon.

"But despite being poor, Brandon has always been the smart one," Casey continues while munching on a chip. "Look at what he achieved. He owns the world, but he just can't see his own worth. Cassius became a doctor to help him, and Oliver spent his whole life building the company. Honestly, for my brothers' sake, I hope Brandon escapes all this. He deserves to live a normal life. Thanks to you, he's beginning to see the light now."

I smile a little. "I didn't do anything. Honestly, it's all him. He decided to finally go out."

She grins back. "That's also true."

"Hey, I don't want to ask this, but it keeps bothering me..."

"Go on, Alayna."

"Do you perhaps know how his family was killed? Does he know the culprit?"

There was disgust in her eyes. "Honestly, Brandon doesn't tell us a lot about what happened that *day*, but we all know that the suspects are inside the Katrakis circle. The family is a vast clan. When Grandfather found out that Brandon and Elga existed, he wanted to make the two of them his successors. But the elders weren't up for this idea since they thought they were the offspring of 'sins.' There's also this rule that those who are already exiled don't have the right to a single cent of the family inheritance."

"But Brandon made all his wealth by himself, right?" I point out. "I'm sure they are all going to leave him alone now."

They should. He suffered all alone. His family was murdered because of it, and he almost lost his own life because of it.

She shakes her head, her expression hardening. "The Katrakises possess unimaginable wealth. We are talking about billions here, Alayna. The family has three heads, and we usually call them 'the elders.' It's a very long story, but my grandfather alone owns one of the biggest banks, shopping malls, and automotive manufacturing industries in Greece, as well as private airlines. Now, can you imagine all their wealth combined?"

I cover my mouth. Brandon's family is *that* powerful. It's almost overwhelming how powerful Brandon would become if he acquired this fortune.

"And Brandon is still going to have this wealth?"

"I don't know, but I've heard he would."

"So that's where the problem lies," I conclude.

"Since Brandon is the son of a prodigal daughter that fell from grace, the elders believe he didn't deserve to receive anything at all, so they were kind of protesting," she explains, disgust never leaving her eyes.

I scowl hard. "And they wanted to eliminate him and his family, is that it?"

"Brandon had already rejected his rights to the fortune, but they felt and still feel threatened."

Things are more apparent to me now. I understand why he couldn't say a word. His blood—his own family—betrayed and literally killed him inside and out. It's hard to believe some people can actually kill a family member.

My poor Brandon. My poor, poor man.

How hard it must be for him. I suddenly want to hold him and tell him that we are still here for him—that *I* am here for him.

"But how about this thing with Lucia—um, I mean Annette? Do you know anything about her?" I ask, suddenly remembering. "She's the reason Brandon hired me. I know her and I know where to find her, but she doesn't seem like a person who could hurt anyone."

She looks at me with a deep frown. "I can't believe you're involved in this, Alayna. I'm really sorry," she says, her face expressing regret. "Annette was the reason why his father left. I don't know what else is the deal with her, but Brandon might know something we don't. She could be a part of his misery."

I fall back on the bed, my knees weak. "I even looked up to her. I was so clueless." I bury my face in my palms, already on the verge of tears.

"It is hard to know everything, Alayna."

I lift my head. Earlier, I remember she said something about three children. She said Brandon's mother gave birth to three children. Who's the other one? Does Brandon have another sibling?

I want to ask Casey that, but I keep the thought in my mind since I probably misheard something. At this point, my head is spinning.

I wipe my face of tears. "There's a lot more I want to ask, but my head is going to explode just by thinking about it."

"I think I've told you enough for one day," she says. "But would you like it if we watched Netflix? I really wanted to watch this new show with someone..."

CHAPTER TWELVE

BRANDON

I throw the last pin on the dartboard, but it doesn't hit the bull's eye. I blow out a sharp breath of frustration. "I can't do it, Ollie. Not again."

"Relax, man." He stands, pulls the pins, and hands them back to me. "When are you telling her, then?"

"I told her it won't take a month, but it's been another week."

I can only connect with her by eating the meals she prepares for me. She'd always leave a note, saying, *"Enjoy your day"* or *"I miss you,"* and I can't even write back.

Oliver sits on the corner of the desk. "You still have to tell her."

"This is too much." I aim for the bull's eye once more and throw the pin. It barely hits the center. I groan. "How am I supposed to tell her that I am going to be away for such a long time?"

"It's going to take a year," Ollie reminds me. "You need a lot of time to completely change yourself. You need to learn everything again. It's like, back to basics. So, you have to tell Alayna about this."

I stop. "Did *he* agree to perform the surgery?"

"Cassius won't let other hands touch you. Whether you like it or not, he's going to be your surgeon. He is smart and the most capable person. He's the most knowledgeable in your case. You've got to trust him, buddy. He's behind all this progress you are having right now. He's the reason why Alayna can hold you and why you can walk outside again. I am just here on his behalf since you don't want to see him."

"You know it's not like that," I say, my voice raised. "It's the fact that he was the first person to know and didn't tell me that Casey was my sister when he was my best friend. You know how devastated I was when I found out about it."

"Well, I'm sorry. I was upset about that, too. If I were Cassius, I don't know if I would have been able to tell you. It was what our father wanted."

"I know, but it's not just that." I sit on the chair and squeeze my temple.

"It's been a year, Brandon. We cannot change it anymore."

"He was getting in the way all the time!" I snap. "He provoked me, and then he touched me. He shut me off with that bloody medication again, Ollie. I almost fucking died. I just can't forget that. He knows that Casey is the only person I have left, and she doesn't even know about it."

"Brandon, he didn't mean to hide it from you," he says, remaining composed. "He's just afraid. No one can know that she's your sister. Her life could be in danger too. What happened last year was an accident. He didn't mean to hurt your feelings."

"It looks like I don't have a choice at all," I say. "I wouldn't want just anyone, anyway." I hate to admit it, but Cassius is the only person I can trust with the surgery. He knows me, and that's enough.

I guess there is no turning back now. I toss the last dart pin I'm holding, and this time, I hit the bull's-eye.

"Your turn."

He puts his arm over my shoulder. "I didn't know that I would get to play this with you, but I'm starving."

"I can do this all day."

"You need to exercise, but why don't we eat first?"

"I'm staying here. I'll wait for you."

"Oh, come on!" He pats my back. "Alayna must've prepared something special."

"Then you bring it here."

"Hey, I thought of something," he suddenly says.

"What?"

"Why don't you just go on a date with Alayna? Of course, it won't be in public. It would be a perfect time to tell her. What do you think?"

"How am I supposed to tell her that we won't see each other for a while after the most fantastic date we ever had, hmm?" I raise an eyebrow.

"So, are you just going to disappear?" He steps in front of me, holding my shoulders. "Come on, Brandon. You can't do that. She'll be *very* disappointed. Who knows, she might meet someone else in your absence," he jokes, but Oliver knows it's also possible.

Over my dead body. I groan. I am fine with anything that I'll be going through, but that's one thing I couldn't let happen.

"You're already seething."

I grit my teeth. "Where can I take her then? You know my condition."

"Is it going to be me again? You have nothing to do tomorrow. What about you take her to Aunt Grethe's villa in Portland? The place is well maintained by the caretakers, though no one has lived there since. It would be far, but it would be private."

"Yes, of course," I mumble.

My mother's villa. I almost forgot that place.

"What do you think? It's a good idea, isn't it?"

I look up at him. "Will you be able to fly us there?"

"And you really can't do anything without me," he says but can't hide the delight on his face. He chuckles. "I wouldn't miss the fun. There won't even be a single person in the neighborhood. Besides, it's a very romantic place. I'd like to fly you there if you allow me to take Betty."

I frown. "Your girlfriend?"

"My fiancée," he corrects.

"Ah, right." I smile. "Of course, you can take her."

"Yes! This is why I like you. The Brandon Lucien I know is still there."

"Only if you take us there."

"Oh well, that's my job." He nods. "I get paid for it. Besides, I'd like to give Betty a tour."

"You can do whatever you want." It's my turn to pat his shoulder. "Hey, I'd like to see Alayna tonight, and I'll tell her the plan. I'll probably join you downstairs to eat."

ALAYNA

Casey has been so much help in the last few days. She's easy to work with, she doesn't brag about her skills and is a good listener. She gets easily fascinated by the simple things I tell her, especially about my culinary experiences. She also speaks about not having a boyfriend for a long time because Oliver and Cassius don't approve, but she respects her brothers so much.

The more I look at her, the more she reminds me of Brandon. They have the same shade of eyes and hair; the way they smile and gaze at people is so similar. She told me that the Katrakis genes are pale-skinned, with blue and green eyes just like Oliver and Cassius, and a lot of them are blond.

I'm always attracted to blonds. My exes are blond, so I wonder why I'm attracted to Brandon. He's so different from any other man I've met. He is mysterious and caring in his way.

A knock on the door interrupts us. Oliver's voice echoes in the kitchen. "Is dinner ready?"

"Yes, I'm just making a sauce." I lift the bowl, showing him.

He sniffs the air. "Smells good."

"I just hope he'll like it. I'll write another note."

"No need, Alayna." He flashes out a sweet grin. "He's going to see you."

"Oh, God. I'll hurry up."

"Easy. You have the whole night," Casey joins in and giggles. "I know you've been waiting for this."

"And she won't just have the whole night. Brandon's free tomorrow." Oliver winks at me, grinning.

"Wow. Really?" My gaze springs from one sibling to the other. "I can't wait to be with him again. Thank you, you two."

I put the sauce in a bowl and place it beside the steak for the final touch. "All done."

"I'll carry it for you, and we can have dinner together," Ollie offers, but Casey quickly holds his arm.

"Hey, you should let her take it to him, you know." Casey rolls her eyes at her brother. "We don't want to disturb them." She lifts the tray and hands it to me. "We can have dinner here, Alayna. We'll be fine."

Brandon is on the couch, busy scribbling notes on his iPad when I enter his room. He puts down the device when he sees me, smiling sweetly as he stands and walks toward me. I stop pushing the trolley and wait for him to reach me. He cups my face and his lips land on mine while I'm still surprised and dazed. Brandon slips his arm around my waist and squeezes me tighter. I pull away.

"Wait..."

He frowns. "What?"

"You can kiss me now, right?"

His expression softens. "I already kissed you last week, if I'm not mistaken. Or was it a dream?"

I laugh. "No. It's not a dream." I slip my arms around his neck, inhaling his sandalwood cologne. He feels warm. "You surprised me. Well, now I'm ready. Kiss me again."

He smiles and dips his face again to mine. His lips are playful in the next attempt. His tongue plays over my lips, parting them. He thrusts his tongue into my mouth, exploring. His breath tastes like mint and chocolate. Both his hands trail down my thighs, and he lifts me, wrapping my legs around his waist.

Brandon's expert mouth goes down my neck, leaving my lips much hungrier for him. The sensation is too much. I moan. He brings me to the couch without breaking the kiss. I sit on his lap and jolt when I feel the hard bulge in his pants... Whoa!

"Brandon!" I moan as he runs his tongue between my breasts. "Your dinner is going to get cold..."

"Hmm, is it?" he whispers, but then he goes back to my breasts until his expert mouth reaches the tip of my cleavage.

"As much as I want to do this, I am starving, and I didn't eat lunch because I've been preparing this since morning," I say, catching my breath.

He stops, frowning. "You skipped lunch?"

"Oh—yeah."

"I don't want you skipping meals for something like this," he says softly.

"I won't. We can do this later. I want to kiss you all over if you don't mind."

"I won't mind," he answers hoarsely.

"Shall we eat now?"

"I'd rather eat you first," he states but lifts me and puts me on the couch.

Brandon walks toward the food trolley and opens the lid. I can't help but admire his pure male beauty. He is sexy as hell.

"No note tonight?" he teases.

I grin. "Do you prefer the note?"

"I prefer you to say every single word. Hmm." He sits back next to me and squeezes me to his side. He kisses my temple. "Your cooking always smells good."

I curl my arms around his waist. "Can I stay tonight? We can watch movies. I'll sleep on the couch."

He hands me a plate with the food I made on it and grabs one for himself.

"Why would you sleep on the couch?" he says.

"Oh, would *you* rather sleep on the couch?" I joke.

"You can sleep in my bed with me," he says simply and begins slicing his steak with a knife. "Besides, it's hard to explore every inch of you if you are on the couch. Unless you prefer the other way. I can make an exception." He winks and eats a forkful of his food.

I gape at him, unable to speak for a moment. What he said makes me so damn warm. His words alone sent intense bolts down to my core.

"But would that be fine?"

"Hmm... This is delicious," he says as he chews. "You haven't made this before. Another improvised recipe?"

I eat a portion of mine and swallow it before I speak again, "No. Actually, it's the sauce."

He stabs another piece with the fork and brings it to my mouth. "Say, ah..."

"What? No!"

"Let me feed you."

My cheeks flare. I hesitate, but he is insisting, so I slightly open my mouth, and when he's about to feed me the steak, he eats it.

"Hey!"

He laughs at his prank, but he picks up a piece using his fingers. "Here."

I immediately eat the food and suck the tip of his thumb.

He freezes, and his expression turns serious. His gray eyes are now watching me hungrily. The palpable tension gives me goosebumps and tickles my insides for a second time.

He shakes his head, chuckling.

"Bad girl," he murmurs and presses a small kiss to my temple. "Let's just eat for now."

I go out of the room for a bit after our little dinner. When I return later, Brandon is sitting on his bed with his legs crossed, holding his iPad. I realize that he's changed the bed covers as well.

He smiles at me. "I just thought it might be more comfortable for you."

"Are we going to sleep now?" I ask. It's kind of early, and I still want to spend more time with him while conscious.

He puts his iPad down. "Would you like to?"

I move closer to him and run a finger over his bedsheets. "Not yet."

"Good." He steps off the bed and takes my hand. "Come, I want to show you something."

Wondering where he's going, I just let him take me. We walk back to his living room, and he opens a door I hadn't noticed before.

I frown. Just how many secret doors does he have? It didn't look like a door at first, more like a part of the wall.

I can feel his hand tightening around mine as he flips on the light. My jaw drops when the place flashes before my eyes.

A wall made of tinted glass is filled with large monitors and computers. Each computer faces another, with at least ten workstations. Bright, neon-green lights illuminate the mainframe. I don't know anything about computers, but I can tell this isn't just a regular office. Then, one particular sight sends chills down my spine.

One side of the wall is like a window into another room. A white room. My whole body quivers as I see the telephone, the desk, and the chair...

I gulp hard. "Gee, Brandon. You could see me in there."

His expression hardens. "Yes..."

"Why are you suddenly showing me this?" I ask but can't take my eyes off the strange view.

I hear his breath quicken and feel his anxiety in his sweaty palms. He's nervous, but he's trying.

"I wanted to show you how I was before I met you," he confesses.

"Before?"

"I never want to use it again after you," he whispers, his voice tortured and vulnerable.

"Is that why you suddenly stopped answering the phone?"

He nods. "You've changed me."

I blow out a sharp breath. I don't know what to say. The tension around us is unfathomable. It must be so hard for him to show this to me.

I clear my throat and decide to lighten up the atmosphere. "What are those computers for? The big monitors? Is this where you work?"

"This is the prototype of the company's mainframe," he explains. "Ollie and I built this ourselves. Some monitors are for the CCTVs, but not just to spy on people. I need to see if someone is going to break in." He turns and gazes at me. "You see, Alayna. I'm paranoid. I want you to know at least this part of me."

"All right, I get it now." I smile slightly. "Did you do all of this because of what happened to your family?"

"I don't want it to happen again."

"But why are the cameras shut down now?"

"I'm not using this room anymore. But you should know that this was the only place I knew I was safe." His body faces me, and he cups my face. I can see the agony in his expression. "When you came into my life, I started to view things differently. I want to live a normal life again."

I lean my face into his hand. "You're giving me too much credit."

His thumb brushes my cheek. "Do you still accept me after showing this to you? Do you still accept me for who I am?"

I weakly smile, but my eyes fail me. Tears rush down my cheeks after the building tension in my chest.

"I do. I do accept you. I like that you're honest and open with me."

He lets out a soft sob. "Thank you. I was worried you wouldn't want me anymore after this."

"I think I received all the shocks a person could handle the first time I met you, but I accept you for who you are. You are a survivor, Brandon. Never forget that."

We walk back to his room holding hands, and then we lie next to each other.

I'd never felt contentment like this. Him lying next to me is more than enough. I wish I could be with him every day like this, but I respect that his situation still demands privacy.

My arms hover around his waist, and I rest my head on his chest. He holds my hand and brings it to his lips.

"I'm free tomorrow," he says. "And I want to go somewhere. Do you want to come with me?"

I smile. "Where?"

"My mother had a villa in Portland. Oliver is going to take us there, and of course, I want to be with you."

"Wow." I look up at him in surprise. "Can you go out that far now?"

"I think so, but I'm still figuring that out. I want to try," he murmurs. His eyes are watching my face intently like I'm some beautiful portrait.

"Of course, I will come." I tighten my arms around him. "Wherever you like, as long as you're with me. But I'm still sleeping here tonight."

He chuckles. "I don't want you to sleep anywhere else."

Silence envelops us for a moment as we relish each other's presence, hearing only the sounds of our breath and heartbeats. He feels so warm, as always, and his body is so firm. His arm holds me safe while his other hand strokes my hair.

He lets me touch the traces of his scar under the thin fabric of his shirt. He feels so incredible, so unreal.

"Are you ever going to tell me what happened to cause this?" I whisper.

"I've never been with a woman in this bed before," he answers instead. I guess he isn't ready to tell another story. Perhaps showing me the room was all he could manage today.

I roll over so I can look at his face. "Have you fallen in love before?"

The question won't hurt, right?

He shrugs. "Yes," he admits, but amused. His answer is followed by a question. "Have you?"

I don't want to answer. It's complicated. "Tell me about her," I ask him.

"I don't think you want to hear it."

"I want to know. It's normal for the present girlfriend to know about her boyfriend's past love, right?"

"Girlfriend?"

"Am I not?" I pout.

He kisses my temple. "Of course, you are."

"So, do you care to tell me?"

"Hmm..."

"Hmm?"

"She was—she was a tomboy..." he starts, his eyes brightening up. Guessing from his facial expression, I can tell that it was a good memory. "There's no feminine side to her gestures. I've known her since we were in grade school. We were childhood friends, and her mother was my mom's best friend."

"So, she's close to your family?"

"Yes, my mother liked her."

"Do you think your mom would like me?"

He laughs softly, and his palm caresses my arm. "You're a good person and an excellent cook, Alayna. Of course, she would. Any mother would."

"Okay, continue your story."

"We never dated." He scoffs. It's a sound of regret, but I let him continue. "She liked me too, but I was a jerk. I dated several girls and even older women, but I never got the chance to tell her my feelings for her."

"Oh, that's—that's sad." My heart twitches. "Then what happened?"

"This?" He shrugs. "*This* happened."

"Life can be unfair. How old were you when all of this happened?"

"You mean when I started to like her or the, uh..."

"Both."

"I was fifteen when I became aware of my feelings for her. I haven't seen her since all this happened to me. I was eighteen."

"What did she look like? Where is she now, and what's her name?"

"Too many questions." He grins. "Hmm, Pauline. She was the prettiest in class, smart, strong since she held a black belt in jujitsu, and she was quite popular. The last memory I have of her is her short blonde hair and the freckles on her cheeks. I guess she went back to Greece."

I suddenly feel envious of Pauline. She sounded like every boy's dream. What if she suddenly comes back here to see him? Would he still feel the same?

"You broke her heart by leaving her without even telling her. You didn't give her closure."

"Would you rather I go back to her? I could look for her if you like," he jokes, raising an eyebrow.

I glare at him. "You are mine. Don't ever go back there or even bring her back here."

"It's your turn. Tell me about your *love* story."

My chest tightens. How can I tell him about the abusive relationship I've been through and the nightmares that still haven't let go of me? I have had tremendous heartache in the past. I'm not sure if I'm ready to tell him. Or perhaps I'm afraid of how he's going to take it.

I don't know how he's going to take it.

"What's important now is you, with me," I say and wrap my arms around him.

"I've just shown you my weakness; now I want to hear yours. I want to be close to you."

"Honestly, unlike yours, nothing is exciting about my life."

"I'm all ears. What can be more surprising than meeting a man who wears a mask?"

I snort. "You even make jokes about that. It's not funny, Brandon. You are more than that. You are strong. You survived all of this, and you are kind, and most of all, compassionate."

Brandon heaves a sigh and rolls to his side, so he can touch my hair. "I sound like the most perfect man in the universe." His thumb brushes my lip.

"Because you are." I gaze into his eyes.

He nuzzles my temple. "Then if you think that of me... Is there something you're afraid of? Everybody is afraid of something. At least, that is what I learned from you."

I hold my breath. "Please don't be surprised."

"Is it very shocking?"

"Promise me."

"I promise." He kisses my mouth. "You must know by now what I feel for you."

"Thanks." I smile. "Well... you are quite right. It is very shocking, but this is different. I did fall in love, yes, but after that, I had always been in a no-strings-attached relationship. Simply, I just don't give myself too much. It's a poison for me to give too much. I can't even believe I'm saying this to you."

He flinches. "What about us?"

"What about us?"

"Is this also one of your no-strings-attached relationships?"

"We're not having sex, Brandon. That's the difference, because... because I thought this could be something real," I confess. "I've never been more willing to try again."

"You've been hurt before, I see."

"Yes, and because of that, I never opened up about this part of myself. But with you, I've broken my every rule."

"Sounds like I'm not the only one with rules." His scowl deepens. "You always surprise me; do you know that?"

"I'm sorry. It's just this... I'm not sure if I can talk about this." I bury my face in my hands.

My heartbeat quickens, and my chest suddenly feels heavy. How am I supposed to tell him the reasons why I can't? How am I supposed to say that because of the man who ruined me... sexually abused me... I've become so ruined?

"It's okay if you can't tell me. I'm sorry I had to ask you." I feel his body pressed to my back and he touches my shoulder.

I shift my head toward him. I didn't realize I was crying until the tears streamed down my face. "I'm sorry."

He freezes. *"Alayna..."*

"I've always wondered when this day would come."

Brandon moves close to me and wipes my eyes with his thumb. "You don't have to tell me if you can't. Whatever that is."

I snivel. "I'd just like to be with you tonight."

"Of course. Come here."

Brandon envelops me in his arms and lays me on the bed next to him. He gazes into my eyes as he caresses my cheek.

He isn't saying anything, and it's only our breaths I can hear. I run my finger over his mask and wonder what he's like without it. Then I realize we aren't so different.

He covers his face with a mask so people won't see the real him, and I've been wearing an invisible one myself since I decided to close off my heart. But slowly, my mask is vanishing because, for the first time, I feel something in my heart that is special again.

I realize I had fallen asleep when I hear Brandon calling out my name. I open my eyes and see his beautiful half-face before me.

"Hey, it's me. It's Brandon. Are you okay?"

It takes me a few moments to digest his words. "Why, what's wrong? Why did you wake me?"

"You've been screaming."

I frown. "I was?"

He nods. "You're having a bad dream, I guess."

"Um, what was I saying?" I ask hoarsely. I suddenly feel in need of some water.

"You were crying. You sounded like you were in pain. Alayna, what were you dreaming about?"

"I have no idea, but..."

"Yes?"

"I didn't know I still do that in my sleep," I mumble, but then I realize I'm not supposed to tell him that. I've always hidden this part of me. I sit up.

Brandon springs up as well. "You've had these before too?"

I shove my fingers into my hair. "Yes. My mother is usually the one who deals with it. I'm sorry, Brandon. Maybe I should go back to my room."

"No, it's fine." Again, he wraps his arms around me. "How long have you been alone?"

"What do you mean?"

"When did you move out and leave home?"

"I don't know if that's—" I pause. "It's been a while. Why the question?"

"And the last time you slept with someone?"

My cheeks flush. "What?"

He gazes at me with a scorching blaze in his eyes. "I mean, in the same room."

I shake my head. "Besides my mother, it's just you—for a while, at least. I've never done this before." I bite my lip hard, still feeling the pounding in my chest. "Sleeping in someone else's bed, I mean."

Brandon releases a heavy breath, and his shoulders relax. "Well, I'm flattered, but whatever this is, if it's constant, it isn't normal, Alayna."

I shake my head. "I don't know what I've been dreaming about!"

"Calm down. I'm just saying that maybe something's wrong and that you should be trying to reach out to an expert."

"You see, I told you about this, and you think something's wrong with me." I feel my voice straining.

"You are certainly overreacting. Come on." He pulls me against him and rubs circles on my back. "It's not what I meant. Look, I've been battling with my issues, so I understand where this is going. All I am saying is that maybe you should pay more attention to this because it might not be good for you."

Suddenly, his touch and the warmth of his body calm my senses. I love how he can be so comforting. "I didn't know this was still happening to me."

"No one was there to wake you before, so you couldn't know," he concluded.

"I had this when—when I was... with my first boyfriend." I look at his face. I almost can't bear the intensity of his eyes.

"Go on," he whispers.

"Not all of us have a nice memory of their first love. I was inexperienced, naïve. I was in love. He was two years older than me."

The muscle in his jaw tightens. "What did he do to you?"

"He *forced* me." I start sobbing.

Brandon shuts his eyes, and when he opens them, his expression is cold.

"Are you okay?" I ask.

"I'm fine," he grunts. "Continue."

Suddenly, I feel weak and quivering. My palms are beginning to sweat. I curl my body and hug my knees. Brandon doesn't move.

I shake my head firmly. "I really don't want to talk about it, Brandon."

"Fuck. How can you keep this to yourself?"

"I just can't, okay?" My voice rises. "I really can't. Please, Brandon."

This is the last thing I want him to know about me. The devil in my past can always find me wherever I am. If I ever say anything to anyone, I'll be in danger...

My devil isn't just an ordinary person. He's a senator's son, and now he's running for mayor. I'll be dealing with a hard wall if I open up about him now.

I close my eyes and let my tears fall.

I know where he is. I've always known. He moved to Seattle with his father.

Brandon harshly runs his fingers through his hair. "Fine. Can you tell me how it ended?"

"No," I whisper. I feel like I'm going to be sick.

He sets his glass down on the bedside table with a harsh thud.

"Then at least tell me his name, and I swear—"

"No! Don't bother. You don't have to dirty your hands for someone like him." I wrap my arms around him and pull him close.

A deep growl vibrates inside his chest. "Alayna, what's his name?"

I shake my head. "No, please. This is the reason I can't tell anybody, or you... I know that you are powerful enough to deal with someone like him, but that'll taint your name."

"I don't care about my name, Alayna. If that's what it takes to destroy this person who forced you, and whatever the fuck else he did to you, I'll crush him. I swear he'd rather wish he were dead."

Shivers run through my spine, and I believe he can do it. I don't know how, but he could. It is in his voice, in his expression. It's dark.

"Please. I can't take it if anything happens to you because of that. I'd lose it if something happens to you because of me... There were things I did that I'm not proud of. You wouldn't wish to hear more of it. So please, don't. It's not worth it."

"But you are. You are worth it." He shifts to my side and cups my face between his palms. He lightly brushes his mouth against mine. "And I love everything about you, however painful your past was. You have accepted everything about me, and so do I."

And I thought he would pity me, or he might take it badly, but no. I find sincerity and compassion in his eyes. I feel like I could tell him everything, and he would still believe in me and care for me. Now, if I'm going to be afraid of something, it's losing him.

"I'm excited about our trip tomorrow," I say, moving on to a new subject. "I can't wait to be with you like this."

"Me too, Alayna."

CHAPTER THIRTEEN

Brandon is still serenely asleep when I go back to my room at four in the morning. I need to pack my things for the trip, and I don't want to disturb him.

I hadn't felt so safe sleeping with someone next to me for a while, other than my mother, but something inside me just doesn't want to surrender all. I had to move out of the room, at least for the night.

The sky is clear and sunny as I go out at six. Oliver is standing next to a black SUV, settling the luggage inside. He's dressed in a casual polo shirt, khaki shorts, and a pair of brown leather topsiders.

"Good morning, Ollie." I approach him. My voice is still croaky.

"Wow, someone's happy," he remarks. Taking my suitcase, he shoves it into the compartment.

"That's a lot of baggage. I thought we were only going to stay for a night and two days?"

"Betty's coming too, but we're going to meet her later." He shuts the compartment door. "You ready?" He grins.

"Yes, where's Brandon?"

"He's inside the car. Get in."

Oh. I didn't notice him. Ollie opens the door for me, and my heart almost melts at the sight of Brandon inside. I smile, biting my lips.

This isn't a dream. I slide into the seat next to him. I can already feel the warmth of his presence. He is casually dressed, like Oliver, only in black.

I instantly want to embrace him, but his expression is impassive.

"I get that you're not used to sleeping next to anyone," he says icily. "But you didn't wake me when you left."

"I'm sorry. I just didn't want to bother you."

"She's right. You need a good sleep." Ollie gets in the driver's seat and buckles his seatbelt. "Guys, I still need to pick Betty up. You don't mind, right, Brandon?"

"No."

I sigh and touch the unmasked side of his face. I shift it toward me and peck his lips. He sniffs my hair. "You smell so good. I've missed you already."

I wrap my arms around him and bury my face in his chest. He smells so divine himself. "Me too."

"Guys, are you ready?" Ollie asks as soon as he gets into the driver's seat.

"Let's go, Ollie," Brandon answers, and Oliver starts the car.

Brandon doesn't seem to mind when Betty sees him for the first time. She's waiting in front of her house, a tall, slender, raven-haired woman. Her hair falls just above her shoulders, and she has almond-shaped eyes and full lips. I remember Oliver told me she is half-Japanese.

I guess Betty knew about Brandon's situation. She isn't

surprised at all to see him. This is yet another time a person other than his family has seen him. She sits in front beside Oliver and smiles pleasantly at us. Brandon doesn't respond, so I greet her back.

"Oh, good morning. It's great to finally meet you, Alayna," she says with a smile. "Thank you for including me on this trip."

"It's great to meet you too, Betty. It was not my idea. Ollie here just doesn't want to have fun without you."

She grins. "He's so sweet, isn't he? I really hope Brandon doesn't mind," she says as she looks at Brandon, who's busy staring out the window. I elbow his side.

He looks at us. "Oh, I'm listening, and yes, anything for Oliver. I don't mind."

He shifts his eyes away again. I rest my head on his shoulder. I love being with this man so much.

Am I in love with him?

He turns his body, so we are almost facing each other. Any woman can fall in love with a man like Brandon. I close my eyes and smile at the warmth of his body against mine.

I open my eyes and realize that I have fallen asleep when the car stops in an airfield. Oliver and Betty are the first to get out. A private jet with "Grethe and Elga Enterprises" written in bold letters on the side is already waiting for us.

"Alayna, Brandon, come on!" Oliver shouts at us from afar. He, Betty, and another guy step into the plane.

"Who's that guy with Oliver?"

"It's his co-pilot," Brandon informs me.

"Ollie can fly a plane?" Gee, that man just has a lot of talents. "Brandon, he can do almost anything. He takes care of you, cooks for you, runs the company, and now he can fly a plane? Add the fact that he still has time to date. Are you sure he's not Superman?"

Brandon laughs softly. He seems very proud of his cousin.

"He's a great man. I've relied on him almost my whole life, and he learned everything just to help me. I owe him a lot."

"Oliver needs you in his life, too. He's also lucky to have you. He wouldn't have acquired all of this knowledge if not for you, right?"

He smiles. "Yes, you have a point."

We land in Oregon after a couple of hours. A Bentley SUV is already waiting for us at the airfield, probably owned by Brandon.

"Good morning, Mr. Katrakis," a man in his late forties wearing a black suit tells Oliver, and his eyes automatically settle on Brandon. "How are you this morning?"

"Good morning, John." Oliver pats the guy's shoulder. "Greet your boss. He's our one and only Chairman of Grethe and Elga Enterprises, Brandon Lucien. Brandon, this is my right-hand man, John."

John gapes at him with widening eyes. He stares at Oliver until he finally turns to Brandon.

"It is a great honor to finally meet the man I've been working for many years. Mr. Lucien, I'm John Harper." Mr. Harper extends a hand to Brandon.

"You've been a good right-hand man to Oliver. It's my pleasure." Brandon flashes a small smile and shakes his hand. "And this is my girlfriend, Alayna."

"It's a pleasure to meet you, Mr. Harper," I say.

"No need for formalities, ma'am. Call me John. Shall I take you to your destination now?" he asks his bosses.

"Yes, please, John." Oliver envelops Betty's waist with

his arm and kisses her temple.

John opens the door for us. Oliver and Betty step in first.

"Your network is a lot bigger than I thought," I whisper to Brandon.

He grins. "I know, but this is the first time I met John. He also knows about Annette's case," he explains.

God, Annette.

The woman I've known as Lucia for years, a person who's famous for her one-of-a-kind recipes and whom I idolized until I found out that she is Brandon's father's mistress. There's a lot more to know about Brandon's life.

"I thought you said you don't trust someone easily, but you entrusted a lot to a person you hadn't seen for five years?" I say matter-of-factly. I don't want to ask about Annette.

"I trust Oliver more. I just don't see John, but I talk to him often."

"Mr. Lucien?" John calls, holding the door.

"Okay, come on. I'm excited about what you have in store for me!" I giggle.

"Of course."

A gray sky covers the city of Oregon. There's nothing in the view except tall trees, and the road is tranquil. A few houses dot the highway, miles away from each other. Only a few people are walking on the streets. I'd never been to this part of the US.

Brandon was silent on the drive. He just kept staring at the streets or the thick gray clouds. I don't want to ask him what he's thinking, but his quietness bothers me.

We turn onto another road. I can see the beach from this side of the road, but it looks dull, probably because of the gray sky.

Why did he choose this place? I was expecting him to take me to a lovely, sunny, dry place where we could stroll around—or at least do something outdoorsy. It's so gloomy in this part of Portland. It's not that I'm complaining; I'm fine wherever he takes me as long as I'm with him.

But an hour later, we head to the coast. The ocean and townhouses are already in sight, so it isn't gloomy anymore.

"Hey." Oliver's voice cuts the stillness.

"Oh, hey..." I respond.

"Come on, we are here. This is where you and Brandon are going to stay," says Oliver as he points to the house in front of us. A lovely, massive luxury house in the middle of the woods.

Great!

"Wow. Is this for real?" I ask in amazement.

He laughs. "Yes, but John, Betty, and I are going to stay in that house." He points out another house—a smaller version of the one in front of us. He seems to notice his cousin's silence as well. "Brandon, are you okay?"

"Yes. I am okay. I'm sorry," Brandon says.

"You've been very quiet," his cousin observes. "Anyway, let's go in!"

"I just don't remember the last time I was here," says Brandon in a low tone. "Come on, baby. Time to unpack." He kisses my cheek and steps out of the car, following Oliver and Betty.

Baby. It's the first time he refers to me with such endearment. I let the word linger in my ear for a moment and follow him out.

"Brandon, John's going to help you with your things. There are also housekeepers we can call if you need one. Your snack is already prepared in the dining room. As for

Betty and me, we're going to our place. I need a shower," Oliver says.

"We'll see you at lunch," Betty says with a smile.

I smile at the sight of them. They look so cute together. I noticed how sweet Oliver is to her; he was always kissing her. I loved seeing them together.

"Yes. Thank you, Ollie, Betty," I say.

"Mr. Lucien, Ms. Hart, shall we go?" John carries our bags inside.

"Brandon, help John with the other luggage," I call to Brandon, who's now speaking to his cousin. "John, I'll carry my bag, thank you."

"Sure. Here it is, Miss Hart." He gives me my knapsack, and I hang it on my shoulders.

Brandon follows us in a hurry as we briefly part ways with Oliver.

"Alayna, are you ready?" he asks softly, and his expression changes. He doesn't look bored or bothered at all. He leans forward and presses a kiss to my forehead. "Come with me upstairs after our snack. I can't wait to finally have you alone," he whispers in my ear, making me shiver.

"Really?" I flash a playful grin. "And what are we going to do?"

"You wanted to know me better, right? You're going to know the real Brandon Lucien, now," he says and winks at me. He walks into the house first, leaving me open-mouthed.

"Oh my God, this place is magnificent!" I gasp as I enter.

The living room is the first thing I see when I step into

the house. The marble floors are ridiculously spacious, and it is so unlike Brandon's mansion in Manhattan. It is so bright!

The interior looks exquisite, and I first think of a spacecraft upon following glass walls with curves and shapes like at an art exhibition hall. The large windows frame a stunning ocean view.

The furniture is modern, unlike in his New York home. The place doesn't have gray curtains, and beautiful paintings of flowers hang on the walls. After all, it is his mother's villa, though it doesn't look like just a villa for me. His mother must have been a cheerful and warm person.

Brandon walks to the huge glass door and stands there, releasing a breath of relief. Circular stairs lead to the second floor, where John took our luggage.

"This place is very different to yours," I say. I stand next to him and stare at the endless seawater.

A smile curls one side of his lips. "My mother initially built this for us, her children, so we could live here when we're older and have a family," he explains, with his eyes also on the view.

"Here... it is breathtaking," I murmur.

"You haven't seen the whole house yet. The bedroom is exquisite too."

"Don't start with the bedroom." I look up at him, smiling meaningfully. "Shall we have brunch now? I'm starving."

"Of course, come. I'll show you around the dining area." Brandon holds my hand and leads the way through another door.

The dining room is also breathtaking; what else did I expect? The interiors are made of glass, which allows me to see the other side from where I am standing. The chandeliers look like white umbrellas, and there's a long, oval-shaped white table in the middle.

Our brunch is already on the table. I haven't noticed a housekeeper around, but by the aroma, it seems to have been prepared only minutes ago. There's French toast, eggs, crêpes, slices of assorted fruits, bacon, sausages, and a pitcher of lemon and cucumber juice. Everything is attractively arranged on the dining table.

"Brandon, why don't you just live here? This place has more privacy, and it's delightful. You won't see a single person around. You are going to live just like Iron Man in this kind of house."

He lowers his face. "Hmm, that is a tempting idea, Alayna, but I have a lot of memories here of my mother and my sister, and I'm not ready yet. I wanted to heal myself first and deal with everything before I settle down." His expression is serious. "The reason I brought you here is that I wanted to discuss an important matter with you, and I want to show you who I am."

I look at his masked face.

"We have had a long day, and I also want to spend time with Oliver and Betty. Afterward, we can have time to ourselves again. Can we eat first, before we start with the real issues?"

I'm nervous about *the issues*, but I'm aware that there is something big behind what he is saying. "Of course."

I choose eggs and crêpes, and Brandon pours me a glass of juice. I didn't want to ask Brandon during a meal, but I'm curious about what he means by the *real* him.

I watch him as he eats, fascinated by him. Brandon is gorgeous, even if I only see half his face.

"What?" He stops.

"You're not aware of how insanely attractive you are, are you?" I rest my chin on my palm, gawking at him.

He smirks. "I was. I was aware, until this." He points to the masked side of his face. He continues to eat.

"Are you ever going to tell me what happened?"

I'm dying of curiosity. I want to know him more deeply. I know it isn't proper to ask him about it over a meal, but I can't help to want to find out more about him. Sure, I know small things about him—stories from his cousins, but none from him. I want to know his side of the story.

I munch on the last of my pancake. I'm waiting for him to answer. All I hear are his heavy breaths.

"Are you finished?" he asks, looking at my empty plate, soaked in maple syrup.

I nod. "Yeah. I'll just drink my juice."

"Hurry. Let's go back to the living room." He gulps down a glass of water, wipes his mouth with a napkin, and places it back beside his plate, then springs up.

I drink my juice fast and hold his hand again, entwining our fingers.

We go back to the living room. Gently, he pulls me to him, and we sit on the couch with our fingers still locked.

"You want to talk about what happened to me?" he asks in almost a whisper.

"Yes, please."

"You see, Alayna, I told you that this is one of the reasons we are here."

"So, you're going to tell me now?"

"Yes."

I smile. "Right now? How should we start?"

"With the root of all, I guess."

"Root? What root?"

He heaves a sigh. Suddenly, his expression turns serious.

"It was *greed,* Alayna. No one has ever wanted me in the family, except for Oliver's side and my grandparents. I'm sure you have heard that from my cousins. My family is very complicated."

Okay, I guess that's the cue. "Yes, I did. I heard from Casey and Oliver. Can you enlighten me as to why?"

"I'm a threat to the Katrakis family. Everything you see and everything I have is because of this very brain." He points to his temple. "I finished a degree online without setting a foot outside, though I built my empire with Ollie's help, of course. I swore to myself that I didn't need them. I still haven't got anything from my mother's inheritance except the mansion in Manhattan and this villa, but it's because this is all I wanted to keep. I wanted to take care of it."

"All your wealth is not from the Katrakises. I got that part too from Casey."

"I guess I don't have to elaborate much, then. Yes, everything is my sole property, Alayna. I worked hard to get it all from that room I showed you. Day and night, I never stopped."

I guess he has all the time in the world because he cannot even go out. If it were me, I'd probably have lost my mind, but his situation didn't stop him from getting what he wanted. He is strong. He's just not aware of that.

"From what I heard, your family still wanted your mother's inheritance?"

"Yes. The Katrakis family is bound by rules, and all of them depend on the family's wealth, except for Oliver's family and mine since we've established our lives outside the circle. Aegeus, my uncle, chose a life without any of my grandfather's wealth to keep his family safe and for the sake of my mother's memory."

I nod. "I'd do the same. I mean, that's what a real family has to be. You care for each other."

"It's not that way for some of them, at least. I don't have concrete proof, but I'm certain." His expression is of deep pain, but he is willing to share it with me. It must be hard for him to go over everything. I can understand how he feels. My father died, and we never even knew who killed him.

I touch his hand. "But you didn't go for your inheritance, right? Are they still trying to take you down despite that?"

"My grandfather still wants me to inherit his fortune, but no one is ever going to let me because of their fucking rules that destroy lives. They believe I'm a bastard."

"But you are not a bastard," I say softly. He should stop thinking that of himself. "Maybe they're just afraid of you. You are stronger now, and that's enough for you to take *them* down."

"You don't know what they are capable of," he insists. "Not when two powerful families in Greece are on their side. They're not going to stop until they kill me, Alayna." He gazes at me, but there's no fear in his eyes, just anger. "I don't know what my grandfather was thinking."

"Do you still talk to your grandfather?"

"Yes, on the phone."

"God, what did they do to you?" I touch his face. "You've been living in hell for a long time."

He draws a deep breath for courage and says, "My—my family was murdered in our own house in front of me."

"And you were there?"

He nods. "They were stabbed. I didn't see it happen because I came out too late, but I saw them lying on the ground, almost dead. The killer burned our house down with us inside, and I was the only one who survived. It almost took my life."

"*Oh no.*"

Dread rushes through me as the images of a murder scene creep into my head. I instantly imagine a young man screaming for his life while his family agonizes, or even worse than that. I shut my eyes in horror.

"Brandon..." I whisper. "That's completely brutal. I don't know how I could go on if something like that happened to me..." I swallow the lump in my throat, which causes my chest to tighten.

"I guess some of your questions have been answered," he says.

"This is why you can't trust anybody. This is why you locked yourself in your room." I keep my tears back. "Is that how you got your scars?"

"Cassius said the incident gave me trauma," he informs me bitterly. "They tried to get me treated; I had surgery, but I freaked out, and my misery didn't end there."

Brandon rams his fist on the table in frustration. I can't do anything for him but hold him in my arms.

"You were just a kid back then. It's not your fault."

"A few days after the incident, I was kidnapped from the hospital," he continues. "Oliver's father thought I ran away, but I didn't."

What?

He locks his eyes on mine. "When I opened my eyes, I found myself in a very dark and foul-smelling room, alone and stripped naked. My arms and feet were tied, and the stitches on my chest were still fresh from the wounds I got when they stabbed me. I didn't know what I was doing there until I felt the excruciating pain in my face. I touched it and found that I was severely wounded."

This is way, way worse than anything I've ever imagined. Whoever did that to him isn't human. They're evil. How could someone do that to a boy?

I sob hard. "Oh, Brandon... You didn't deserve any of that. You didn't do anything wrong." I wrap my arms around his neck, and I pull him into a tight embrace. "I'm so sorry all of this happened to you."

"They left me there because they thought I was dead," he goes on. "But I heard them, those people who did this to me, Alayna. Before I lost consciousness, I heard *them*: Annette and another one who's called Marcus. I know what they did to me. They poured acid on my face and burned me with a lighter. This face."

He lets go of me and looks into my eyes, touching the side of his masked face with his palm.

"No one ever heard me scream," he goes on. "They left me to bleed to death, but I did not die. Uncle Aegeus found me. I cannot think about it anymore. I can't—"

"You didn't die because you have to make everything right again. I'm so sorry for what happened to you. You don't have to talk about anything like this anymore. Not with me."

"I want you to see what's behind this thing," he murmurs. "But I'm afraid of what you might think of me."

Oh my God. Is he taking off the mask?

I instantly catch his hand to stop him from removing it. His fingers are quivering. I know he is afraid, and it isn't the best time for him to reveal everything. Maybe later, or tonight, or perhaps another day.

"I would love to see you, Brandon. I just don't think now

is the right time." I kiss his mouth softly. "But I did mention that you are beautiful, right? Whatever happened to your face doesn't reflect how great a person you are."

His eyes soften. "This is what I love so much about you. You lift me all the time. I don't know what I've done to deserve you."

I smile. "You make me happy. What else should it be? You are mysterious, but you're kind, you're generous, and you're honest. But you are hurting too, so I want to take care of you."

"I should be the one who's protecting you and taking care of you, but I can't if I'm like this," he murmurs.

"But you are getting better," I remind him.

"I am, but it's not enough." He sighs, staring back at me. "I think I should give you a tour first. I'll show you our room."

"Of course. I'd like to see it."

Brandon and I go upstairs, and he leads me to an open bedroom. I'm not exactly sure if it is a bedroom; it has no walls or doors, but it is so spacious. At the center stands a king-sized bed.

On the right side, there is a glass room containing a massive CD and music collection, while the other side has an abstract mural and a floor-to-ceiling bookshelf. I can't believe no one was using the house.

"This is stunning. Are there other rooms? This space almost occupies the whole floor," I ask while walking to the glass enclosure.

"There are other rooms, but this is the best." Brandon appears behind me and wraps his arms around my waist. He smells my hair and kisses me softly. "Would you like to unpack before our afternoon snack? I'll give you time."

"I'd love to shower first." I gaze into his eyes and put my arms around his shoulders.

"What's wrong?" he asks.

"I was just thinking. I can't imagine myself anymore without you. It's like you're already a big part of my life."

"Likewise," he whispers, but there's a heaviness in his voice. "You don't know how much you changed me."

"But why do I have a feeling that I won't be seeing you for a long time?" I ask. "All of this means something, I know, but you're not going to leave me, right?"

Brandon hurls out a sharp breath, but his expression hardens. "I will always belong to you no matter what."

I nod and tiptoe so I can reach his height. I rest my head on his shoulder, embracing him so tight it hurts. I start the kiss this time, and he returns it by cupping the back of my neck and just breathing.

He is slow at first, teasing my lips, sucking them one after the other. His other hand trails down my waist, slipping it inside my shirt and then gives my back a soft squeeze.

He pulls back a little, leaving me cold and with lips still wet. "Why don't you take a shower now?"

"Ugh!" I moan in protest. I haven't even recovered from the kiss yet. "God, you are such a tease."

He chuckles sweetly. "Do you want me to join you?"

"You can't do that."

"What? I will let you peek."

My eyes grow wider than they already are. "No, you won't!"

He laughs at my reaction and kisses my forehead. "You're so cute. Maybe next time. Go on."

Eventually, I obey and make sure I'm clean everywhere, just in case he makes such a move again. I come out wrapped in a bathrobe and find Brandon sitting by the window, holding a book.

By the look of his glistening hair, he's already had a shower. He's changed into a white shirt and charcoal-gray sweatpants.

"I thought you'd be waiting downstairs," I say, approaching him.

"I changed my mind," he says, his eyes still on the book. "You've been in the bathroom for an hour." He reaches for my hand, brings me close to him, and sniffs my hair. "I love how you smell."

"I love how you smell too."

"I want to spend more time with you, but I might not be able to stop myself the next time you show up wearing nothing underneath," he mutters almost harshly. He leans over. "And your nipples are peeking out."

I look down at my chest and see that one of my breasts has spilled out of the bathrobe. I feel my cheeks burn and cover myself.

He moves me aside and stands up. "I'll wait for you in the living room." He gives me another peck on the lips, then marches to the stairs.

The rest of the day is perfect. Brandon and I have the house to ourselves. We talk a lot about his childhood. We binge on food and shows, with our legs tangled together like a normal couple. It feels too good to be true. I wish for the day not to end.

The following day, Betty is already in the dining room when Brandon and I go for breakfast. But she has a concerned expression on her face.

"Brandon, Alayna," Betty says, forcing a smile.

"Hey. Where's Ollie?" I ask.

"He's making a call," she says. "Come, sit, and have breakfast."

"You go first. I'll just check on Oliver," Brandon tells me.

"Are you sure?"

"It won't take long." He kisses my temple before he leaves.

Betty smiles at me again when we are alone in the dining room. I sit and start putting food on my plate.

"So, what do you think of the hot spring?" Betty abruptly asks. "I'd like to go this afternoon."

"Hmm." I take a sip of my hot chocolate drink. "I've never been to a hot spring before, but it does look nice in the pictures."

"Let's go together, but of course, we'll ask the boys—"

"You two should go first." Ollie suddenly walks in and kisses his fiancée's head. "Brandon and I will come after."

I frown. "Why? Is there something wrong?"

"I'm sorry, Alayna. I know that this is supposed to be his vacation, but we just need to do something important... Some work that needs attention." Ollie pulls a chair next to Betty and sits. "Oh, John will take you there, of course."

"That's fine, Ollie. But where's Brandon?"

"He's talking to Cassius," he says simply and begins filling his plate with food. "Don't worry, it's nothing serious."

"At least we can have some girl-bonding time, Alayna!" Betty suggests cheerfully. "I want to know you better, and I don't have many girlfriends here. Besides, when we marry..." She holds Oliver's hand and grins sweetly. "We're going to be real sisters. It's tiring to speak English all the time. I heard you can speak fluent Japanese."

"Hai, dekimasu!" I answer, bowing my head.

"Sugoi!" she says. "We should teach Oliver."

Oliver chuckles and feeds her the crêpes. "You speak too much."

"Hey!" she complains with a mouth full of food.

I laugh at the sight of them. They look really cute together. Betty is pleasant company, after all. I already imagine myself relaxing under the spring water with her, probably asking her about Japanese cuisine because I love their food so much.

"Okay, okay. I'm going to the hot springs with you," I say.

"Yes!" She raises her arms in victory. "I can't wait."

CHAPTER FOURTEEN

BRANDON

Damn. This is bad timing. Just when I thought everything was going my way, another fucking issue arises. But this isn't just any problem. This is about Alayna's and everyone's safety. I can't believe they've tracked us this far.

I call Cassius, and he answers right away.

"Thank God!" he breathes out. "I thought you weren't going to call. Have you read my message?"

"Yes, but did you find out who the sender is? Oliver got it as well. I'm freaking out right now, and we still don't have a trace." I rake my fingers through my hair.

"No, it was sent anonymously. Did you tell Oliver the plan? What the heck is wrong with you? You know that it is still dangerous for you to go out that far, and you went there with Alayna?" His tone is furious.

"I know, but I was planning to tell her about our plan—your plan."

"I just got back home, Brandon," he complains. "Mother's going to kill me if I leave again. You know the risk. Alayna could be in danger too, and my brother and his fiancée. Tell Alayna everything tonight, and when you are done, you're coming with me to Athens."

I grit my teeth. I can't imagine Alayna getting hurt because of me. What happened before can't happen again.

"Whoever the hell they are, they know where we are! They know that I'm here."

"Did you tell Alayna about the hot spring?"

"Yes, I'll ask the girls to visit the resort today."

He exhales in relief. "Good. I'll try to track the IP address again, but I have a feeling they used a private network. Listen... I'll see what I can do to fly back there, and I'll take care of the girls first. But stick with Oliver while I'm away, no matter what. Do you understand?"

I guess I have no choice but to follow his lead. "Yes, yes. Thank you. I understand."

He hangs up.

I clench my fists hard as I scan the photos Oliver and Cassius received from an anonymous sender. It's a picture of the four of us in front of the villa. It was taken yesterday.

Please, not again.

I could never forgive myself again if something terrible happened to Alayna.

ALAYNA

Something doesn't feel right about Brandon after his talk with Cassius. He's dejected and cold when he comes back.

What could they have possibly talked about?

Oliver and Betty have already left, and Brandon is still silent. We are now in the bedroom, and he's staring vacantly at the ocean stretching outside the window. The view is stunning, but Brandon's mind seems somewhere else.

"Hey..." I say. "What's wrong?"

"Nothing." He turns to face me, takes my hand, then brings it to his lips. "I love you, Alayna," he whispers out of the blue and pulls me against him, crushing me in his arms. I almost can't breathe.

"Brandon, are you okay?"

"I don't think I ever told you how I feel about you yet, but I do. I love you, Alayna. Never forget that."

The normal reaction of a person would be a delight at hearing those words. I mean, of course, I'm happy. But why does it feel like he's going to disappear? Like a lover saying his goodbyes?

"Brandon, can you tell me what's going on with you?" I slightly move away from him so I can see his eyes. "You're making me nervous."

"Why? I can't tell you how I feel?"

"It's not like that, but—"

"I just can't imagine myself without you."

I can't explain the emotion he is projecting, but something is troubling him. I can sense his restlessness.

"Where else will I go?" I ask. "I don't think I'm capable of leaving you unless you ask me to."

"I won't." He smiles weakly. "Except today, with Betty. I will go after you, but I'm afraid I have to tell you to pack all your things because we're not going to stay here tonight."

My eyes widen in shock. "What? I thought we would be staying here for a few days. This place is amazing."

"Yeah, but something came up." He brushes his thumb on my cheek.

"Is this about Cassius? What did he say to you? I heard you speak to him."

He scowls. "Cassius has nothing to do with this."

"Is it work?"

He shakes his head. "Don't worry. We can still come back here, and I'm taking you to some place I know you'll like tonight."

I smile. "It doesn't matter where you're taking me as long as it's with you. I need to pack my things then."

"Do you need help?"

"Of course."

Still dispirited, we started to get our things ready for tonight.

From the very start, I completely understood how secretive Brandon was. I never fully expected anything from him, given his situation, but rather accepted everything he was to be able to make our relationship work.

Now I don't want to pressure him into telling me everything. It's his privacy. But I still wish he would learn to open up to me.

Brandon glances at his wristwatch. "We still have time. Come with me."

"Where?"

"Just come." He grabs my hand.

Brandon pulls me to a stairway I haven't seen before. It's narrow and hidden inside a door. I'm guessing it goes down to the back of the house.

"Where does this lead? Hogwarts?" I joke.

"You'll see."

When we reach the exit, there's another pathway to a

garden house at the tip of the trail. But before reaching the miniature house, we walk on the field, among the daffodils.

I inhale the pleasant scent as the petals sway with the wind.

"You wanted to show me this?" I ask as we walk.

"It'll be a waste if you don't see this." He smiles. "This place is well maintained by the caretakers. I didn't want to abandon what my mother cherished when she was still alive. Do you like it?"

"I love it! I don't understand why you want to leave. You could stay here forever."

"Then, will you come back with me here?"

"It doesn't matter where you're taking me, as long as it's with you." I make him stop to kiss his nose.

I have fallen deeply under this man's spell. I have never felt so happy and so alive in a relationship before. But getting to know Brandon has made me realize that I must've forgotten how it feels to love someone again.

I hear him purr in my ears. "Alayna, I have to tell you something later."

"And I'm not allowed to ask what it is now?"

"Not yet, no. It's something important that I need to tell you... or *show*."

Lowering his head, Brandon seals my lips with his in another lush, wet kiss. My hands move to his hair, sliding through his scalp. Just before this leads to more, my phone vibrates in my pocket.

"Is that yours?" he asks.

"Unfortunately." I pick up my phone and check my screen. "It's Betty. She texted me."

Brandon laughs lightly, and the sound sweeps almost all my irritation away. "It's all right, love."

"It's *not* all right!" I complain. I go to my inbox and read her message anyway.

Sorry, Alayna. Change of plans. I need to go to town first. Is it okay if we could just meet there?

"Well... I think I need to get ready."

"Why?" He frowns, then glances at my phone, and I let him read the message. "She didn't tell you if she's with Oliver?"

"But that was the plan, right? Betty and I go alone, and then you and Oliver go?"

Brandon's shoulders relax. "It's time to go, then."

CHAPTER FIFTEEN

BRANDON

I contact Cassius after Alayna leaves with John.

"Where are you now, Cassius?" I ask as soon as he picks up.

"I took an immediate flight. Expect me there in ten hours. How're the girls?"

"Alayna's going to town now with Betty."

"Good. What you need to do is wait," he instructs. "I already told Oliver to call for security to escort you. You okay?"

"I'm fine," I assure him. "No one's tried to harm me up to this point."

"Don't be so sure," he warns. "You still need to be watchful. The security will be there in an hour. Did you tell Alayna?"

"Not yet."

"What? Brandon *that* is the plan. You're there because you're supposed to tell her."

"But she's not ready yet, and I can't if she's—" I pause,

massaging the back of my neck. "She likes it here, Cassius."

"She's never going to be ready." He exhales. "But there's nothing we can do about that for now. Just stick to the plan and don't go out alone."

"Thank you, Cassius. I owe you this time," I finally say, after the long cold war we just had. I have to admit that he has been there for me ever since my tragedy, just like Oliver.

There's a long pause at his end. "It's all right." He hangs up.

I head back inside while I spot Oliver walking in my direction.

"Ollie?"

"Heard anything from Cassius?" he asks.

"Yes, he's on his way here. We can expect him in ten hours. What's the plan?"

He scratches his head. "I don't have a good feeling about this. I can't even say anything in detail to Betty, but she's excited to see the spring and—"

"Hold on." I raise a finger. "What do you mean she's excited to see the spring? Didn't she leave an hour ago?"

"*What?*" His eyebrow rises. "What are you talking about? Betty's inside."

"What do you mean she's inside?" I yell. "She texted Alayna earlier, and Alayna already left with John—Fuck!"

Oliver's face turns white. "What?"

Alayna...

My chest tightens, and my head turns blank for a moment.

This is their plan. Their target is Alayna. But how could this happen?

I try to reconnect my memory to see if I missed anything strange yesterday. There was no one around the house when we arrived. I had Oliver instruct them to have everything prepared before and make sure no one skulked around during our stay.

There's no one else around but the five of us. And if I were to suspect anyone in our circle, it would be John or Betty. They're the only persons I met recently—persons I can't utterly trust.

But if it's John, then Alayna's in trouble.

With shaking hands, I dial Alayna's number straightaway, but the call redirects to voicemail. I try again and get the same outcome.

"Fuck! Fuck! Fuck!" I curse repeatedly. My vision is beginning to get blurry, and the throbbing in my chest increases as if there's a ticking bomb inside.

I try to call her phone for the third time, but she isn't picking up.

Oliver grabs my shoulder. "What are you doing?"

I look at his face. I almost want to yell and tell him my suspicion about his fiancée, but I keep my thoughts to myself. I will not stoop that low when I have no evidence.

"They've got Alayna. She left with John after receiving a text from your fiancée. There's no one else... It's just *us*!"

"Brandon, it's not Betty, I can assure you."

I want to trust him, but his words aren't enough when Alayna may already be in danger. "I have no time to talk about anything right now, Ollie. I've got to find her."

"Goddammit!" he swears, coming after me. I rush toward the driveway, getting into the driver's seat and buckling up.

Oliver slides into the passenger seat. "Betty's phone is missing, and she's been looking for it since yesterday."

"Call John. If he answers, then he's not our suspect. Alayna's still safe. We'll talk about *that* later."

Anxiously, Oliver pulls out his phone and presses the speed dial. After several attempts, his right-hand man answers and puts the phone on speaker.

"John, are you with Alayna?"

"Yes, Mr. Katrakis. I left with Miss Hart a few minutes ago," he answers.

"Did you arrive in town?" Oliver asks.

"Not yet, sir, but we're almost there. Is there something wrong?"

Good. If they're near the town, then she's still safe. "John, this is Brandon," I say. "Give me your exact location, stop the car right now, and wait for us. Why is her phone out of coverage?"

"Brandon, what's wrong?" Alayna speaks softly. "I forgot to charge my phone."

I shut my eyes with the relief of hearing her voice. John isn't the mole. That leaves Betty.

"Alayna, baby, listen to me. You can't go to the spa."

"Why? Betty's waiting for me there."

I scowl at Oliver. He shakes his head.

"Betty's phone was stolen, Alayna," Oliver answers her.

"What? How can that be?"

"I'll tell you later," I say. "Just stay with John and don't leave the car. We'll be there."

I hang up and shift the car to a higher speed.

"Do you think they're on the move?" Oliver asks me.

"What else would it be? My enemies are on the run now, Ollie."

"*Our* enemies," he corrects. "I know that you suspect Betty, Brandon. You have every right to, and I can't blame you for that, but she's not a bad person. I know Betty and her family."

I grip the steering wheel hard. "And you have to understand that we can't drop our guard."

"Of course." He looks away, and his jaw twitches.

"And I won't be able to forgive myself if anything happens to Alayna."

I clutch my chest with my free hand. I was wrong for not thinking this through... for trusting something so easily. Betty could've asked Alayna about the change of plan herself. She is next door, but Alayna received a text instead. Suddenly, I feel the burning pain inside me again. But nothing is more grievous than realizing that I have involved Alayna in my war.

ALAYNA

Chills travel down my spine, making me colder than I already am.

How can someone steal Betty's phone when there's no one else in the house but us? How can they know that I'll be meeting her at the resort?

Oh my God! The traitor must be in our circle.

Is it John? No. John spoke to Brandon and Ollie and told them where we are.

How about Betty? We don't know much about her. However, she wouldn't do anything that obvious. No sane person would betray us by using their own phone number.

I jolt in fear when someone suddenly knocks on the window a few minutes later, but relief floods through me as I find Brandon standing outside.

I push the car door open, and he instantly catches me in

his arms, holding me tight against him.

"I'm all right," I assure him, wrapping my arms around his body.

"You are certainly not all right because of me. I thought I'd lost you," he says breathlessly.

I gaze into his eyes. "You didn't, so don't worry, okay? What happened back there?"

"Brandon." Oliver appears behind him and hands Brandon the car key. "We don't have much time. Hurry up and leave. I still need to go back to the house. Betty's still there. But will you two be all right?"

I feel Brandon's arm tighten around my waist. "I'll keep her safe."

"You too, okay?" Oliver briefly hugs his cousin.

Brandon nods. I look over my shoulder and give Oliver and John a small smile before stepping into the other car.

"Where are we going, Brandon?" I buckle my seatbelt.

"Somewhere safe." He brushes his thumb over my chin. "Do you trust me?"

"Always."

Brandon revs the engine to life, then pulls out of the place.

After almost an hour's drive, we stop in front of a traditional Japanese wooden gate with two pointed roofs and calligraphy etchings on each side.

"Did we just escape to Japan or something?"

"This was a dojo. Come, let's get inside." Brandon takes my hand and leads the way. It's even more surprising that he opens the gate by pushing some blocks of wood like a combination code lock.

"Dojo? Is that where people practice martial arts or something?"

"Yes."

Entering is like passing into another world. The open gate reveals one of the most beautiful places I have ever seen. On the vast land in front of us stands a Minka: a house in handcrafted natural wood with a triangular roof and cherry blossom trees around it. Finding it is like traveling to early Japanese civilization.

Brandon walks in first through the house's largest entrance, and an old woman in a kimono appears at the doorstep. She doesn't look Japanese at all.

"Lydia." Brandon embraces her.

Lydia's eyes seem to sparkle—like a mother's gaze at a long-lost son. "Brandon, my child. It's really *you*."

"Oh, Lydia. I've missed you."

I almost want to cry at their reunion, though I haven't the slightest idea who she is.

She pulls away first and cups Brandon's face. "Cassius isn't lying. You're really here."

Brandon grins. "Lydia, I want you to meet my girlfriend." He pulls me next to him. "This is Alayna. Alayna, this is Lydia."

She swiftly turns her eyes to me in awe. "Oh, my boy is all grown up. It's a pleasure to meet you, Alayna."

We shake hands, and she squeezes my palm softly.

"The pleasure is mine, Lydia."

"Lydia is Lennie's sister," Brandon explains.

Ms. Lennie has a sister! No wonder they look alike. Only Lydia is probably younger.

"I used to go anywhere Lennie went. Brandon was just a little boy back then," she says heartily and gazes up at Brandon. "You grew up so tall and so handsome. Come inside. You are safe here."

"She knows what's going on?" I whisper to Brandon, but Lydia hears me.

"Oh, dear. I always look after Brandon, even if I'm far away. I talk to Lennie almost every day." She speaks slowly, making her voice sound even gentler.

"I'm glad Ms. Lennie has you."

"No, I'm glad she has *you*." She touches my cheek. "Come in, come in! Let me show you your room first. You don't have to take your shoes off. You are my guests."

When we get into the inner part of the house, all I can say is a big wow!

The house's structure, though old-fashioned in appearance, doesn't seem fragile. The doors are latticed screens, covered with white paper, and the flooring is pure wood.

"I wish I could take a picture."

"You can't; her husband didn't want it to be like a tourist spot," Brandon whispers. "He is Japanese."

"Oh, I see," I whisper back.

"Lydia, where is Kenjiro?" Brandon asks.

"Ah! You can guess where he is at times like this. His way of living is still the same. He's in the training camp with his new karate students. He won't be back until next week. It makes him happy, so I let him." Lydia stops in front of another door. "This is going to be your room, or do you want separate rooms?"

"*No*," Brandon and I say in chorus. "We're fine here. Thank you, Lydia."

"I know, I know." Lydia smiles meaningfully. "If you need anything, just tell me."

"Thanks, Lydia. I'm sure everything you have here is enough."

She strolls back to where we came from.

Brandon slides the door open. "Ladies first."

I step into the room and sit on the floor; there are no chairs but thick comforters with glossy blankets instead.

"Did I mention they have a hot spring here?" Brandon adds when he sits across from me.

"Do you mean I can still try it here?"

He chuckles. "Of course. I planned on bringing you here anyway."

"Is this the place you were telling me that I'd like?"

"Do you like it?"

"I love it!"

"Hey!"

To his surprise, I jump to get on his lap, but he falls out of balance, so I flip on top of him.

"Sorry..." I was going to get up, but he yanks me back.

Brandon assesses me with his gray eyes, and we are both suddenly quiet. He brushes his fingers over my hair and tucks the strands behind my ears. "You're so beautiful," he whispers out of the blue. "Such beauty doesn't deserve my ugly face."

My heart melts at his insecure words. I can't stop myself from kissing his mask. *"You're* beautiful, Brandon," I say softly. "Inside and out. I wish you'd stop thinking like that about yourself."

He tightens his arms around me, and I rest my head on his chest. For a long moment, we stay like that, just enjoying the moment.

"Come with me." He gently puts me aside and stands up.

"Where?"

He holds my hand and pulls me to my feet. "Just come."

The moonlight is the only source of light in the hot

spring, but the beauty of the clear water still stands out. The spring water falls into a rectangular marble pool. Around it are bamboo parapets and cherry blossom trees. The lights are warm and almost solemn. It's so peaceful here.

Brandon walks close to the water first, then he pulls off his shirt, revealing his broad back. Gradually, he strips off his pants. My throat dries up, but oddly my mouth salivates at the sight of his immaculate buttocks. I remember seeing him the first time this way, and his body is exactly the same as I remembered.

He slightly shifts his body to face me, preventing my eyes from looking down. "Come, Alayna," he invites softly and steps in the spring water.

I take my clothes off, letting them drop to the ground before I stride into warm spring water. I blow out a breath of relief, shutting my eyes as the soothing liquid touches my skin. I follow Brandon to the middle of the pool.

"Beautiful, isn't it?" Brandon says in his deep, soft voice as he walks behind me and touches my bare shoulders. He wraps his arms around my body.

"It's wonderful," I whisper, smiling.

He buries his face on my neck and kisses me. "I need to tell you something."

"I expected that," I say, knowing what he wanted to show me. "I'm ready."

I spin around and look up at him, and to my surprise, his face is already bare.

The breath catches in my throat. My stomach churns. I shiver, the warmth of the water unable to stop a feeling of iciness. My knees feel frail, and my cheeks tremble.

Brandon's expression is wounded... disgusted... dark.

"Your... your mask," I murmur.

I tear my gaze away and look down. Honestly, I'm not sure how I should feel. I'm confused. I don't want to offend him, but I don't know if it's all right to look at his face.

His face...

It has severe burn scars. A portion of the right side has irregular fibrous tissues. It seems to have been sliced several times. The cuts go from his forehead down to his right cheek. He doesn't even have an eyebrow there; it's as if there's no more flesh but only dead skin. I remember him telling me about the acid poured on his face.

"Even I can't look at my face in the mirror," he croaks.

"It's not like that," I say breathlessly.

"Then look at me, Alayna..."

I swallow, and bit by bit, I look up. I haven't noticed that I'm already crying until my tears stream down my cheeks.

"Oh, Brandon..."

"Doesn't this monstrous face scare you?" He laughs bitterly. "Tell me, because I don't mind. I'm scared of it myself."

"No, believe me, no." I shake my head firmly. "It's the opposite. It makes me love you more..."

At my words, Brandon begins to sob.

I raise my hands but halt for a moment. "May I?"

He slightly nods.

And with his permission, I touch the side of his face that is damaged. Carefully, my finger trails his scars, and they are strangely soft. Brandon's breath hitches.

"Does it still hurt?" I ask.

"Sometimes."

"Is it hurting now?"

"No," he says hoarsely.

"This doesn't look that bad," I say truthfully, smiling a

little. "You're still so beautiful to me."

"Oh, Alayna." He takes my hand and takes it to his mouth; he pulls me and presses me against his bare body, his skin to my skin. He continues to sob on my shoulder. "I can't live like this anymore."

I slide my arms around him. "Whoever did this to you, they will pay dearly," I promise. "How could someone do this to you and still live with themselves?"

"I think I already told you why I had to hide," he reminds me, probably referring to his illness—the illness that caused him to detach himself from the world, afraid that someone would harm him again.

"But you have to fight back."

"Yes, but this is also why we are here, Alayna. And why I'm going to tell you this. Listen to me..." He pulls away a bit and gazes intently into my eyes. "I have to go back *home* and get some treatment."

I frown. "What?"

"Because you are right. I have to fight back, and I can't be like this forever. I have to go and fix everything, Alayna. It's so hard for me to say this, but I have to—"

"*Leave*?" I stop him from finishing his sentence. "You have to leave."

"Yes, I need to go to Athens. Where my mother came from. I wouldn't be able to protect you if I'm like this."

"Until when?"

"I'm not sure. Cassius said it may take a year."

"What? That's a very long time—"

"Alayna, I want to love you in every way. I want to give you more, but I can't if I'm still like this. And what happened today isn't something I can take lightly. They already did it once, and I lost my family. I cannot afford to lose anyone."

He cups my face. "Not you."

"It's not your fault, what happened before. You didn't know." The tension building in my chest finally bursts out. I finally cry. "When are you leaving?"

"Tomorrow. Cassius will come here to take you back to Manhattan, and we will leave as soon as I know you're safe."

"That's so soon..." I know I can't do anything about it anymore. Brandon is going to leave. And I can't be the one who stops him from achieving his goals, even if it's painful for me.

"Wait for me." He wipes my tears away. "I'll come back to you. So please, Alayna, will you wait for me?"

"Y-Yes..." I sniff hard. "I love you, Brandon, and if you think this is what's best for you, I will wait."

"I love you." He brings me back to his arms and kisses my temple. "I love you so much."

"How can I do my job if the Master isn't even there?" I ask.

"You can still stay at my house and do your job, even if I'm not there. What happened today can happen again, so I have to keep you safe."

"You still haven't told me what happened. I was going to meet Betty in town."

Brandon grunts. "Oliver and Cassius received photographs of us when we arrived at the villa yesterday. The sender is anonymous and can't be tracked. Then Betty said her phone was stolen today—if that really is the case. But I have a suspicion, though I hope I'm wrong for Oliver's sake."

I frown. "You suspect Betty?"

"I don't know much about her, but she's Oliver's fiancée, so I let her come with us. But that's what I'm going to find out. It could be one of the housekeepers. I don't know." He blows out a worried breath. "But whoever sent you *that* text wanted to take you away from me. This is how it happened ten years ago, before my family was slaughtered, Alayna. And it'll kill me if I lose you too."

"You won't lose me." I tighten my arms around his body. "I'm not leaving your side unless you tell me to. Even if you're away, I will still be here. Just come back to me no matter what."

"Of course, Alayna." He kisses my forehead and smiles. "I'll come back to you."

After that promise, he lowers his head and kisses me. This time, his lips aggressively coax mine. I groan as tiny bolts of electricity rush inside me. His kiss grows demanding. I tighten my arms around his neck, and my nails dig into his back. He thrusts his tongue into my mouth, and his mouth devours me... possessing me.

He grips my waist, and leisurely he slides his hand up to my breast, pinching my nipple softly.

"Ahh..." I can't help but moan loudly.

"Shh..." He laughs. "Come. Let's get you out of the water."

I shiver with the anticipation that he wants this to lead to something more. He takes my hand, but I stop. I cover myself with my arms. "I've never walked in this state outside."

"No one will come here. I promise," he assures me. "Come on."

Brandon emerges from the water, and his erect shaft stands before me. I had no idea he would be this big. I feel the space between my thighs moisten. "Brandon..." My throat dries up, and my eyes widen.

He takes me again, heaves me out of the spring, and presses me against his large frame. His eyes assess me, and he frowns when they travel down my belly.

I gasp as I realize what he is looking at; I had completely forgotten about it. I try to cover the imperfection on my body, but Brandon grasps my wrist.

He asks angrily, "What is this?"

He sees it now—my own insecurity...

"What happened to you, Alayna?" he insists.

These are my scars from cigarette burns. I've had them since I was eighteen. "It seems we're not so different," I say bitterly.

"Is this..." He pauses. His expression darkens to fury. "Is that what I'm thinking? Who did this to you?"

"I don't want to talk about that."

"Oh, baby." He suddenly bends down and touches my waist, then starts kissing my stomach.

"Brandon!" I hold his head to maintain my balance as my arousal increases.

He presses soft kisses on my scars, making sure his lips touch each of them. We stay that way for a long time, but I need more of him. I'm willing to give all of myself to him now.

"Brandon, please... Please come up here, please..." I beg, and he complies.

"No one will hurt you again, I promise." Brandon claims my mouth again in a deep kiss. We sigh and pull on each other's mouths as if we can't get enough.

I have fallen on him like a ravenous madwoman. I'm touching him and grinding myself against him. I have never felt so good with a man, given my issues in the past. His expert hands and touch have only made me want him more.

My head is spinning, and I'm still gathering my thoughts when he gradually glides his hand between my legs.

"Brandon, are you—"

"Shh. Do you trust me?"

"Yes..."

A playful smile curves his lips. Carefully, he lays me on the tiles, and without warning, he cups my cleft. His thumb presses my clitoris gently, then he thrusts his finger into me.

"Oh gosh..."

Round and round, he hits my spot as if he knows my body better than I do.

"You're so wet... Look at how your pussy throbs." His grin is playful as he continues to thrust his finger into me.

He has never spoken to me like this before; so raw and rough. I bite my lower lip hard, and my eyes flutter with each stroke. He moves so slowly inside me, massaging me.

"Ahh..." I moan. I'm ready to beg for more, but it's as if he knows my body; he softly touches my very sensitive spot.

"Oh gosh!" I cry in pleasure, but as I'm on the brink of orgasm, Brandon pulls his fingers out again and brings them up to his mouth, licking them with his eyes glued to mine.

Damn. That's insanely erotic.

"How could you do this to me? Making me lose myself, mm?" he whispers, his voice raspy.

"Please..." My body arches with yearning. I'd be willing to give more if he asks me to. I've suddenly become too greedy, but I can't force him to do something he might not be ready to, given his complicated condition.

"What, baby?" I sense the amusement in his expression.

"I want more..." I whisper.

"Are you sure?"

I nod. "Y-Yes... but if you are... if you want to..."

His gaze softens. "Of course, I want to. You have no idea what I want to do with you right now."

"Then I'm sure... I want this, Brandon."

My throat dries up.

But as fast as he moved seconds ago, it seems like forever before he lowers himself on me, so I part my legs farther with him between them.

"Now, please..."

And he answers my plea without hesitation. Brandon thrusts his beautiful cock into me. At first, I feel slightly sore because of his size, but it's like my whole body has fallen into a pool of pleasure. His shaft is throbbing inside me, filling me and hitting every sensitive nerve. He feels so firm, so powerful... so perfect.

"Fuck! I knew you'd feel this good," he murmurs harshly, and at his next fierce thrust, his mouth savagely claims mine again. I tangle my fingers in his hair, and I feel his muscles working.

"Brandon..." I call, but he rams into me relentlessly... fucking me.

He groans in response, sounding rough. "You feel so fucking good."

I shut my eyes, relishing the boundless pleasure he's giving me. It has been a very long time since I felt genuinely aroused. I have been in senseless relationships where sex didn't give me much pleasure at all—more like a dull act couples do to kill time.

However, sex with Brandon for the first time makes me feel so alive. It makes me feel that I'm wanted... that I'm loved.

At the back of my mind, I want to ask him if he's okay, but I keep my words unsaid because I don't want him to feel differently about himself. I'm only worried that our actions might be hard for him. He has never fully recovered, and he has not been this intimate with someone in ten years.

Nevertheless, he was right when he told me he can satisfy a woman. Brandon tenses up, quickens his pace, and grips my waist tighter so he can pump me. I cry as my orgasm finally takes over me, and the tremors spread to my toes. After several more thrusts, Brandon pulls out of me and spurts on my belly.

At that moment, I wish I wouldn't ever have to get up; I wish I could just stay like this with him forever, but my heart warns me of an uncertain future. It's as if Brandon has read my mind; he hoists me up so my legs wrap around him. In one ferocious thrust, he pulls me down and is inside me again.

I wake up in the middle of the night after a terrifying dream, and when I open my eyes, Brandon is staring at me.

He wipes away my tears. "Are you okay? You were crying."

"Hey..." I bury my face in his chest and embrace him. "I thought you left without saying goodbye."

"Alayna, I'll never do that to you. But are you sure you're okay with this?"

"I am okay with this," I whisper. "I'm happy that you wanted to finally do this."

"Then what are you worried about?"

"We don't know what's going to happen. Everything is going to change."

"My feelings for you will *never* change."

I force another smile at his vow. "You should have decided to do this a long time ago, you know?"

A soft murmur escapes his lips, and he embraces me. "It

will be torture without you."

"That is why you have to heal fast," I tell him. "I'm looking forward to seeing you succeed." But I then laugh softly between tears. "Is this going to be our last night together?"

He does not bother to reply because we both know the answer. I hear him weep, so softly—like a child.

The next morning, Cassius finally arrives at Lydia's house. He gives Brandon a brief hug, then pats his back as if they've longed to hold each other for a long time. It is a short but emotional greeting. They have fought long enough, and they are each other's best friends.

Cassius flashes a weak smile when he sees me. He isn't the Cassius I met before. He has shadows under his eyes—the mark of a sleepless night.

"Hi, Alayna," he says with a weak smile.

"Hey."

"Are you okay? Are you ready?"

"Yes. How about Brandon?"

"I'm safe here," Brandon answers slowly. "No one knows I'm here except Cassius and Oliver. I asked him not to tell his fiancée, and he understands."

"But there's another sudden change of plans," Cassius says. "I'm supposed to take back the two women, but we should be more careful. Oliver's coming here alone in a while to get you, and John flew back to Manhattan with Betty last night. You know my brother, and for him, family is more important."

Brandon agrees with his cousin, then faces me. "Don't leave Cassius's side, do you understand? I already ordered additional security for your safety."

"Don't worry about me. Where is Lydia?"

"Lydia's inside preparing breakfast. I don't want you to leave on an empty stomach."

"Great, because I'm starving," Cassius says, chuckling. "I've been flying back and forth. I'm getting sick of it."

Brandon taps his shoulder. "Then you go first. You have another flight later."

After our breakfast, everything seems normal. The two cousins talk a little more with Lydia, mostly about their childhood. I already know that Brandon and Cassius were best friends since grade school, but I haven't seen them speak without roaring in each other's faces.

I gather from their conversation that Lydia was once Oliver and Cassius's nanny, and she used to live with them in Athens. Brandon is laughing, carefree, enjoying Cassius' inside jokes. Lydia reminds them how much of a headache they were as kids. Until it's time to finally say goodbye.

"Ready to go, Alayna?" Cassius asks as he carries my suitcase. He's by the gate with Lydia.

"Yes, I just need a few more minutes," I say.

I throw my arms around Brandon's neck. This time, I cannot hold back my tears. I cry so hard that I'm crushing him, but he doesn't mind. "I know. It's hard to do this, but promise me that you'll come back healthy, okay?"

"I should be the one saying that," he whispers painfully, almost inaudibly. "I'm the one who's leaving."

"I can take care of myself. Oliver and Casey are with me." I hold his face. His beautiful eyes are swollen, just like mine. "Promise you'll come back."

"I'll come back. Just go, Alayna. Before I change my mind."

I brush away my tears with the back of my hand. "*I love you.*"

"I know." He presses a lingering kiss on my forehead. "Go. Cassius is waiting."

God. This is more painful than breaking up. I turn away from him, tempting to look back, forcing my feet to walk away.

"Shall we?" Cassius asks.

I sob even more.

"Are you sure you want to go?" he asks again. "We can still leave later if you like."

"What's the difference?"

"Just imagine how hard this is for him," he says softly.

"I know that, Cassius. He's the one who's leaving." Damn. My tears just can't stop, but then I turn to Lydia. "Thank you for everything, Lydia. You really have a nice home."

"It's my pleasure, my dear." She touches my face. "I'm glad you like it here. I wish we could spend more time together."

I hug her. "I wish, too. Take care, Lydia."

She strokes my hair affectionately. "Of course, dear. Now, go on."

I release her and walk outside with Cassius. I glance in Brandon's direction once more, but he has already turned away as if the world had slowed down.

I guess this is it.

Goodbye, Brandon.

CHAPTER SIXTEEN

Six months later
Athens, Greece

ALAYNA

I found Brandon, Alayna," Oliver says, reappearing at our table.

We are now at the annual family reunion in the Katrakis Manor in Athens. Hundreds of guests have attended, and I spot a sea of blond heads. Ollie said some guests are from the Stavros and Dragoumis family and others are close friends. Everything around us looks luxurious. I'm glad I listened to Casey; she had me wear her sparkly, emerald evening dress. As usual, Oliver is very handsome in his designer tuxedo.

I feel my face brighten up, but my heartbeat quickens. I gulp the champagne and grimace at it. "Where is he?"

"I suggest we wait for the party to finish. He's... occupied."

"Alayna? Ollie, Casey!" Cassius suddenly appears with a bright grin across his face. He is dressed in a white designer tuxedo, and his blond hair is brushed back.

With open arms, I embrace him. "Cassius, it's good to see you."

"It's only been six months, but it seems like forever." He gently strokes my back, then releases me. "When did you arrive?" he asks, looking at his siblings.

"This afternoon," Casey answers and hugs her brother as well.

"Where is Brandon? Can you take me to him?" I almost plead. "Is he all right?"

I haven't heard from him in the last half-year. He didn't answer any of my calls. I can understand the situation he's in, but I'm dying inside, waiting for him to return my voicemails, texts, or even emails. I'm freaking out, anxious that something might be wrong.

"He still needs a few more operations, but he's perfectly fine," Cassius informs me. "But you. You look stunning!"

I smile a little. "Thanks."

"Cassius, where's Dad?" Ollie asks.

"He's with Grandfather. I'm joining you tonight instead. Have you eaten?"

My stomach churns. I haven't taken any food since breakfast. I won't be able to eat until I see Brandon.

"Alayna didn't eat lunch," Casey says. "Please convince her. She won't listen to us."

"I don't have an appetite. I came all the way here to see Brandon," I insist.

"We all know that, but we don't want you to collapse before you see him," Cassius says.

"I spoke to him briefly earlier, and I told him you're here.

Let's just wait until he's free," Oliver says. "I heard he's giving a speech tonight. He's probably getting ready."

I roll my eyes. "Fine."

"Alayna, I'll get something light you can eat," Casey offers. "Oliver, can you help me?"

"Of course."

Ollie stands up but stops when someone on the stage begins to speak.

"Good evening, everyone." A very beautiful, blonde woman in a shimmering red evening dress says on the microphone. "On behalf of the Stavros family, I'd like to thank everyone for letting us celebrate with you. My mother wishes for me to do this under the spotlight."

She laughs, and more pleasant laughter echoes in every corner of the hall.

"I've fought with her about coming here," she goes on, "but here I am. She even wants to offer everyone a song, but I'll cut this introduction off. I'd like to invite someone on stage. A person that is so dear to me..."

The lights go dim, and a spotlight hits a particular table in front of the grand hall. And I can't be wrong. *He* is too familiar, and he's looking in my direction.

Dressed in an impeccable blue Armani tuxedo, Brandon shifts his attention away from me and gracefully marches to the aisle. A version of him I haven't seen before. He had his medium-length wavy hair trimmed into a short, classic cut. His flawless face is more defined now, with light facial hair on his angular jaws that makes him even sexier. He radiates power, with everyone's attention on him.

"Let's welcome one of the grandsons of Petros Katrakis, Mr. Brandon Katrakis Lucien!"

A round of applause erupts at the woman's dramatic

introduction.

Brandon walks on stage and greets the woman with a peck on the cheek. She blushes and looks at him with yearning.

My heart sinks, and I tear my gaze away. I'm not sure what's happening anymore, and everything around me turns blurry. I'm certain that he saw me, but he ignored me.

"Excuse me, I need air." I stand up and storm out of the place.

"It's me! Have you forgotten about me?" I scream from the top of my lungs, but there's no sound coming from my throat. There seems to be a wall dividing me from him as I ram my fist on the invisible surface.

"No! Please, come back! It's me! Brandon, it's Alayna," I cry hard, but it's no use. He can see me from the other side but remains still. Seconds later, a beautiful woman steps closer to him, and she slides her arms around his waist.

My heart shatters into a thousand pieces.

"Who is she, Brandon?" the woman asks, looking at me with blank, soulless eyes.

"No one."

"No! It's me, Brandon. It's Alayna!" I shout, but there's still no sound coming from me.

He sneers at me, and I watch him hold the woman's waist and kiss her cheek.

"No!" I yell in anguish. I can't breathe. I bang the wall once more with all my remaining strength, but I'm too late.

Brandon and the woman stride away.

"Come back, please!" I sob. "Oh, please don't leave

me..."

"Alayna! Wake up! Alayna!" I snap back to my senses and see Oliver's concerned face.

"Ollie?" I whisper.

His shoulders relax. "Thank God."

I feel my breathing slow down, but I taste the dryness in my mouth. "I'm dreaming again, aren't I?"

"Yes, are you okay?"

I look up at him, and whenever Ollie is here like this, I can't help but pour out my emotions.

Ollie doesn't have to say anything, but I know he moved into the room next door a few months ago just to check up on me. I have been like this almost every day since we returned from Athens. I haven't had a proper night's sleep since then.

It is this very reason why I have become anxious about sleeping at night. I've had panic attacks during my sleep, and I'm aware of some. I first found out that I had these episodes a few years ago when Mom was waking me in the middle of the night. I was always screaming as if I were in pain.

But unlike before, the episodes in the past few weeks are clearer. I'm aware of my nightmares. I dream the same thing every night. It is always Brandon and the woman with him in Athens. I guess no one knew about this until Oliver started to see through me. I'm in my most vulnerable state whenever I'm alone at night.

"Why can't you tell me what's wrong, Alayna? I want to help you, but I can't if you don't tell me what's going on. You've been like this for a long time now," he murmurs.

"I'm sorry, Ollie." I touch my forehead. "You can just ignore me or go back to your room upstairs, so I won't disturb you again."

He sighs in frustration. "Come on, Alayna. We've been living together for almost a year. We're friends, and I'm worried about you. This isn't something I can ignore anymore. We have to tell Cassius. Maybe he can help you."

"My case is different from Brandon's. I'm fine, Oliver. They're just nightmares." I try to convince him; or myself.

He holds my hand. "You are sweating unusually. You are panting, and for God's sake, your skin feels cold. You are hyperventilating, Alayna," he says pointedly. "These are obvious indicators that you need to seek help. I may not be a doctor, but as Cassius's brother, I know about this. Am I wrong?"

I jerk away from him and step out of bed. He's trying to figure me out, and he isn't wrong. "Leave me alone now, please."

Silence. But Oliver remains by my side.

"All right!" I throw my hands up and fold my arms across my chest, shaking my head. "Let's say you're right, but I was like this before, Oliver. This isn't new. If you think that it's because of Brandon, I'm telling you that it's not."

"I didn't say it's because of him, Alayna."

"It's because of him... I'm... I'm like this *again*."

Oliver steps close to me. "I understand if you can't tell me what's going on with you, but at least tell Casey."

"I don't know."

He rubs my shoulders gently. "You need to get back to sleep, and I'll stay here with you. Is that all right?"

I sob under my breath. Eventually, I nod. "Yes, please."

"Are you okay?" I ask Oliver when I find him in the library.

I place a cup of coffee on his desk. He has been working nonstop at his computer.

He picks up the cup and takes a gulp. "I'm all right."

"Ollie, you've been working all day. You already missed lunch."

"I'm okay, Alayna," he assures with a small smile. "Don't worry."

I walk behind him to see what he's working on. He is typing codes of letters and numbers I can't understand, but I know for sure that this is a computer program.

I step away quietly, so I won't disturb him anymore. When I head back to the door, he shouts aloud, "Yes!"

He stretches out his arms and groans as he relaxes on the seat.

"What happened?" I ask curiously before exiting.

"Brandon created this program last year, and there was an upgrade with the operating system recently, so some functions aren't working. There's no better programmer than him, so I tried to contact him, and he sent me the full new version today. But converting it to fit into another program is another beast, and it took me five freaking days." He gulps his coffee again. "Thanks for the coffee, Alayna."

"Oh, wow." I march back to his desk. "You spoke to him?"

"Well... I... Yes... Earlier today."

"How is he? Did he ask for me?"

Oliver can't answer right away. It's obvious that, as usual, Brandon refused to speak to me again.

"I'm sorry, Alayna. I'm sure Brandon's just busy. Oh, I forgot to tell you. Tomorrow will be his fourteenth operation."

I never stopped counting the days from the time he left,

and one year has almost gone by. "How many operations does he need?"

"It should be seventeen or eighteen, I think. Don't worry, Alayna. It will be over soon."

"I'm tired of waiting like this, Ollie," I say honestly. "I don't know what's wrong with him. I haven't been able to think straight. Can you just tell me the truth? Is there a chance that he might not want me anymore?"

"Oh, please don't think like that." Oliver swivels his chair to face me. "Brandon loves you. He's there because you led him to the right path, and now he is close to getting better. Let's give him more time and wait."

I grit my teeth. "But I'm tired. I'm tired of listening to sentences that seem to be scripted. That's all you and Cassius say to me. Why can't he make just a single call when Cassius can all the time? I want to speak to him, Ollie. If you just let me talk to him..."

"I'll try to tell him, Alayna," he says wretchedly. "I'm sorry if you feel that way."

"You told me *that* before, and you had every chance to let me know he spoke to you today." I finally find the strength to leave the room.

As expected, Cassius phones me at nine in the evening. It is always at the exact same time. We talk mostly about what's going on with him in Athens, never about Brandon. But I'm fed up with all their secrets. I have to know what's going on with him through Cassius.

"He's often outside, but I don't know where he's going," Cassius explains.

"Is it okay for him to go out alone now?" I ask, staring at the ceiling of my bedroom.

"He's not alone. He usually has ten guards chauffeuring

him around. Our grandfather has him working on something he doesn't tell me about."

"Sounds like typical Brandon." I bite my bottom lip. "He's very secretive. But is that all you can tell me? Is he preventing you from saying anything?"

"It's not like that. He's just very, very busy, I promise that's all. Why don't we talk about you instead? Oliver told me you were hospitalized the other day. Why didn't you tell me something's bothering you?"

"It wasn't anything to worry about."

"Alayna, Oliver told me you lost consciousness. How can I not worry about that?"

I guess Oliver really told him all about it. Including the fact that I could've been dead by now if it wasn't for him.

"If you could just let us help you," he coaxes.

I shrug. "Talking to me like this helps. I'm really okay, Cassius. And I listened to Oliver's advice about teaching freshmen Italian and Greek cuisine at a training center in Midtown while Brandon's still away. I guess I forgot to tell you. I started working part-time there the other day."

"That's great, Alayna. I wish I could be there for you, but things got busier around here. I'll try to fly to Manhattan once I clear a schedule. Brandon still needs me here."

"Yes, he needs you more." Cassius being with Brandon is the one assurance that he's not all alone—if that's still the case. He probably has some blonde next to him now. "And I'm with Ollie, so you have nothing to worry about. By the way, Casey and I are going to see another new movie tomorrow."

He laughs. "But don't spoil the whole thing for me. The last time you watched *The Archer*, you told me the entire freaking ending."

"I won't!" Finally, I genuinely laugh. Whenever I speak to him like this, it's as if all the agony and longing in my heart do not exist. The feeling never lasts, but for a short moment, I feel like I'm alive again.

"Can I talk to you tomorrow?" I ask.

"I'll call you, Alayna."

"Promise?"

I can sense his smile. "I promise."

One year later

BRANDON

"Are you ready, Brandon?" Cassius sits next to me and hands me a glass of champagne.

"Thank you. I'm more than ready."

"Are we going straight to the mansion?" he asks and then frowns as he takes a sip of his liquor.

"No," I simply answer.

"But why? Alayna's waiting."

I shake my head. "No. I can't." I gulp my drink. "Please..."

"Why? What's going on?

"It's nothing." I empty my glass and lean back, closing my eyes, putting on my headphones.

It's going to be a long day...

CHAPTER SEVENTEEN

Athens, Greece
Twelve months earlier

S o, you have returned," my grandfather stated, and his once powerful voice turned rough, almost inaudible. His blond hair had turned gray. He might be old, but his eyesight and his memory were clear as crystal.

"My grandson," he called as he looked upon me. He was sitting on his favorite padded wooden chair. I stood in front of him.

"Yes, I have, Grandfather." My respect for him did not change. He was the only person who favored me in the family.

"Yes, yes." He forced a smile. "You know that I've been waiting for you to accept what's rightfully yours, finally."

"I did not come here for that," I said. "I came here to regain my old self." I wasn't interested in his fortune. I returned to make everyone pay and to bring myself back to who I really was. I was my mother's son and a brother to my sisters. "But I do have one request to make."

"What is it? I'll be happy to do anything to make up for my failure to you and your mother."

"I need your help—your power... your voice. I know that you still have it in you, and I have a plan."

"I heard a woman made you come back home. Is this true?" he answered instead.

I gritted my teeth. "I wanted to protect her, but I decided to come back here. It will be easier if you leave her alone."

"I did not ask about her because of that. Our family has become greedy, and you must know that while she's still with you, she isn't safe. She will be a target."

I clenched my fists. "I'm well aware," I said quietly.

"They killed your mother and your sister." He suddenly began to cry. "And I did nothing. I was blind, so I'm going to help you, my grandson. This is my promise to you. I'm going to protect you with everything I have. Your request is granted. Do whatever you think is right."

"Thank you, Grandfather."

ALAYNA

"Alayna? Alayna, it's Cassius! It's Cassius!"

Casey dashes to the door, but I remain still as my heart is pounding abnormally just from hearing Cassius's name. It means *he* is here too.

Brandon... They have announced that he's returning today. I should be excited, thrilled... but instead, I'm afraid.

I follow Casey, but my knees feel frail, like they were about to fail me. Then suddenly, Oliver squeezes my shoulder.

"Alayna?" he mumbles, his eyes worried. "Are you okay?"

"I don't know," I say. I don't think I will ever feel right.

"You're going to be fine." Seeing Oliver like this has always comforted me.

After he broke up with Betty for some reason, Oliver was always there when I was crying at night, despite his own problems. He was there when I fought against my nightmares. He waits until I fall asleep to make sure I'm okay.

"I'm okay, really." I fake a smile.

"No, you're not okay. You're bothered. I can see it."

"Ollie, you know exactly what happened that day." I hug myself as I try to stop myself from crying again. I am getting tired of it. It's as if the massive pain in my chest never stopped.

"Don't overthink it for now. He's finally here. You can be together again. You should be happy," he says, then smiles faintly. "Now, shall we go and greet him?"

"I'm ready."

"Good. For now, let's just welcome him."

A white Aston Martin stops in front of the mansion. In a couple of seconds, Cassius gets out of the car. It has been half a year since we last saw him. Casey rushes toward her brother and embraces him. Even if I was lonely as hell, I can't help but smile at the sight of them.

"Look at you! You gained weight," Cassius jokes.

Casey pouts and slaps him on the arm. "You didn't even come home for a year, and that's the first thing you're going to say to me?"

"Oh, come on, you knew how busy I was." Cassius

scratched his head. "Why don't you give me something to eat now? I'm starving."

His eyes wander until they meet mine. His expression turns serious, and I realize something I'm not sure I can take. Brandon is not with him.

I heave a sharp breath and shut my eyes.

"Where's Brandon?" Casey asks the same question that's in my mind.

"Can we just go inside first?" Oliver suggests. "I'm sure Cassius is tired, Casey."

"What? I just asked where Brandon is—" she says but stops. "Sorry."

I grab Ollie's arm. Suddenly, I feel out of air. I knew it. I knew Brandon was avoiding me.

"Casey..." Ollie calls out again. "Let's see if they've prepared lunch."

She averts her eyes from mine. "Okay."

"I'll give you two a space to talk," Oliver mumbles in my ear. "You should talk to Cassius."

"Thanks."

Oliver takes Casey back inside. Now it's just Cassius and me. I want to hear any excuse Brandon would've told him. However, Cassius stands still.

"Hi," I say, low-spirited.

"Hi... Are you okay?"

"Same as always." I shrug. "... and you?"

He smiles faintly. "Good."

"Where's he?"

"He's here. In Manhattan. He's back, but he went to the office first."

I nod. It's not like I didn't anticipate this. If I were important to him, he would be here to see me. It turns out I was right, and everyone else was wrong.

Simply, I'm not his priority anymore. For the millionth time, I shed quiet tears and bury my face in my hands.

"Come here." Cassius's arms wrap around me. "I'm so sorry, Alayna. But he's coming here tonight. This is his home. We just have to wait for a few more hours. You'll get to talk to him again."

"Oh, God." I sniff. "I don't know anymore, Cassius."

"Maybe he just needs some time."

I raise my head. "Time? I've given him enough time. You know how long I've waited for him, but he's been indifferent to me. You saw how he was in Athens—"

"Stop thinking about what happened in Athens for one second," he snaps. Cassius rarely snaps, and he draws a deep breath to compose himself. "Please, Alayna. There's nothing we can do for now but wait."

"Why do I feel like you're not telling me everything?"

"Ask him whatever you want to ask, and if you are right, you can tell me or tell Casey. We are here for you. But please do remember that Brandon's still hurt, and he's lonely. He just went through a lot the past year. I know how much he longed for you. It's too early to doubt him now."

I cry hard. It seems there will be no end to my agony. I'm already losing hope. My head suddenly feels so light.

"Alayna? Alayna? You don't sound fine."

"No, I'm... I'm all right..."

My vision turns from fuzzy to dim. Unwittingly, I shut my eyes and succumb to darkness.

BRANDON

Athens, Greece

"Okay, take a deep breath. This might irritate your skin a little, but it's normal. You have to be very, very careful." I looked at Cassius's eyes as he started to remove my bandage.

The procedure and the medication took four months. I had eleven operations and three plastic surgeries. Cassius said that my cheekbones were dislocated—the reason why the flesh wounds were always raw. It got infected because it wasn't treated immediately. He said I was lucky it did not spread to the other part of my face. I still had more operations to go for my ribcage and the scars on my chest.

"Are you ready?"

I nodded. *"More than ready..."*

Cassius started to carefully undo the bandage.

"I was waiting for this moment, buddy—all my life. I waited for this," he said.

"I know, and I've been such a prick to you," I admitted.

"Heard something from Oliver? Did you talk to Alayna? Do they know about this day?"

"No. I talked to Oliver, and they seemed fine."

He stopped. *"Are you saying you didn't talk to her?"*

"You know that there's a threat to her life. You heard what they said. The enemies are smart. We have our grandfather and his fortune, but they are too many."

He sighed sharply.

"It's sickening that I have the same blood. That's how they knew about you being here and doing well. Are you going to show yourself? It's Aunt Agatha's fortieth birthday next month, and you are invited because Grandfather is

going as well. There will be a private meeting with the heads of the family. My father is coming. You are the legal head of your family. I heard they were going to talk about Grandfather's will."

"Are you coming?"

"Dad wants me to go. Oliver is flying here next month."
I smirked.

"Of course, I'll come. I can't wait to see their faces when they see me. It's funny; it's a masquerade party," I joked.

"Maybe Alayna's right after all," he said suddenly.

"Right about what?"

She was right that everything would change if I took this path, and I was slowly changing. This heavy burden I'd been carrying my whole life. Starting with justice for my family and the people who wanted me dead. They already took my family's life. I won't risk any more lives for me. Not Oliver, not Casey, not Cassius, and not Alayna.

The place I call home has become unfamiliar to me. A lot of things have changed. The lights are too bright; they almost hurt my eyes. I stroll into my living room and turn them off, slumping on the couch. My back and my neck are killing me.

It's funny that I barely want to step foot into this house now when I couldn't even get out of here before.

It's been a long day, and I still have jet lag. I close my eyes to get a bit of rest, but the lights are turned on again.

"Hey!" I complain.

"I see now that you're here..."

I force my eyes to open and find Cassius in my living

room. "Cassius, what's going on?"

"Where were you?" he answers me with a question, his voice stern.

"Can you turn off the light? Why are you still here?"

"I was waiting for you. Where have you been?"

I smirk. "I don't think I like the sound of your voice."

"I don't think I like how you act either. You're turning back to your old self," he remarks.

I force myself to sit and scratch my head. "Where is this coming from? You were fine earlier."

"Yes, until I saw Alayna," he says firmly. "She's in pain. She's not like she used to be when I first met her. I told you many times in Athens, and you promised me you'd get back to your fucking senses."

I press my temples with my fingers. Damn, my head. It just won't stop pounding. "I'll see her tomorrow, so what's the big deal?"

"I don't know what the hell is wrong with you anymore. You stood her up in Athens, may I remind you? I know that you suffered, but she suffered too."

"I'm aware!" I shot back. "But I can't face her right now, Cassius—"

"Finally, some truth." He shakes his head incredulously. "You don't want to see her anymore. Is this about Pauline?"

"No." I avoid his eyes.

"Then what's bothering you now?" he exclaims. "You've got what you wanted. I fixed your face, but if you're going to be like this, I'd rather have your burned face than your attitude!"

"I don't want to talk about this now, Cassius." I stand up, raising my hand in surrender.

"I told you back in Athens, Brandon, and I'm serious. I'm

giving you a chance. *One last chance*, Brandon."

My chest tightens. He is serious. I know he likes Alayna. I always knew, but I could do nothing about it. "What right do you have to give me a *chance*? I told you I'll talk to her tomorrow."

Cassius's jaw and fist clenched in unison. "She's not here..."

Wait. What?

"Where is she, Cassius?"

No, no, no. She can't be outside alone. She's not supposed to leave the house.

"I took her to my clinic. She lost consciousness."

I ball my fists. "Then what the fuck are you doing here?"

"Good. I guess you still worry about her, but it's fine. She's not alone." His tone calms down.

At that moment, I realize again there are only a few people in the world I can trust; besides Oliver, Cassius is one of them. We had a misunderstanding in the past, but he is an ally. And I need him now for Alayna. He will keep her safe, so all these conversations are pointless. At the end of the day, Alayna will still be on Cassius's side.

Because that's all that matters. Her safety.

CHAPTER EIGHTEEN

ALAYNA

"No, no! Please, no!"
"Please come back."
"Don't leave me again."
"Please come back to me."
"I'm okay with it. Just come back to me."
"No. No. I'm not a burden."
"You said you would come back."
"Don't leave!"
"Brandon, don't leave."
"No!"
"Alayna? I'm here. I'm here."
"No. You are not."
"Please don't be like this, Alayna."
"Brandon, just tell me you won't leave!"
"Ahh!"

"Alayna, wake up!"

I open my eyes, and it isn't Brandon but Cassius in front of me. His hands are cupping my cheeks, and his expression is one of concern.

"Cassius? Why what happened?"

"You had a nightmare... I guess." He brushes my tears with his thumb. "So, this is what Oliver's talking about. Alayna, how long has this been happening?"

"He doesn't want me anymore," I answer instead, and I don't know why I'm not getting tired of it. But it's just too painful.

"That's not true. He's just in bad shape right now. Here, drink this." Cassius helps me sit, then hands me a glass of water and a capsule. Quickly, I take the medication. I look around the place. I'm not in the mansion.

"Where am I, Cassius?"

"You're in my clinic. You fainted. Oliver and Casey know you're here, so you only need to rest. Try to hydrate yourself more." He puts the glass back on the side table. "And you'll be staying here for a few days. You need some time away from the mansion."

I feel my chest cramping again. "But I've been away from him for a long time."

"You need to rest, Alayna," he insists. "This is not good for you anymore. Let him rest too. Both of you are just tired."

"Please take me to the mansion!" I beg. "I... I need to know what he has to say. I can't stay here like this. He must be home by now so—"

He hugs me abruptly, and his body feels so warm that it briefly calms my senses. "Stop, Alayna... Please."

I clutch the fabric of his shirt. "I can't take this anymore, Cassius."

"This is why we are here. Oliver, Casey, and I... I am here for you, so please calm down, Alayna."

"I've been dreaming the same dream every night," I confess. "It started when he returned from Athens. I went all the way there to see him, but he was with another woman. Tell me, Cassius, did he find someone else? Is that the case?" I ask. I can't think of any more reason but *that*.

"He didn't find someone else; I can assure you."

"The woman at the party... Who is she to him?"

"It's Pauline."

"So that's her. Oliver wouldn't tell me." I laugh bitterly. I pull away from Cassius. "I know her. Brandon told me."

"Yes, she's Brandon's childhood friend."

"Don't cover up for him. I know she's his ex. She's his first love. Did he forget all about me because he reunited with her?"

"I told you, that's not it. They were best friends, Alayna. Brandon feels he has some sort of responsibility for her. It's not anything more than that."

"But *you* are his best friend, Cassius," I point out.

"Don't come to such conclusions for now. Brandon misses you, even if he doesn't say it. But if you are right, I will be the one to confront him. I promise." Cassius tucks the strands of my hair behind my ears. "Now, why don't you go back to bed? It's only past three. I'll have the nurse look after you."

I hang on to him. "Are you going to leave?"

"No, I'll be right outside, Alayna."

"Stay here. I don't want to sleep alone."

He brushes his thumb across my cheek. "Are you okay with that?"

I nod. "Yes. As long as I know someone's with me."

"Okay. I'll sleep on the couch."

I smile a little. I lie back on the bed and roll to my side so I can see Cassius. He brushes off the invisible dirt on the couch and leans back.

"I always knew you were a good person," I say.

He laughs, looking at the ceiling. "People tend to judge me by appearance."

"Are you admitting that you look like a bad guy?" I joke.

"Yes, a good-looking bad guy." He glances at me and flashes a grin.

I giggle. "Thank you for staying with me."

"You're welcome. Now, sleep. I'll be here until you wake up."

"Good morning, Alayna. Breakfast in bed?" Cassius places a tray of toast and a glass of milk on the bedside table.

"Sure. Thanks, Cass."

"You're welcome." He grins. "Oh, your color is back. I think you'll be fine tomorrow."

"I can't thank you enough for this treatment, and I'm sorry. I've been a mess."

"You'll be fine. You just need to clear your mind and"— he picks up a piece of the toast and hands it to me—"start fresh, you know? I suggest you eat your breakfast. I'm taking you out later."

I take a small bite of the toast. "I thought I'm not allowed to go out?"

"I didn't say you're not allowed to go out," he says, smiling. "Casey wants to see you. She called me this morning."

"Oh." I nod. "I just realized one thing. I don't want to meet anyone right now. It's kind of exhausting."

"Then, would you rather stay here?"

"Yes, and actually, I have one favor to ask you. I know that you won't allow me, but I need this to move forward."

He sits on the edge of the bed. "What is it?"

"First of all, thank you for not leaving me last night, and you're right. I'm just tired, and maybe I need more time to clear my mind. I know Brandon just arrived, and I still have a few more months in my contract, but I'm thinking of going on a vacation."

"Hmm. I believe your contract does say you're entitled to vacation leave. That's a good decision, Alayna. Where are you planning to go?"

"Home. To Lawrence." I shrug. "But I still want to talk to Brandon and clear things with him. Only then can I move on."

"Are you sure about that? I'm not going to stop you, but I wouldn't advise it either. I worry more about the aftermath, but of course, it's still your decision," he states with understanding.

"I need to know if he still cares for me or not, and I need your help to do that because I really feel like he doesn't want to talk to me."

"Unfortunately, Brandon is being difficult right now. Not just with you, but with everyone else," he says honestly. "I'm not trying to be negative here, but what will you do if he says something else?"

"If he wants to really break up, you say?"

He nods slightly.

I look down at my lap. "Then I'll let him go. It's all I want. His clear answer."

Cassius doesn't speak right away, thinking maybe, but then he says, "Okay. I'll help you talk to him. I'll call Oliver."

I smile at him, grateful for how understanding he is.

BRANDON

Athens, Greece

My grandfather tossed the glass of wine. Deep inside, I was grieving. I promised him that I would protect the family because he knew I could be trusted. But right now, I might've failed him. What I was doing wasn't enough.

"How?" he howled as if someone had died again. "How could you not tell me such information? Since when have you known about it?"

I wouldn't have wanted to believe it myself.

"I was wrong for not telling you." I clenched my fist. "But I thought we agreed that you would let me do these things my way. You got into my private files, Grandfather. Did you think I'm doing nothing?"

I know that it will hurt him, finding out a family was killed by his own flesh and blood.

"Helen lost her life because her son murdered her. He made her transfer everything to his name then killed her. I didn't mean to get into your files. I trust you, my boy, but you should've told me about this. Oh, Helen, my sister," he whimpered. "What did they do to you? Oh! Why did you not tell me about this sooner?"

I swallowed. "Even before, they already owned half your

properties. When your brother Euricius died of a disease, he had already transferred everything to Helen. What are they going to do next? And what is this that I found out? There was a reason you wanted me to have the rest of your fortune. You want to invest it in my company so you can secure it. So you could have it back at the right time?"

"You know that I decided to give my fortune to you since you were a child. Don't say that, Brandon!" he bellowed.

"I want to trust you, but how could you do this to us? At the end of the day, this is all about fucking money!"

"Watch your language, Brandon! That was a long time ago! I regret all of it now, and I need your help. I already told you this, my boy."

I shook my head.

"I'm going to present myself publicly at the party this weekend. Now that your properties are under my name, please don't think that I'm doing this because of you. I'm doing this for my mother and Elga."

He nodded; his eyes filled with guilt.

"After all these years, what this family is fighting for... worth nothing." He looked at me with sincerity. "I do not wish for us to fight. You are all I have. I'm so sorry, Brandon."

"I don't wish for us to fight either," I mumbled, surrendering. "All I want from you is your trust."

"Of course, I trust you." He forced a smile. "What is your plan now?"

"To start with the root of it all. I can't get rid of the root because it's a foundation. But if I get rid of the stems, I might have a chance."

"Your father's mistress," my grandfather said. "Annette. Your Uncle Alfio's half-sister."

CHAPTER NINETEEN

BRANDON

It's the second day Alayna hasn't come home.

Things have changed. The house. The people. And me. I can go outside, yes. I can finally face people, but the constant pain in my chest is still there. It didn't go away, and I will probably have it until I die. I guess one year just isn't enough.

A knock on the door interrupts my thoughts. "Come in."

"Master Brandon?" It's Lennie. She pushes the trolley inside. It's unusual. Normally, she will only leave the food at the door. Seeing her smile at me like this makes me realize that my decision might have been a good one after all.

"Lennie." I walk toward her and embrace her small frame. This is the first in many years I've held her like this. Lennie is a mother to me, so being able to embrace her this way is pure joy.

"Look at how you grew up, my master," she says kindly, holding my arm as she studies me.

"It's *Brandon* to you, Lennie. I've missed you."

"I always believed this day would come." She touches my face fondly and smiles. "I never lost hope that you'd finally walk out into the world and look at you now. But what happened?" Her expression becomes concerned. "I heard Alayna collapsed. Did you get to meet her?"

I groan inwardly. "We didn't have a chance. She was already away when I came home. It's my fault."

"My dear boy. You might have your reasons, but I saw how Alayna suffered," she states with some severity. "Why wouldn't you speak to her?"

I can't look at her eyes because of it. I was ashamed, but everything I did in the past year, I did for everyone's well-being. "I didn't know what else to do, Lennie."

"And whatever is bothering you, you can't tell her?"

"Not at this time."

She nods and smiles faintly at me. "Well, I hope you know what you're doing."

"Brandon?" Oliver abruptly appears at the slightly open door.

"Yes, Oliver?"

"Is this a bad time?" he asks, looking from me to Lennie.

"We're fine here, Oliver," Lennie says. "I just brought our master his dinner."

"Oh, thank you, Lennie." He walks inside. "I've been looking for you, man."

"It's a pleasure to have you back, Master. I'll come back to fetch the plates later." Lennie excuses herself and exits the room. Oliver closes the door after her.

"Why? What's going on?" I ask, moving behind my desk to sit.

"Same old. You've been drinking?" Oliver picks up the

empty bottle of beer on my desk.

"Leave it," I tell him. "That's from last night."

"What are you doing here?" he asks. "Alayna's with Cassius, Brandon."

"I'm aware."

"Then why are you still here? You're not going to see her, are you?"

"We'll talk when she gets better."

"And if she doesn't?" Ollie demands. "She's been waiting for you a whole damn year. You didn't speak to her even once, Brandon. I'm tired of covering up for you or of giving her your paltry excuses. I thought when you returned, everything would go back to what you two had. Can you tell me the truth? Do you still want her or not?"

I sigh. I can't believe I have to answer to everyone for this. "She can't be with me."

"Why not?" he demands.

"I have my reasons," I say. "I will tell you everything, but please, Ollie, give me some time to fix this."

"By pushing Alayna away?" He rakes his fingers through his hair. "Is this how you fix things?"

"I said I have my reasons, Ollie!" I snap.

"Whatever goddamned reason you have, Alayna still carries all the weight. Anyway, I'm going to see Cassius," he says. "If you still have a spine, just see her once and tell the fucking truth about why you can't be with her."

ALAYNA

Three days later, I ask Cassius if I can go outside. He allows me but tells me he has to bring me back to the clinic. He's also being extra careful, so he comes along.

Honestly, I'm getting used to his company. Cassius is very accommodating and endlessly patient with me. After we shop for a few things at the mall, we stop at Starbucks.

"Oliver's on his way," he says, then takes a sip of his Frappuccino.

"I've been thinking." I look at him. "I just thought of this last night."

"What is it?"

"I want to leave tomorrow. I want to see my family."

"We already talked about this, and of course, you can, Alayna." He grins. "It will help you unwind."

"But there's still something else I want."

He puts the cup on the table. "Hmm. Go ahead."

"I still need to tell Brandon about this. I want to tell him formally because he's my boss, and if you can take me there..."

"What?"

"You don't need to stay with me," I continue. "I just want someone to be with me while I travel. It's too much, I know, and Kansas is very far away and—"

He chuckles. "Of course, I can take you there. I have time, but I have patients waiting for me, so I can't stay long."

"I just don't want to be alone," I repeat. Honestly, I don't know what's gotten into me, asking him for a favor like that. I'm having these mixed emotions because of him.

The lump in my lungs lightens, and the rapid beat of my heart slows down. Brandon doesn't want me anymore, so I guess it's time for me to clear my mind of him. He's hurt me enough. It's like I've died inside. I'm done with this stupidity.

But I know my life must go on. I have a family to support. I have to grab anything that will bring me peace.

"Did you tell Oliver that I need to speak to Brandon?"

He checks his wristwatch. "Yes, and they should be here by now."

My eyes widen. "What? Now?"

He nods. "Yes. I asked Oliver if he could convince Brandon to see you. But are you sure you can tell him—"

"Tell me what?" Someone suddenly says behind me, and I jerk as I recognize the voice. It's the voice I've been dying to hear for what feels like a million years. I look over my shoulder and see Brandon standing there. The tension inside me starts to grow, and my heartbeat accelerates.

The reality is all clear to me now. Brandon can walk outside his comfort zone—without his mask. I've already seen him once without it, but this is my first time seeing his face up close.

He's splendid... beautiful... mind-blowing... perfect. There are no other words I can think of to describe how magnificent he is. He's like a brand-new person and almost regal in his tailored dark blue shirt and charcoal-gray trousers.

It hurts even more to see him like this because I know he isn't mine anymore.

Brandon pulls a chair across from Cassius and sits in it. He gazes sharply at both of us, but I can't look directly into his eyes, so I shift my gaze. I can already feel the tension between us with no words spoken. I can't believe Brandon can act as if nothing happened, but I feel his eyes watching me.

"Alayna, how are you?" Oliver speaks to cut the stillness. I almost didn't notice him because of Brandon's unnerving presence.

"I'm all right, Ollie." I smile a little.

"I don't have a good feeling about this," Cassius whispers to me.

"It's okay," I whisper back. "I'll tell you now."

"Do you think this is the right time?" he asks.

"You know that we can hear you, right?" Oliver interrupts.

"Let's get this over with, shall we?" Brandon says. "Why do I need to be here? Can't this wait, and we'll talk about it in the house later?"

Cassius grunts. "What the fuck did you just say?"

"Come on, Cassius. I know that something's going on here." He looks back and forth from me to his cousin shrewdly.

"Maybe or maybe not," I say. I'm suddenly flaring up. What the hell is his game?

His jaw tightens.

"What is it you want to say?" Oliver asks. "Cassius said you have something to tell us."

"First," I begin, "I want to use my vacation leave so I can go to my family," I announce, avoiding Brandon's eyes, which never leave mine.

"That is not what you want to tell me, as per Oliver," Brandon presses.

"I'm not finished," I shoot back. I don't know how I got this courage. Maybe because Cassius is sitting next to me, but my chest is getting heavy again—as if the pain there really never faded.

"I think you both need to talk alone," Oliver suggests.

"No, I'm saying this with everyone here." I look at Oliver and at Brandon again. "What I want to say is I just need a vacation. I'll come back, but I cannot continue working in that house."

"What?" Cassius and Oliver exclaim.

"This isn't what we talked about, Alayna," Cassius hisses.

"And I'm not going to talk about anything private anymore. I'll try not to let my private life interfere with my work. I hope you all understand what I mean."

There. I said it. It sounds simple, but inside I want to burn.

Oliver glances at Brandon, then back at me. "What are you saying, Alayna? Aren't we all friends here? Besides, your contract still isn't over."

I shake my head. "I don't think I can be friends—"

"I'm going with her to Kansas," Cassius suddenly declares, cutting me off.

"What?" Oliver cries. "What the hell is going on?"

"I need to unwind so I'm going with her," Cassius explains. I want to speak up, but he holds my hand under the table, assuring me that it's okay. I understand what he's trying to say.

"Wait, wait. What the hell is going on here? *Alayna?* Are you okay with this?" Oliver asks again, and there's still nothing from Brandon. However, his eyes have darkened, as if he might explode at any moment.

"Don't ask her," Cassius says. "Of all people, you know what she's been through, Ollie. You were there."

"That's true, but this is something else."

I clench my fist under the table. I can't say anything. I suddenly feel restrained.

"I can't believe I came all the way here just to hear this piece of crap, Cassius," Brandon mocks.

Oliver grabs his cousin's shoulder. "Brandon, you promised."

Clearly, he doesn't care about me, no matter what Cassius does to provoke him. "I didn't ask you to come here."

His expression hardens. "Because I have to say something—" He looks at me. "To you, at least, but I am expecting to speak with you *alone*."

I laugh mirthlessly. "If you're going to say something I already know, no, thank you. I'm not interested in hearing it."

"Did you not hear what I said?" he bellows. "I said I wanted to talk to her... alone." He grits his teeth and is seething under his breath. He glowers at Cassius and Oliver.

"No one is standing," I say.

Brandon squeezes his temples with his fingers, then rams his fist on the table. The people around us look in our way.

"Fuck!" he curses. He stands and buttons up his suit. None of us make a movement. "I told you I don't want to share, didn't I?" Furiously, he storms out of the coffee shop.

Oliver remains seated. "I thought you wanted to talk to him?"

"He did not come to talk. He came here to bring a storm."

"Are you two even serious about what you are saying?"

"I'm only taking her there," Cassius says truthfully. "I only said that because I'm fucking pissed at him."

Oliver's shoulder relaxes. "Don't scare the hell out of me like that," he scolds, shaking his head. "I asked Brandon to come so they could talk. I don't know what the hell is going on with him because he won't tell me anything. I just hoped that he'd tell Alayna."

After another minute, Brandon comes back. He grasps

my wrist and tugs at me. "Come!"

"Ouch! Brandon, what are you doing?" I cry.

"Just come!" he snarls.

Cassius stands up in a panic. "Hey, you're hurting her!" He's about to reach for my hand, but Bandon stops him with a glare. Cassius withdraws.

"Come with me," he says again, then drags me outside and shoves me into his car.

I grab the door handle, wanting to get out. I can't be alone with him right now. Not when I'm still trying to compose myself. Cassius is right. I'm not emotionally ready. I push the door open to get out, but Brandon prevents me.

"Let me go, Brandon," I order, shaking the handle; it just won't open.

He shuts his eyes, gripping the steering wheel hard. "Stop."

"Let me out!" I scream.

"Hey!" he shouts back and catches my hand. "I said stop! You need to calm down."

"Don't do this to me. Let me out. I... I need to breathe." Then there it is again. I'm out of breath. My eyes are getting fuzzy. I clutch my chest and groan.

He shifts his body to my side and grabs my hand. "Alayna?"

"Don't touch me!" I shove his hand away, but he cups my face.

"What's going on with you?"

My breath quickens. "I... I need to... I need to go out. I need to get away from you..."

Unexpectedly, he wraps his arms around me and rubs circles on my back. "Isn't this what you want? To talk?" he murmurs as if he's talking to a child. In my heart, I know what was happening, but my mind is messing with me. I don't know what I'm doing anymore.

"Let me out, Brandon," I plead, and my stupid eyes just won't stop crying. "I don't want to talk to you anymore."

"Shh..." he hushes me. "Tell me what's going on."

I struggle against his arms. "It hurts to be with you."

Brandon pulls me close. My heart knows I longed for him and how badly I waited for this moment. His fingers stroke my hair tenderly, but I know he isn't mine anymore.

"I hate you. You ignored me." I pound his arm repeatedly. "I hate you!"

"Breathe, Alayna," he whispers, still caressing my back.

I let out a deep breath. I'm beginning to calm down. The rapid pounding of my heart slows. I let him comfort me.

"Good. That's good," he says.

I bury my head in his shoulder. I miss him. I badly miss him. But I hate him just as much. He did this to me.

"Just say it," I sob. "Just say that you don't want this anymore—that you don't want me, instead of making me wait."

I raise my head and search for his eyes. And it's an almost painful sight. He is so, so beautiful that it hurts. I attempt to touch his face, the side where he wore the mask, but he shuts his eyes and snatches my wrist.

"Not today. You need to rest."

"If you can't say it, let me say it for you."

"Don't. You don't deserve—"

"Stop it! Stop it!" I shove him away, but he brings me back to his arms. I can't keep having him like this. I'm tired of waiting. Why couldn't he just tell the truth? Why couldn't he tell me that he doesn't love me anymore?

"I just want this to stop," I declare. I should have done

this before.

He kisses my temple. "I'm so sorry, Alayna."

"You're free now, Brandon, but don't ever think that I'll forgive you. After this day, there will be no more us."

I shut my eyes, and everything turns dark.

I'm back in the clinic when I regain consciousness. I remember what happened before I passed out, and the pain is still here. But it's different now. I ended everything. Now I know which path I'm going to take.

"That was really brave of you." Cassius strokes my face. "I thought I'd never see Alayna again. The *real* Alayna."

I sit up. "Because you were right, and it's over now. I no longer have to torture myself by waiting. Thank you for everything, Cassius."

"You made me worry back there. I thought something had happened to you. Are you okay?"

"I'm okay." I touch his hand. "Will you take me to Kansas?"

"I think I already said yes."

"No, it's not what I mean. Maybe stay a little bit? I'll show you where I grew up?"

He smiles. "Maybe."

I finally smile, and I know for sure that this time, I didn't force myself. I embrace him. "Thank you, Cassius, for being there."

He hugs me back. "Always."

CHAPTER TWENTY

BRANDON

A few hours earlier

Cassius, I need a favor. We are still in front. Come here and take Alayna."

He and Oliver come in a flurry. I step out of the car and open the door on the passenger side.

Cassius rushes to her and gently shakes her shoulder. "Alayna? Alayna, can you hear me?" He caresses her flushed cheeks with his thumb, but she doesn't respond. "What happened to her?"

I curse under my breath. The way he holds her is too familiar. I fucking want to tear his arms off, but I calm myself. "She fainted."

"What did you do?"

"We never had a chance to talk. She was crying the whole time," I say.

"God, I think she needs to give this a rest. You just

couldn't wait until she's ready," he snarls and looks at his brother. "You both know it's not good for her."

Oliver doesn't answer, but he nods.

"Alayna?" He touches her face. "Oh, God. Are you okay?"

"Don't wake her. She fell asleep."

"Don't tell me what to do because you can't take care of her!" Cassius snaps. "I'm taking her from here." He envelops Alayna in his arms and tries to lift her legs, but she grunts painfully.

"Let her sleep," I insist. "Take the damn car and take her back to your clinic." I throw the keys to him, and he catches them.

"Brandon. Are you sure?" Oliver asks. "Are you going to let it end like this?"

"Take her before I change my mind," I order, ignoring Ollie's statement.

"Yes, but I will not take her just because you told me so. I can't believe that after the hardship we've been through, you have not changed." Cassius shuts the door, turns, and gets into the driver's seat. He takes off, speeding down the road.

"Are you sure of what you just did?" Oliver asks again.

"It's fine, Ollie."

"But why?"

"It will be a rough ride next time. I won't even have time for myself."

He scowls. "What do you mean?"

"A year ago, I found Alayna because she's an acquaintance of my father's mistress. I put her in danger. She doesn't know how dangerous that woman is."

"Is that what you've been doing in Athens?"

"I've been investigating. Grandfather thinks Annette is our uncle's daughter, but she's not. Annette is Helen's bastard. Her firstborn. Uncle Alfio and Annette are half-siblings."

"What?" He scratches his chin.

"Come with me. I can't talk about it here."

As soon as we return to the mansion, I go to my desk and pull out some documents from my drawer.

"This is the information about our families, registrations, records that might help us."

Oliver opens the first binder, looks at the first page, and says, "This is our family tree."

"Euricius, Petros, and Helen are the Heads of Katrakis. Surely you already knew that," I continue. "Euricius was the eldest with one son, Estevan. There are five grandchildren: the twins Carmelo and Constantine and their three older sisters who are married to the Stavros family. They lived inside the compound. You'll always see them in family gatherings. However, Euricius transferred half his fortune to Helen when he passed away, but the twins didn't take what was left of their fortune for some reason.

"Petros, our grandfather, is the second head of the family. But now that Euricius and Helen are gone, he is the head of the Katrakis family. He owns the other third of the Katrakis's fortune. Our grandfather was just greedy in his younger years. He liked to use his money for everything, and because of it, he almost lost all his children. I lost Mom because of his greed. You already know our family's story, so I won't explain this much further. This is what you needed to hear.

"Helen, the youngest, and her son Alfio were accused of my mother's murder, but this was never confirmed."

"He's one of your suspects now?" His question sounds like more of a conclusion.

"A dangerous accusation, but yes, Ollie. I have been connecting the dots, and it all leads to him and Annette."

"Hold on." He scowls hard. "Not just Annette or some unknown Marcus, but him?"

"Unfortunately, Alfio plays a big part in all this."

Oliver smiles mirthlessly. "He's despicable, and what's worse is, his blood runs through our veins."

"Listen to this, Oliver: Even with a piece of substantial evidence, it's going to be hard to take him down. He is protected by people from high spheres, politicians, and businessmen. He wanted to take our grandfather's wealth for his illegal businesses. Drugs, gambling, and sex clubs. He's the leader of an organization—like a mafia. I'm still looking for information on it. His sons, Charlie and Silvanus, are helping him."

"And you're their greatest threat," Oliver concludes. "You are wealthy even without the Katrakis fortune. Uncle Alfio could be one of the reasons for your mother's and sister's deaths. This is what everyone knows but refused to do anything about. They are afraid of Alfio. He'll do everything to take you down. But where is Annette in the family tree?"

"Betrayal runs in the family," I answer. "Before her husband, Helen had an affair outside the family alliance when she was sixteen, and Annette is her daughter. This is what I found out about her. Annette is a famous chef, there's no doubt about that. We even found Alayna because of her.

Her origin is Greek and Italian. A long time ago, our grandfather said Annette went to Alfio's second wedding. I saw the copy of his marriage registration, and Annette's name was listed as a witness using the Katrakis name. This is evidence."

"And no one suspected it since it's a closed-court ceremony."

"Yes, and so Annette is Helen's illegitimate daughter, Alfio's half-sister," I continue. "I found this proof from my informant. I couldn't tell you because there are people I needed to protect. Uncle Alfio won't let us take this secret to the public, so we have to be careful."

Oliver scans all the papers I presented to him. "I'm not sure how you got this, but I'm amazed, Brandon."

"But I can't be so sure if she's one of our culprits. Something's off."

"What do you mean?"

"I can't tell for now. But Alayna's information about Annette is right, Ollie. Her current address is correct, and she's still using her fake name. I know where to find her now. I know where she lives. One thing is for sure. Alfio is helping Annette. They're helping each other, and my father could be their ally."

Six months ago, Uncle Alfio introduced himself to me in Athens. He acted as if I was his favorite nephew and talked about doing business with my company. Never in my life am I going to acknowledge him as family. I promised to take him down—and everyone who caused my family's death. I'm powerful enough to bring him to his knees.

"I'll show you another thing," I suddenly say and pull at a drawer. I pick up a small envelope and toss it on the desk. "Open that."

Oliver opens the envelope and draws out the content.

"Pictures?" He frowns.

"Yes. Please, take a look."

He picks up one of many and stares at it. "Who is this late-forties lady, I guess?"

"That's Alayna's mother. There are pictures with her siblings in there too, in Kansas."

"What?" Oliver spreads out the photos on my desk and scans each one. "Wait." His expression stiffens.

"Did you notice?" I say, referring to the man in the gray hood approaching Alayna's mother and some of her siblings on the street at different days, places, angles, and shots. I'm sure it was just one person, but he hid his face with a black face mask.

"Fuck," he curses. "They're getting close."

I massage my temples with my fingers. "Yes, that's why I sent additional security to Lawrence. They know about her family now, whoever the fuck they are, and this... This is already a warning, Ollie," I say pointedly.

"And you have these photos taken how?"

"I sent someone to look after them."

Oliver shuts his eyes. "Is this why you couldn't face her? She doesn't even know you're doing this."

"I can't, and it doesn't matter. She can't know, and you know why. First Alayna, now her family... She's not safe with me anymore."

"Do you know who's after them?"

"No."

"God!" He slams his fist on the desk. "Why didn't you tell me this sooner? Alayna misunderstood! I misjudged you."

"I wasn't sure at first until this. I can't let them get hurt because of me."

"But don't you think it's too late for that?"

"This is why...." I stop, and Oliver puts a hand on my arm.

"Is this why you broke up with her?"

"I don't want to, Ollie. But I have to so they will leave her and her family alone..." I whisper.

"Oh, man." He rubs my back. "But letting her go with Cassius... It's not okay, don't you think?"

I shut my eyes. "She's safe with him. If there's a person other than me who can protect her, it's Cassius..."

"But you can protect Alayna now. This is why you left for a year—to get better, right?"

"Yes, I can," I say tersely, "but how about her family, Ollie? Some things are uncontrollable, and I can't be there for her if what I'm afraid of happens... I'm not weak anymore, but I'm not that strong," I admit.

He nods, understanding our current situation. "But she's going home to Lawrence."

"As long as Cassius is with her, she's safe," I repeat. "He shouldn't leave her alone, and you should tell him that, but he has to know his place." I clench my fist.

"He likes Alayna, and Alayna thinks you don't want her anymore."

"I know," I growl.

"Man, do you still know what you're doing? One wrong move, you might lose everything..." he remarks with concern.

"I'd rather lose everything, but I have to keep them safe. Oliver, what happened to Mom and Elga can't happen again."

"Then this is it? It's over with you and Alayna?"

"For now."

BRANDON AND ALAYNA'S STORY
WILL CONTINUE IN THE SEQUEL OF
THE BILLIONAIRE'S MASK SERIES

THE BILLIONAIRE'S REVENGE

MASK TWO

COMING SOON

ABOUT THE AUTHOR

Margarette Grey writes contemporary romance stories featuring hot billionaires and clumsy heroines. She loves the thrill of reading gripping romance novels at night, kissing alpha males in her dreams, and writing about them in the morning. She makes her home in The Pearl of the Orient Seas, where 'leisure time' means indulging in drawings, watching anime, Korean dramas, and Netflix series.

www.margarettegreyauthor.com